Colin Wilson is one  and popular writers at wo er in 1931, and left school ears working in a wool stics factory and a coffe was published in 1956. It claim and was an immediate bestseller.

Since then he has written many books on philosophy, the occult, crime and sexual deviance, plus a host of successful novels which have won him an international reputation. His work has been translated into Spanish, French, Swedish, Dutch and Japanese.

By the same author

COLIN WILSON

The Janus Murder
Case

PANTHER
Granada Publishing

Panther Books
Granada Publishing Ltd
8 Grafton Street, London W1X 3LA

Published by Panther Books 1985

First published in Great Britain by
Granada Publishing 1984

Copyright © Colin Wilson 1984

ISBN 0-586-05972-5

Printed and bound in Great Britain by
Collins, Glasgow

Set in Times

For Jackie – with affection

ACKNOWLEDGEMENTS

As with its predecessor, *The Schoolgirl Murder Case*, this novel owes a great deal to the help and technical advice of friends. Chief among these was Sergeant Donald Rumbelow of the City police force. I am also grateful to Bill Waddell, curator of the Black Museum at Scotland Yard, and to Geoff Martin, Scenes of Crime Officer at Notting Hill Police Station, for reading the book in typescript and commenting on it. Other friends who gave help and advice are: Donald Seaman, Christopher Fry, Bill Hopkins and Jackie Noble.

CW

ONE

Saltfleet never discovered what it was that had awakened him. His sleep had been so deep that for a moment he felt confused, wondering where he was; he was in a single bed, and the window seemed to be in the wrong place. Then it came back: he was in the house of his brother-in-law Gerald, in Ladbroke Terrace Gardens, not in his own bedroom in Thames Ditton. In the other single bed, Miranda was sleeping peacefully, her bare arm resting on the eiderdown. He could hear the occasional sounds of traffic in Ladbroke Grove and Holland Park Avenue. But that was not what had awakened him. The beating of his heart told him that something had touched his policeman's sense of urgency.

He slipped out of bed and crossed to the window, the thick carpet yielding like a lawn under his bare feet. The square below was deserted, its grass and trees looking like a stage set in the bright moonlight. He raised the casement softly, and leaned out. As the heavy drone of a goods lorry died away, he heard the footsteps from the opposite pavement. Through the railings of the gardens, it was impossible to see anyone. But the steps were those of a woman, and they sounded brisk and unhurried, like a businesswoman setting out for work. What aroused his detective instinct was that they seemed to start in the middle of the square; yet he had heard no sound of a closing door to suggest where she came from. When the sound faded around the corner, he closed the window quietly, and got back into bed.

He knew it would be difficult to get back to sleep. For the past week he had spent at least an hour every night thinking about Geraldine. She was his only child; and on her fifteenth birthday, a week ago, he had discovered that she was no longer a virgin. The thought still made his heart contract with a morbid emotion that was like a bruise. He knew it was stupid, that it happened to other people's daughters; he even knew that half the girls in her class at school were no longer virgins. Yet it still revolted and distressed him. She was not like other people's daughters. With her long, slim body that sunburned so easily, her blond hair that came halfway down her back, her sudden bursts of affection that made her fling her arms round his neck or curl up on his knee as he sat in his armchair, it was hard to think of her as more than a little girl.

On the previous Friday he had returned home after a long but satisfying day in court; the judge's summing-up had made it clear that the Sansini brothers would be found guilty of demanding money with menaces, grievous bodily harm, and abduction of minors. They were London's worst criminal gang since the Krays and the Richardsons, and it had cost Saltfleet and his team six months to build up the case against them. Geraldine's birthday party started at half-past-four, but it had been impossible to get home until seven. He had carried her present – a music centre – up to her bedroom, then went downstairs to look for her. In the lounge, eight or nine teenagers were watching television, but Geraldine was not among them. They told him that Miranda had driven someone back to Hampton. He went into the garden and called Geraldine's name, then walked down to the river to see if she was in the dinghy – she loved to lie in it listening to pop music over earphones. The boat was empty. He stood there for a while, relishing the shadowy calm, and the autumn smell of the river. He was passing the boatshed, on his way back to the house, when its door opened, and Geraldine came out; she was followed by a boy. They looked startled and embarrassed; the boy, who had bristly blond hair, avoided Saltfleet's eyes. Geraldine said: 'I was just showing Charlie the speedboat.' When he told her there was a present in her bedroom, she hugged him; but the gesture lacked spontaneity.

As they went into the house, he opened the door of the shed, to make sure the light had been turned off. The seat cushions and the life jackets had been laid on the floor behind the speedboat, forming a mattress with a pillow. Saltfleet picked them up in his arms and tossed them back into the boat. As he did so, something fell to the floor: a pink rubber contraceptive. He stared down at it, feeling the bottom fall out of his comfortable sense of well-being. He took a paper handkerchief from his pocket and picked it up; its moist state made it obvious that it had been used recently. The image of Geraldine that came into his mind was painfully explicit; he felt a flood of nausea and incredulity. He screwed up the handkerchief and hurled it into the wastebin.

Geraldine was in her bedroom, the door wide open. She saw from his face that he knew. He had a curious feeling that even if he had looked the other way, his emotion would have telegraphed itself to her like a radio signal.

He was changing into casual clothes when Geraldine pushed open the bedroom door. She stood with her eyes averted, looking very slim in her white party dress. For a moment he felt that his suspicion was absurd. Then she said, 'I'm sorry,' and he knew it was true.

'How long has it been going on?' His voice felt thick in his throat.

'About a month.' She was quiet and submissive, as she used to be as a child when he was annoyed.

He found it hard to think of anything to say that would not release an explosion of pain and anger. He said finally:

'You'd better go down to your friends. They'll wonder where you are.'

She said, 'Yes,' and went quietly. She always had a certain dignity and self-possession.

And now, a week later, it was still unresolved. Miranda, he discovered, had suspected for some time. The day after the party, she and Geraldine had a long talk. Apparently Charlie had not been the first. It had happened six months before with her previous boyfriend David, a shy young man who seemed to be interested only in model aeroplanes and computers. She had surrendered her virginity on the hearthrug in his home, when the family was out at the cinema. After that, David had become very possessive and talked about marriage; so she threw him over for the more experienced – and casual – Charlie.

Saltfleet found it an impossible situation. If she had been a few years older, the solution would have been a flat of her own; but she was obviously too young. He thought of making her promise to abstain from sex for another year or so; but Miranda pointed out that this would only make her furtive and dishonest. Apparently she and Charlie some-times made love three times a day; she could hardly be expected to stop completely. Miranda took it all with her usual sensible calmness. But her solution outraged him: to send Geraldine to the doctor to be fitted with a contracep-tive device. The thought of consenting to his daughter having sex in boatsheds and on hearthrugs filled him with a fury of total rejection.

The move to his brother-in-law's house had been planned months before, and it was too late to change the arrange-ment. Gerald was a wealthy stockbroker who liked to spend September in the Caribbean. It suited him perfectly to have a policeman to stay in the house, and it suited Miranda to be close to the West End shops for a few weeks. Geraldine was to move in with the Fitzmaurices, who lived a few doors down the road in Thames Ditton, and whose daughter went to the same school. A week ago this had seemed a marvellous arrangement; now it seemed like a trap devised by fate. Geraldine had a key to the house; it was like presenting her with a honeymoon cottage.

When faced with a baffling case, Saltfleet had a habit of emptying his mind, then trying to see it with fresh eyes, as if looking down on it from above. Now he tried it with the present situation. It brought a flash of insight, but no comfort. Looked at from a sensible point of view – the view of someone who was not involved – it was straightforward enough. Geraldine was a normal fifteen-year-old, living in a quiet suburb. She was old enough to bear children, but she was expected to go to school and do her homework every evening. She wanted to enter the adult world, to start living. So it was natural enough for her to experiment with sex. He could still recall the delight he had experienced as a nineteen-year-old Police Constable, having his first love affair. Her name was Greta Barlow, and she was Miranda's best friend. He still felt a stir of excitement as he remembered making love to her behind the tennis club, and under a weeping willow by the Thames at Maidenhead.

He also remembered his shocked disbelief when he found out that she was also sleeping with a police sergeant named Fison. It was the same feeling of betrayal he now felt about Geraldine. Miranda had been kind and sympathetic. Suddenly, he had realised she was the kind of girl he had always wanted: quiet, shy, but self-contained. She belonged to herself – which was why he wanted her to belong to him. Her father was a high official in Customs and Excise; Miranda was the kind of girl who played squash at the country club and knew the South of France. Her family had frowned on the idea of her marrying a policeman; but the first time they kissed, both knew there was a chemistry that made them perfect for one another. Again and again, after his marriage, he had marvelled that he had found a girl who was so close to his ideal. When he was working on a

11

difficult case, he often felt that he was doing it for her, like a knight fighting for the honour of his lady.

And that, he now realised, was the problem. He had seen Geraldine in the same way: as a younger version of his ideal woman. So it felt exactly as if it was Miranda who was having an affair. When he found himself picturing Geraldine lying with her naked legs open, the image blurred into Miranda. He could still remember the shock he had experienced as a teenager when he read the *Morte d'Arthur* and realised that Guinevere had been unfaithful with Lancelot. Yet was it Geraldine's fault that she had failed to live up to an ideal that was inside his own head? Pure Guineveres were probably imaginary. His years on the Vice Squad should have taught him that women were made of flesh and blood . . . Yet he was still unable to argue himself out of the sense of outrage and revulsion.

He lay awake thinking about it for more than two hours, but he was still no nearer a solution when he fell asleep.

Miranda said: 'There's something going on down there.'

He opened his eyes, reluctant to emerge into the daylight. She was standing by the window.

'Where?'

'I think they've found a body . . .'

'What?' He was out of bed and across the room, leaving the continental quilt behind on the floor. She was right. The canvas screens in the garden below were unmistakable. As he watched, a squad car drew up; he recognised the Divisional Detective Inspector who climbed out: Fitch, from Hammersmith.

He said: 'Damn.'

'What is it?'

'Something woke me in the night, and I forgot to check the time.'

'A noise?'

'I don't know what it was. But I went to look out of the

12

window.'

'Does it matter?'

'It could.'

He was dressing quickly. Miranda said: 'Here's another car.' He went and stood beside her, buttoning his shirt.

'That's . . . whatsisname – the Coroner's Officer.' He pulled on his sports jacket. 'I'll be back in a few minutes.' He glanced at her regretfully as he left the bedroom; the sunlight was outlining her parted legs through the thin material of the nightgown.

The iron gate into the garden was almost opposite his front door. A dozen or so onlookers were standing by the railings, trying to see what was happening. The policeman at the gate said: 'You can't go in there, sir.'

'Chief Superintendent Saltfleet, CID.'

'Oh, sorry, sir.' He stood aside to let Saltfleet pass. He should have asked to see identification, but Saltfleet's air of authority was enough.

Fitch glanced at him in annoyance, then recognised him. 'Hello, sir. What are you doing here?'

'Staying in the house opposite. What's happening?'

'Sailor's been killed – stabbed to death. Polish.'

The Scene of Crimes officer was kneeling by the body, which was covered with a blanket; he had just finished outlining its position with pegs and string. The Coroner's Officer, a Police Constable, was standing well back, waiting for him to finish. The Scene of Crimes Officer was only a Detective Constable; but until he was satisfied that no clue had been overlooked, his authority was absolute. The only other person present was Fitch's assistant, a Detective Sergeant. At this stage of the investigation, the less people who trampled the ground, the better.

The body lay under a plane tree, whose leaves were just beginning to fall. Bushes of laurel, hydrangea and rhododendron isolated this part of the lawn like a backwater, and overhanging trees meant that it was not overlooked by the

13

surrounding houses. This explained why Saltfleet had seen nothing from the bedroom window in the night. He thought: whoever killed him chose a good place . . .

He asked Fitch: 'Any idea how they got in?'

'Not yet. Could have climbed the railings . . .'

Saltfleet strolled across to the far side of the garden, then walked along the edge of the lawn. Opposite the central flowerbed, there was a gap in the bushes, and the trampled ground and broken twigs suggested that it was some kind of an entrance. He knelt carefully on the lawn, taking care not to obliterate any marks, and peered through the branches. The railing on the far side looked bent, but the gap was not large enough to admit a man. This point was halfway along the garden – approximately the spot where the footsteps had started in the night. Saltfleet moved forward cautiously, trying to avoid touching the branches, and reached out for the railing. When he tugged, it moved inwards. It could then be pushed aside to make a fairly wide gap. When he pushed it back, it slotted into a space in the horizontal tie. The edges of the tie showed bright metal, although it was rusting over; someone had carefully removed a small portion with a hacksaw.

He went back to Fitch, who was dictating to the Detective Sergeant. The blanket had now been removed from the body, and the Coroner's Officer was giving it a preliminary examination. The dead man was short and heavily built, with close-cropped red hair, and the high cheekbones that Saltfleet associated with Slavs. The lips were drawn back from the teeth in a wolf-like grimace of pain. The trousers were around the knees, and the thighs were brown with dried blood; so were the genitals, the naked stomach, and the front of the green seaman's jersey. The man had bled a great deal; it had run down his left side, blackening the grass underneath.

The Scene of Crimes Officer looked up from his

notebook and recognised Saltfleet. He was a burly, black-bearded young man; Saltfleet recalled he was from the Notting Hill station.

'Hello, sir. Didn't realise this was your patch.'

'It's not. I'm staying in the house over there.'

The Constable knew perfectly well that F was not one of Saltfleet's divisions; it was a polite way of establishing territory, of pointing out that, even if Saltfleet *was* a Chief Superintendent, he had no official business there.

'I don't suppose you heard anything in the night, did you, sir?'

'No.' Saltfleet saw no point in mentioning what had happened; he had seen nothing. 'But I think I've found how they got in.'

He showed the Constable the loose railing, and watched him examine the sawed metal with a magnifying glass.

'Ever seen anything like that before?'

'Can't say I have, sir.'

'I have. When I was on the Vice Squad. Somebody sawed through a railing in Chelsea, so it could be lifted up. When it was back in place, it looked perfectly normal.'

'Prostitute?'

'Yes.'

'And when was that, sir?'

'Oh . . . about 1965. Why?'

'Things have changed a bit since then, sir. In this area particularly. It's all more free and easy, so they can advertise. And that means most of 'em can afford a room or a flat – even a maid. They don't need a public garden.' He backed out cautiously on to the grass. 'That's more likely been done by a teenager – looking for a place for a quiet fumble.'

'There must still be a few amateurs around.'

'Yes, but most of them hang around the foyers of the big hotels.'

15

He was making a sketch in his notebook, so Saltfleet left him alone. The photographer had now arrived and was taking shots of the body; after that, he would smooth out the muscles of the face and take more photographs, to show to possible witnesses. The police surgeon and the fingerprint expert should be along soon. There would be no point in fingerprinting the dead man – since his identity was known – but it should be worth examining the railing for prints, as well as bloodstains.

Saltfleet looked at his watch; it was just after eight-thirty. Miranda should have made the coffee by now. It was pleasant to be able to look at the scene of a crime without involvement, knowing he was free to go whenever he liked. But because the autumn sunlight was warm, and there was a smell of lavender in the air, he felt an inclination to stay for a few minutes longer.

If the killer had left by the sawed railing, he would have to walk past the flowerbed. And this was an obvious place for someone in a hurry to throw a weapon. Saltfleet walked slowly round the bed; it was planted with collarette and cactus dahlias, with dwarf lavender around the edges. But the flowers were too dense to catch a glimpse of the centre. Then, on the far side of the bed, he noticed a trampled flower. Stooping down and pushing the lavender aside, he could see a man's footprint in the damp soil.

The Scene of Crimes Officer came and stood behind him. Saltfleet glanced at his boots, then at the footprint.

'Have you looked in there?'

'Not yet.'

'Somebody has. Look.'

The Constable got down on his knees and examined the footprint. Then he circled round the bed until he saw a way clear among the flowers. He tiptoed in, moving with surprising lightness. After a moment he said: 'I think we've got something.'

'The knife?'

'No.' He crouched and carefully moved the flowers aside. 'But it's been here.'

By taking a long stride over the lavender, Saltfleet could see what he was looking at. A dahlia stalk had been broken in the middle by an impact, and the leaf had an obvious bloodstain; because the dew on it was wet, the stain was still red.

Fitch came over. 'Found something?'

'The place where he threw the knife. But it's gone. He must have thrown it away in a panic, then decided to come back for it. There's his footprint.'

Fitch said warmly: 'Nice work, Evans.'

The Constable coloured, and glanced at Saltfleet. 'Thank you, sir.'

Saltfleet said: 'Well, I'll be off. If you feel like a cup of coffee, you know where I am – number eleven.'

Fitch said: 'Thanks. I might well do that.'

Saltfleet turned to the Constable. 'By the way, do you happen to know if Elfie's still operating in this area?'

'Elfie? No, I don't know the name.'

The Detective Sergeant said: 'You mean the redhaired prostitute? Elfie . . . what's her name . . . Yes, she's still around.'

'Oh, that one,' Fitch said. 'The one who organised the protest. Yes, she's still around all right. Think she might be able to help us?'

'No, I shouldn't think so. I met her when I was working on the Thames Nude murders . . . thought I might look her up. See you later.'

The smell of frying bacon met him as he came into the house. Coffee was percolating on the stove. Miranda said: 'I've just been talking to a policeman – he was making door-to-door enquiries.'

'Did he tell you what it was all about?'

'He said they were investigating a murder.'

'That's right.' He sat down at the kitchen table, and she

17

poured him coffee. 'Some poor devil of a sailor.'

'How was he killed?'

'Stabbed to death.'

'For money?'

'I don't think so. My guess is that there was some kind of sexual motive.'

'Why?'

'His trousers were pulled down.' He decided not to elaborate before they ate breakfast.

'How horrible.' She gave a grimace of disgust. 'Do you think there's much of that kind of thing around here?'

He could see she wanted reassurance. 'No more than anywhere else. Plenty of prostitution, of course. Do you remember the Thames Nude murders in the mid-1960s – Jack the Stripper? He used to strangle prostitutes and leave their bodies on the foreshore of the Thames. Several victims used the same pub in Portobello Road.'

'And why do you think this sailor was killed?'

He shrugged. 'Perhaps some kind of a quarrel. Perhaps they were on drugs. There's only one thing that puzzles me.'

'What's that?'

'He threw away the knife in the middle of a flower bed as he left – obviously in a panic. Then he came back for it – probably realizing it might have fingerprints. Now you'd think he'd just crash his way into the middle of the flowerbed, find it, and then get out. But he tiptoed in, taking great care not to leave an obvious trail. Why should he do that?'

'Perhaps he didn't want you to realise he'd come back.'

'But why? What difference could it make? There was a body lying a few feet away. If he wanted to cover up his trail, why didn't he drag it into the bushes, where it might not be found for a day or two? And remove the seaman's papers, so it couldn't be identified? Then it might not have been found until the trail had gone cold.'

'He was probably in too much of a hurry.'

'No, he wasn't – or he'd have trampled into the

18

flowerbed . . .'

'Then what do *you* think?'

'I don't. I just get a kind of feeling . . . a feeling of something a bit odd . . .'

She placed his breakfast in front of him. 'You don't have to think about it. It's not your case, and you're supposed to be on holiday.'

He took the hint, and dropped the subject. In fact, at this stage of a murder enquiry, he never tried to think his way to a solution; he tried to allow his instincts and intuitions to operate. Sometimes, these amounted to something very like second-sight. In the Thames Nude case, for example, he had experienced from the beginning a curious certainty that the murderer would never be caught – that he would commit suicide when the chase got too close. And later, when their chief suspect committed suicide, and the murders ceased, he had tried to explain to himself how he had known. He reasoned that a man who killed women in the throes of his own sexual pleasure – strangling them as they performed oral sex – was somehow different from the usual sex killer: that there was an element of the spoilt child about him. And such a man would become subject to hysterical self-pity when he felt the police were getting close. Yet the next time he had to deal with a sex killer – the child-rapist Jones – he had to admit that there was again the same element of the spoilt child about him, the feeling that his own desires mattered more than anything in the world. And Jones was definitely not the suicidal type. Saltfleet had to admit that his intuition could not be explained in logical terms: it was simply a strange way of *knowing*, a kind of contact with the mind of the murderer, like accidentally being connected to someone else's telephone conversation. In the present case, his intuition told him there was something odd about the man who had returned for the knife.

He was drinking his third cup of coffee, and reading the *Telegraph* when the doorbell rang. Miranda called from the hallway: 'Who could that be?'

'Might be Fitch, the DDI from Hammersmith. I told him to come in for a coffee.'

Miranda opened the door; he heard her say with surprise: 'Hello, Francis!' A man's voice said: 'Hello, my dear. What a pleasant surprise.' He recognised the precise, slightly nasal tone of Aspinal, the pathologist from University College Hospital. Miranda said: 'Gregory's through there.'

Aspinal came in, followed by Fitch. He was a tall, thin man, with a sardonic mouth and a manner that always reminded Saltfleet of a caustic public school master. Many of Saltfleet's colleagues disliked him; but throughout the dozen or so cases on which they had worked together, Saltfleet had always found him trustworthy and helpful.

'Nice to see you, Gregory. Do you know George Fitch?'

'Of course. Sit down. Coffee for both of you?'

'Black for me,' Aspinal said. 'I had rather an exhausting night last night.'

Saltfleet refrained from asking about it; Aspinal was unmarried, and had a succession of beautiful mistresses. Saltfleet was not sure whether he envied him or felt sorry for him.

'How about a spot of brandy in it? That might do you good.'

'What an excellent idea.'

Saltfleet brought in the cut-glass brandy carafe from the sideboard in the front room. Aspinal stopped him as he started to pour it into his coffee. 'Do you mind if I have a separate glass? If I'm not mistaken, that's Remy Martin, and it seems a pity to spoil the taste.' Without a word, Miranda disappeared, and returned with brandy glasses.

'For you?' Saltfleet held the carafe above Fitch's cup.

'Oh, thanks. In my coffee. Not too much . . .'

Fitch was obviously slightly overawed by the house; but, since this was a social call, he had decided to drop the 'sir'.

He was one of those detectives who looked prematurely aged and slightly overweight, as if the years of struggle to become a Divisional Detective Inspector had not been entirely worth it; he looked tired, or perhaps merely discouraged. But the smell of the brandy obviously cheered him.

Aspinal asked: 'On holiday?'

'Until next Wednesday. We're looking after the house for Miranda's brother.'

Aspinal smiled at Miranda. 'You must be delighted to have a murder on your doorstep – something to keep Gregory occupied.' He was always mildly flirtatious with her, and she recognised it for what it was: a form of courtesy.

'Don't say that! I'm hoping to get him to go shopping and visit a few theatres.'

Saltfleet smiled at her. 'It's a promise.' He turned to Fitch. 'Any idea about motive yet?'

Miranda sighed and said: 'Excuse me.' When she had left the room Fitch said: 'The doctor here thinks it could be jealousy.'

'Only a guess.' Aspinal lowered his voice, in case Miranda was within hearing. 'I've only encountered three similar cases – with mutilation of the genitals. All involved jealousy.'

Saltfleet said: 'I didn't notice any mutilation.'

'Only attempted. But it was there.'

'And if he was a Polish sailor – presumably on shore leave – he wouldn't have much time to get involved in a love triangle.'

'That's what we've got to find out.' Fitch opened his notebook. 'We've traced his ship – the *Stefan Batory*. It docked in Tilbury on Thursday with sulphur and copper ore. The Tilbury CID man should be there now.'

Saltfleet asked Aspinal: 'Why didn't he scream?'

'He was stabbed in the heart. He must have died instantly.'

'What was the angle of the wound?'

Aspinal chuckled, and slapped Saltfleet lightly on the shoulder. 'Good, Gregory, very good.'

Fitch's face betrayed his bewilderment.

Aspinal said: 'It was upward, from below the ribcage.'

Saltfleet said: 'Aha.'

Fitch looked from one to the other, waiting.

Saltfleet explained: 'It's not easy to stab somebody in the heart – the ribs tend to divert the blow. Do you remember Johnny Berman?' Fitch shook his head. 'He was an East End gangster who was doing a complicated double-cross. We got a tip that his boss – a man named Royce – had him murdered. The body turned up a few months later in a wood near Oxshott. It was badly decomposed, but Francis was able to establish that he'd been stabbed in the heart from below – at an angle – with a long-bladed knife. Royce's right-hand man was a Corsican named . . . Alfredo something. We checked with the Corsican police – Renucci, that was his name . . . We checked with the Corsican police and found that Renucci was suspected of several gang murders in Marseilles, and that the victim was always stabbed in the heart from below. He'd perfected an upward thrust of the knife so it went in just below the ribs. We couldn't pin it on Renucci, but we got him deported for another crime . . .'

Fitch said: 'You think this could be a gang murder?'

Saltfleet shrugged. 'It's possible. This sailor could have been involved in some racket – drug-smuggling, perhaps. But that's not what I had in mind. I was thinking that if he was stabbed in the heart from below, the killer must have been someone who knew how to use a knife.'

'You say it's a Corsican method?'

'I'm not sure. You'd probably find it's common to brigands and bandits in the Mediterranean area.'

Aspinal said: 'If I remember rightly, the Greek brigands used to go for the windpipe with the same kind of blow.' He made an upward jerk with his hand.

The doorbell rang; they heard Miranda open the door. A moment later, she looked into the kitchen. 'Inspector Fitch. They want you to ring the station.'

'Thank you, ma'am. I wonder if I could use your phone?'

Saltfleet said: 'There's one in the next room.'

When they were alone, he asked Aspinal: 'Any ideas?'

'It's a puzzling one. I might be able to tell you more when I've done the PM. But I doubt it.' Saltfleet pushed the brandy decanter towards him. 'Ah, thank you. Just a little. The answer probably lies in the dead man's private life. He may have had a mistress in London, or a male lover. He may, as you say, have been involved in some racket – drug-smuggling, even spying. In which case, the sexual aspect is a deliberate red herring . . . You're lucky it's not your case.'

Saltfleet smiled, shaking his head. 'I almost feel it is.' He reached behind him and closed the kitchen door. 'I'll tell you something I haven't told Fitch. Something woke me up in the night – our bedroom overlooks the square.'

'No one else seems to have heard anything.'

'I don't know whether I did. I just woke up. I don't even know what time it was.'

'Did you look out?'

'Yes. I went to the window. It was bright moonlight, but I couldn't see anything. I heard something, though – a woman's footsteps . . .'

'Running?'

'No, no. There was nothing odd about them. Just normal footsteps, walking briskly, but not in a hurry.'

Aspinal shook his head. 'I don't see how it could have been a woman – Fitch showed me the footprint in the flowerbed. Unless, of course, there were two of them. Are you going to tell Fitch?'

'I don't see any point. It might send him off on a false

trail – looking for a woman. And I don't . . .'

The door opened and Fitch came in.

'I'll have to leave you, gentlemen.'

'Anything new?'

'Not much. Our man at Tilbury says this chap left his ship at about two o'clock yesterday afternoon. He had a reputation as a loner – usually went off on his own. They think he was going to try to pick up a woman. And the murder weapon could have been his own knife. Apparently he usually carried a kind of flick knife – the kind they use in the Baltic for gutting fish. His mates say he always carried it – ever since he got mugged in Glasgow. It wasn't in his pockets.'

Saltfleet asked: 'How about money?'

'He had a hundred pounds from the ship's purser before he left. He still had eighty in his wallet.'

Fitch drained the remains of his coffee. 'Thanks for that – just what I needed. I'd better be off.'

Saltfleet went with him to the door. 'I'm going to try ringing this woman Elfie – do you want me to sound her out? She knows everything that goes on around here.'

'Oh, thanks. You know where to contact me – or my Detective Sergeant – Lawson.'

'So long as Scottie doesn't think I'm interfering.' Chief Superintendent Scottie MacPhail was Fitch's boss at the Yard, and was inclined to be resentful of poaching on his territory.

Fitch grinned. 'I shan't tell him if you don't.'

In the kitchen, Aspinal was finishing his coffee. Saltfleet said: 'It's strange about the money.'

'Strange?'

'If he was really involved in some racket, they'd have taken the money to make it look like robbery.'

Aspinal stood up.

'Do you want me to ring you if I find anything interesting at the PM?'

24

Saltfleet said: 'No thanks.'

'Are you sure?'

'Quite sure. It's not my case, is it?'

TWO

When they came back from shopping, three hours later, Geraldine was sitting on the doorstep. He felt a surge of delight, followed by an immediate chill of caution.

'What are you doing here?'

She kissed him. 'I got bored with Thames Ditton so I thought I'd come and see you and Mummy.'

They went into the kitchen, and Miranda unloaded her purchases on the table. Geraldine opened the refrigerator and poured herself a glass of milk.

'I'm dying of hunger . . . Are you doing anything nice this afternoon?'

'We thought we'd go to Regents Park and have tea there.'

'Oh good! Can we go to the zoo?'

'I expect so.'

Saltfleet said: 'I'm not staying for lunch. I've got to meet someone. I'll be back in about an hour.'

In the garden opposite the screens had been removed, and there was no longer any sign that anything had happened. He wondered what they had done about the bloodstains on the grass: probably covered them with leaves. By this time Aspinal should have finished the post-mortem.

As he walked towards Portobello Road, his thoughts turned back to Geraldine. He understood why she had come. She felt as he did: a sense of misery, a desire to heal the breach between them. But there was nothing to be done.

They were not lovers; they could not kiss and start all over again. The situation was maddening because there seemed to be no solution. At least he was grateful to her for making the effort.

The George was crowded. He recognised Elfie in the corner of the saloon bar; she was seated at a table with two other women. The red hair was unmistakable. But as he came closer, he realised how much she had changed. She had been attractive, almost beautiful, in a hard brassy way, with her high cheekbones and full lips; now, he realised, she had turned into a middle-aged woman, slightly overweight.

'Hello, Elfie. Can I get you a drink?'

'Hello, Greg!' She had a pleasantly hoarse voice, too low for a woman. 'Nice to see you.' It struck him with surprise that she meant it.

'Your glass is empty.'

'All right, thanks. A gin and tonic.'

'How about your friends?'

The two women shook their heads. 'No thanks.'

When he returned with the drinks, they were gone.

'Hope I didn't drive them away?'

'They were going anyway. Cheers.'

The bitter felt pleasantly cool and sharp in his throat; the morning's shopping had made him dry.

'How's Joe?'

'Not too bad. We're married now, you know.'

'Yes, I heard.'

'He's got a bad back – has to spend a lot of his time lying down.'

The idea was incongruous; 'South American Joe' was one of the toughest pimps he had ever encountered, and was notoriously belligerent.

They talked about old times and mutual acquaintances. She still had the same vitality, and the aggressive honesty that had always appealed to him. But he was saddened by how much she had changed physically. When he had last seen her, sixteen years ago, her figure had been exceptional, with big, rounded breasts. The orange-gold hair made every man look at her; but it was the hips and thighs that drew surreptitious glances. She used to wear tight skirts, and had a disturbing way of turning her body from the hips that drew them tight across her thighs, and made the pubic mound stand out. Joe used to slap her rump and say she had a gold mine inside her knickers. In fact, she had often made more than a hundred pounds in an evening. Now the breasts were as large, but no longer jutted under the material of her blouse; the waistline had gone, and the skin of her neck was mottled. Only the face had not changed; but then, that had never been pretty, with the big, masculine jaw, the uneven teeth, and the bridge of the nose that had been slightly flattened in some quarrel.

He had told her about the murder on the telephone; but he decided not to mention it unless she raised the subject. He wanted her to trust him; she was more valuable as an ally than as an informer. As she drank her second gin, she told him about the campaign she had organised among the local prostitutes, to protest against police harassment; they had occupied a church and stayed there for a week.

He said: 'But surely, there aren't many of them left on the streets now?'

'Oh, not now. This was ten years ago. It's changed a lot since then.' She chuckled. 'Most of us didn't realise what was going on at first. I came up behind Joe one day when he was reading a magazine, and I saw this picture – some girl with her pants down and her finger inside herself. I said: "Christ, where'd you get that?" and he said: "Bought it at the newsagent at Notting Hill Gate." Couldn't believe my eyes, so I sent him out to get some more. They were all the same – full of women showing everything they'd got. So we all started advertising in these magazines instead of in shop windows. And of course, we've never looked back. Some of 'em can make a thousand quid a week.'

'But the rooms must be expensive.'

'Fifty quid a day on average. But when you can charge between twenty and a hundred quid a time – depending what he wants – that's nothing. And of course, a lot of them share, so it's only twenty-five a day.'

'Two in one room?'

'Not at the same time. You get a lot of part-timers now – housewives from the suburbs who do it for a bit of pin money. Perhaps two of 'em get together, one does mornings, the other afternoons.'

He asked casually: 'You still involved?'

'Oh yes. Joe won't let me retire yet. I specialise in what we call domination: thigh-length black boots, black cloak, bull whip, the lot.'

Saltfleet roared with laughter at the image this evoked; she laughed with him. He said finally: 'Well, I'm glad it's going so well.' He meant it.

'Oh, it's all right. Funnily enough, I don't really enjoy all this domination stuff. The other day I had to walk up and down some bloke wearing high heels, and I slipped and nearly castrated him – there was blood all over the place. It nearly put me off for good.'

'How did he react?'

'He didn't mind. What bothered him was when *I* looked upset. He wanted to believe I'd done it on purpose, to make him suffer. As soon as I called him a contemptible pig, he cheered up no end . . .'

Although he laughed with her, a stab of pity and protectiveness made him think of Geraldine; it was a sudden recognition that women are too vulnerable. She noticed the shadow that crossed his face.

'Does that shock you?'

He made the first excuse that came to hand.

'Oh no. I was thinking of that poor devil of a Polish sailor. Somebody had tried to castrate him . . .'

'Did they . . .' The way she stared into her drink made

him aware she was leaving something unsaid. He let the silence lengthen. She said: 'He was in here last night, you know.'

'Are you sure?'

'Those two women I was talking to when you came in . . . He tried to pick them up in here.'

'How do you know it's the same man?'

'Foreigner with close-cropped red hair and arms like an ape . . .'

'He tried to pick up *both* of them?'

'That's right. Said he liked two women at the same time.'

'Why didn't they?'

'They didn't like the look of him. They thought he was a bit kinky.'

'In what way?'

She shrugged. 'It's a certain type, isn't it? A bloke who wants two women at the same time probably wants them to take off all their clothes and kneel at his feet. He wants to feel he's the lord and master.'

'A sadist?'

'Probably. He's certain to want something a bit peculiar. He might want them both to go down on him at the same time.'

He decided not to press for further elucidation. He sipped his beer thoughtfully.

'That probably explains a lot. In fact, it's *got* to be the answer. He wanted something a bit peculiar – as you say – and he ended up dead.'

'That sounds right to me.'

'Then I've been thinking along the wrong lines.'

'What did you think?'

'The angle of the knife wound made me think it was a man who was accustomed to using a knife – perhaps a Corsican or a Lascar. Can you think of anyone of that type in the area?'

She thought for a moment. 'No. Nobody.' It struck

Saltfleet that her own husband had always carried a knife. She seemed to read his thoughts. 'And it's not Joe – he's got a bad back.'

He smiled. 'I'm sure it's not Joe. Did your friends say anything else?''

She pulled a face at him. 'Why are you interested, anyway? You told me you were on holiday. Can't they do without you?'

This semi-aggressive teasing convinced him that she had something more to say. He said: 'Wouldn't you be curious if somebody got murdered outside your bedroom window?'

'No. It happens every night.'

'What else did your friends say?'

She sipped her drink, enjoying making him wait. He was, after all, a copper. She said finally: 'When they left, he was talking with a little blonde tart outside.'

'Did they know her?'

'No. Not her name, anyway. They've seen her around.'

'Have you seen her around?'

'Yes.'

'Do you know her name?'

'No.'

He looked at her, and she stared back at him. She was obviously telling the truth.

'Can you describe her?'

She made a contemptuous grimace. 'Not a professional. Little pale-faced thing with eyes like a frightened rabbit.'

'When you say not a professional, do you mean she does it to pay the rent? Or for fun?'

'At a guess, I'd say for fun.'

In his Vice Squad days, Saltfleet had come across a number of young girls who had become prostitutes because they thought it romantic, as some boys dream of being bandits or pirates. Most of them were middle class.

'Working-class type?'

'Hard to say – I haven't talked to her. But I'd say no.'

31

'Any idea where she might be found?'

She shook her head, frowning. 'She must live in the area . . . I'll tell you who might know, Terry Nash.'

'Where can I find him?'

'Her. Want to hang on while I phone?'

She was gone before he could reply. That was typical of Elfie. When he had first known her, the local police regarded her as uncooperative and bloody-minded. But in the Thames Nude case, he had quickly realised that she could be as useful as half-a-dozen men on the beat, and set out to win her trust. It had paid off: a tip from Elfie had helped them track down the chief suspect, the man who had later committed suicide.

She was back almost immediately. She said: 'You're in luck. Come on.' She picked up her glass and drained it.

He followed her out.

'Does she know the girl?'

'Yes.'

The house was in a back street off Westbourne Park Road. Elfie gave three quick rings. The girl who answered the door wore a neat maid's uniform with a white apron; she had a pale face and jet black hair, worn straight. As she led them upstairs, he caught a glimpse of bare thigh above the black stockings.

They followed her into a kitchen. Elfie said: 'Terry, this is Inspector Saltfleet.' That was his rank when he first knew her. 'He's an old friend.' The girl's handshake was cool and firm. She was not pretty, with her snub nose and wide mouth, but she had the mobile face of a natural comedienne.

Saltfleet said: 'This is a murder investigation.'

'Yes, Elfie told me. That Polish chap.'

'You've heard about it?'

'It was on the local news at midday.'

'He was seen talking to a blonde girl with a pale face. Elfie thought you might know her.'

She nodded. 'That sounds as if it might be Rosie.'

32

'Any idea of her other name?'

'Afraid not.'

'Or where she lives?'

'No. Except she's a patient in a loony bin.'

He stared in surprise. 'Are you sure?'

'That's what she told me.'

'Did she say where?'

'Somewhere at the back of Stanley Crescent, that area.'

'About a hundred yards from the scene of the murder.'

She wrinkled her nose at him. '*She* wouldn't be mixed up in anything like that.'

She spoke with such contemptuous conviction that he asked: 'How can you be sure?'

'She's just not the type. She wouldn't say boo to a goose.'

There was a sound of a door closing, then footsteps descending the stairs. Terry said: 'Excuse me', and opened the kitchen door. Saltfleet was startled to see a figure dressed entirely in yellow, wearing a black rubber mask that covered the entire head; it looked like a monster from a Hollywood horror film.

Terry said: 'Hello Moira. I didn't think you'd be finished yet.'

'I'm not. He's taking his time.' The accent was West Indian. As she came into the kitchen, Saltfleet saw she was naked under the thin rubber suit. She reached up with both hands and wrenched the mask off her head. Then she noticed Saltfleet.

'Oh, sorry. You waitin' to come up?'

Terry said quickly: 'No. This is a friend of Elfie's.'

'Good.' She collapsed on to a kitchen chair. 'I need a cup of tea.' She looked warm; the brown face was beaded with sweat.

Terry switched on the electric kettle.

'What have you done with him?'

'He's strung up.' She chuckled. 'He'll be all right.'

Elfie said: 'Moira, this is Inspector Saltfleet.' She added

33

quickly: 'He's not here on official business.'

Terry said: 'He's asking about Rosie.'

She grunted contemptuously, and took a cigarette from a packet on the table. Saltfleet tried to keep his eyes off the pink nipples that stood out under the transparent rubber; it had never struck him before that a rubber suit could be so attractive. He struck a match for her, and she nodded her thanks. She asked: 'When the next one due?'

'Not till half-past-three. It's them two rabbis.'

She sighed. 'They're all right. They're nice.' She asked Saltfleet: 'Rosie in trouble?'

'Oh no. But she was seen talking to a man who was found murdered this morning.'

She nodded listlessly; she was obviously tired. She said after a pause: 'She wouldn't kill nobody.'

'So Terry says.'

Terry said: 'Anyone else like tea? No?' She handed the black girl a mug of tea. 'Want me to see he's all right?'

'No. He'll be OK.' She tasted the tea, then sighed, and unzipped the rubber suit down to the waist. Saltfleet observed that, without their covering, her breasts no longer seemed sexually exciting. He asked her conversationally: 'Do you know Rosie?'

'Oh sure. She been here.'

'Has she?'

Terry said: 'She was talking about turning professional.'

Moira nodded wearily. 'She be no good.'

He asked: 'Why not?'

It was Terry who answered. 'She's a masochist. She likes being beaten. She probably go and get herself killed or robbed or something.'

Elfie said: 'I told you. She's kinky. You've got to treat this like a business. It's not a way of getting kicks.' For some reason, this struck all three women as funny, and they burst into laughter.

34

'Any idea of her address?'

Still laughing, Moira said: 'I've got it in my phone book somewhere.' She turned to Terry. 'You know where it is.' Terry nodded and left the room. Saltfleet looked at his watch, and realised with a shock that it was almost three o'clock. He had promised to be back in an hour. He was wondering whether to ask if he could use the telephone when Terry's voice called: 'Moira, quick. I think he's dead.'

The two women rushed out of the room; Saltfleet followed them. The door at the top of the stairs stood open. Against the opposite wall there was a large wooden crucifix; a man in a yellow rubber suit hung on it, suspended from the wrists, his head slumped on his chest. A limp penis was hanging out of a hole in the suit.

Saltfleet supported the man under the armpits while the women loosened the leather straps that held him. He was a grey-haired man of about seventy; the mouth hung open and spittle ran from the corner. He did not seem to be breathing.

Saltfleet helped to carry him over to the huge double bed; Terry knelt over and placed her ear against his chest.

'It's all right. His heart's beating. He's fainted, that's all.'

Moira breathed a sigh of relief. 'Thank the Lord.'

With the instinct of many years, Saltfleet observed automatically the contents of the room: the bright silk cushion-covers, the knick-knacks on the mantelshelf, the glass animals on the dressing-table, the picture of the small black girl with ringlets on the windowsill. Above the bed was a raffiawork doll with a black face and pointed teeth, whose fierce brown eyes seemed to glare at them. The man on the bed stirred.

Moira said: 'He's waking up. Get out, quick.'

Saltfleet tiptoed out of the room and down the stairs. Terry was giggling again. She said: 'We do have fun, don't we?'

In the kitchen, Elfie said: 'I'll have that cup of tea after all.'

Terry asked him: 'One for you?'

'No thanks, I've got to go. Did you get the phone number?'

'Oh yes.' She took the notebook out of the pocket of the maid's apron. 'You'll find it under R.'

He found the word 'Rossy' scrawled in a childish hand, followed by a Notting Hill telephone number. In brackets opposite was the word 'Mori'.

He copied down the number. 'Any idea what Mori means?'

'Mori? I think it's death in Latin . . . momento mori.' She looked over his shoulder. 'Ah, no. I think it's the name of the bloke who runs the place.'

'Ah, thank you.' He wrote down the name. 'Elfie, thanks for all your help. I'll let you know if there are any developments. Let's meet again soon. I've got to dash now – I promised my wife and daughter I'd take them out to tea. See you later.'

From the telephone box on the corner, he rang the Hammersmith station and asked for Detective Sergeant Fitch. The man on the desk said Fitch was at Tilbury. He promised to call back later. He started to dial Miranda's number, then decided it could wait for a moment. Instead, he rang the Notting Hill number. When a female voice answered, he said: 'Could I speak to Dr Mori please?'

'I'm afraid Dr Moro is engaged at the moment.' She emphasised the name like a schoolmistress correcting a pupil.

'Could you tell me when he'll be free?'

'I'm afraid I can't. Could you leave a message?'

'I'm a police officer, and I wanted to ask him some questions.'

'I see.' The voice was very sharp and controlled. 'I'll give him your message.'

Saltfleet suppressed his rising irritation.

'I need to see him as soon as possible.'

'You want me to make you an appointment?'

'Yes please.'

There was a long pause – he sensed she was deliberately keeping him waiting – then she said: 'Monday morning is the soonest he could manage. Half-past ten.'

Keeping his voice level, Saltfleet said:' 'I want to see him now.'

'I'm afraid that is quite impossible. He's very busy.'

'Would you mind bringing him to the telephone?'

'I've told you that is impossible. He's with a patient. I suggest you ring back in an hour. He may be free then.'

'Could you give me your address there?'

'You don't have it?'

'I wouldn't ask you for it if I did.'

'I'm afraid I am not authorised to give you this address. You will have to obtain it through the proper channels. Goodbye.' She hung up.

Saltfleet chuckled and said: 'Bloody bitch.' It controlled his rising anger.

He looked up 'Moro' in the London telephone directory; there were only two, and it was obvious that neither was the one he wanted. He dialled the operator, and asked for the Subscriber Clerk for the Notting Hill area. When the man came on the line he said: 'This is Chief Superintendent Saltfleet, CID. I've got a telephone number here and I need the address.'

'Yes, sir. Could you give it to me?' Saltfleet dictated the number. 'What police station are you ringing from?'

'I'm in a public call box. But if you like, you could ring the operator at New Scotland Yard and give her the number. I'll get it from there,'

'Oh, that won't be necessary, sir. Would you hang on a moment?' After a pause, he dictated the address: 'It's the Institute of Sexual Science, 1 Lansdowne Gardens, West

Eleven. The subscriber's name is Dr Robert Moro.'

Saltfleet thanked him and hung up. Then he rang Miranda.

'Look, darling, I'm sorry about this, but I think I've turned up a lead . . .'

'Yes, I thought it must be something of the sort.' There was no suggestion of reproach. Although they had been married thirty years, the sweetness of her temper never ceased to surprise him.

'I've got just one more call to make. I'll try and get back in half an hour or so.'

'Oh don't hurry. We're both watching a film on television.'

A taxi stopped a few yards beyond the telephone box, and a passenger climbed out. Saltfleet said quickly: 'Thanks, darling. See you soon.'

He climbed in and asked the driver to take him to Lansdowne Gardens.

THREE

It was one of those quiet roads with private walled gardens and an air of permanent desertion. The taxi dropped him on the corner, outside a house with a high, yellow-distempered wall. The green door looked very solid, and there was no bell beside it. He tried the handle, expecting to find it locked; but it swung open easily. The tall Victorian house was detached from its neighbours; like the garden and the unmowed lawn, it had an air of casual neglect.

He mounted the steps to the portico. Above the front door, on a wooden plaque, there was a Latin inscription: AMORI ET DOLORI SACRUM. A brass plate beside the door read: Institute of Sexual Science. Director, Robert Moro, MD. When he pressed the doorbell, it rang in the hall; almost immediately, the door was opened by a broad-shouldered youth.

'Is Dr Moro in, please?'

The youth looked at him blankly, as if he had spoken in a foreign language. He had a lean, cadaverous face and spiky hair; if he had been older, Saltfleet might have taken him for a punch-drunk boxer. When Saltfleet repeated the question, he nodded vacantly, and stood aside for him to enter. A woman's voice called from the stairs: 'Who is it, Frankie?'

It was unmistakably the voice he had spoken to on the phone. As she came down the stairs, the first thing he saw was red stockings; after that, a tight black skirt and tailored white blouse. She was in her mid-twenties, with blond hair that was drawn back from her ears. She snapped at the youth: 'How many times do I have to tell you *not* to answer the door?' She turned to Saltfleet. 'What is it?'

'I'm Chief Superintendent Saltfleet of the CID. I want to speak to Dr Moro.'

She obviously recognised his voice. Face to face, she was less sure of herself, but the control was still there. 'I'm afraid that's impossible. He's busy.' She made it sound like a secretary answering the telephone.

Making his voice deliberately flat and neutral, Saltfleet said firmly: 'Please tell him I want to talk to him about a murder.'

She stared back at him coolly, calculating how far she could go on obstructing him. He noticed that she had a bruise on her left cheek. She said finally: 'Wait here, please.'

She turned her back on him and went up the stairs. Looking at the calves in the red stockings he thought: Infuriating bitch. But lovely legs.

The youth continued to stand like a sentinel, with one hand on the door latch. Saltfleet looked into the blank face with mild curiosity; the youth continued to stare back for a moment, then turned his eyes away and looked into the distance.

Down the corridor, a door opened, and a woman with long, dark hair looked out; on the upper half of her body she was wearing only a bra. She peered curiously at Saltfleet, then smiled and closed the door again. Saltfleet studied the youth out of the corner of his eye, trying to decide what created the effect of subnormality. The shoulders were very broad and powerful, but there was nothing else to explain the ape-like impression he produced; his body was well-proportioned, and the face almost good-looking. Saltfleet decided it was some indefinable emanation of the personality.

From the top of the stairs, the girl's voice said: 'Would you come up.' As soon as he moved away from the door, the youth closed it. There was something slightly eerie about the motion, as if he was some sort of mindless guardian.

She led him into a large room at the top of the stairs; it had probably once been the drawing-room. She said: 'Dr Moro will be with you as soon as he's ready.' Her voice implied that the wait might be a long one. She closed the door behind her with a sharp click.

The room seemed to be a combination of office and museum, with glass cases round the walls. The windows overlooked the garden, and the crescent beyond, with its autumnal trees. The furniture was pleasantly old-fashioned, and the huge mahogany desk looked as if it was too big to be manoeuvred through the door. Behind it, above the mantelpiece, hung a large, brown-tinted photograph of a mild-faced man with drooping eyelids, a scrubby moustache and a Semitic nose.

Saltfleet moved slowly from one case to the next. They contained a mixture of exhibits that he found puzzling; the typed notices attached to the glass were in German. The one that drew his eyes contained various items of old-fashioned ladies' underwear, including red silk camiknickers trimmed with white lace; there was also a rawhide whip, a pair of riding boots with spurs, a pair of old brass handcuffs, and a Mauser pistol. A photograph at the back of the case showed a middle-aged woman with heavily mascara-ed eyes and a sensuously painted mouth; the type that would once have been called a vamp. The photograph in the next case was of a pockmarked man with a Kaiser Wilhelm moustache, its ends arrogantly twisted upwards. The exhibits included a length of chain, some rope, a coil of rusty barbed-wire, several knives, a set of burgling tools and an enema. A small case further on contained only one exhibit: what was unmistakably a severed human hand.

He was studying this so intently that he was startled when a voice behind him said: 'I must apologise for keeping you waiting.'

A small, grey-haired man was holding out his hand. Behind the rimless glasses, the eyes were sharp and friendly. He was casually dressed in a baggy grey tweed suit, and wore a spotted bow tie.

'My name is Moro.' His handshake was firm and strong.

'Chief Superintendent Saltfleet, CID.'

'Won't you please take a seat?' It was said with such courtesy that it sounded as if he was offering an expensive cigar. Saltfleet sat in the chair facing the desk.

'This is a fascinating place you have here, doctor.'

He could see he had said the right thing. 'Thank you.' The eyes gleamed with pleasure. 'These are exhibits from the Institut für Sexual Wissenschaft in Berlin – I rescued them before the Nazis burnt it down. I was assistant to the late Dr Magnus Hirschfeld.' He gestured at the photograph over the mantelpiece. 'He was one of the great pioneers of sexual science. He built up a remarkable collection of exhibits. These, for example' – he pointed to the nearest case, which contained a suit of clothes, a cleaver and a coil of rope – belonged to Georg Grossmann, the cannibal murderer. He used to lure girls up to his room, butcher them, and eat the tenderest parts of their bodies. The rest he sold for meat.'

'What about those?' Saltfleet indicated the case containing underwear.

'Ah, that woman is actually Colonel Wilhelm Moeller, the German intelligence officer who was also a Russian spy. The great love of his life was a Russian courtesan who used to allow him to wear her underclothes – he had those under his uniform when he was arrested.'

'Who is that?' He pointed to the photograph of the man with the Kaiser moustache.

'A pervert named Grau who terrorised Berlin in the 1920s. One of his more unpleasant habits was to break into houses and force women to strip at gunpoint. Then he used to chain them up and administer enemas. One interesting point is that the gun was never loaded – he had a horror of loud noises.'

'And this?' He pointed to the severed hand.

'The hand of the Algerian sex murderer Hassan Ouargla, who killed boys. He was sentenced to be dismembered alive, and the Bey presented the museum with his right hand.'

Saltfleet said: 'Incredible.' He was surprised to find that, after thirty years of experience with homicide, he could still feel nauseated.

'Ah, human nature is incredible, my dear sir.' Moro gestured expansively, his eyes radiating enthusiasm; he might have been speaking of works of art rather than sex criminals. 'But now, please tell me what I can do for you.'

'I'm investigating a murder.'

'Most interesting.' Moro looked pleased. 'What kind of a murder?'

'A sex murder.'

'Even more interesting. And you want to consult me? Please describe the circumstances.'

'The victim was a Polish sailor. He was found early this morning in Ladbroke Terrace Gardens.'

'That is nearby, is it not?'

'Just across the road. The man had been stabbed to death, and there had been an attempt to mutilate the genitals.'

Moro's manner became very serious. 'And in what way can I help you?'

'A few hours before he died, he was seen drinking with a blonde girl in a pub in Portobello Road. Her description fits one of your patients. A girl called Rosie.'

'Ah, now I understand. You want to speak to her.'

'If I may. Is she here now?'

'Yes.' He reached out for the intercom on the desk, then stopped. 'Before I send for her, there is something I must say to you.' As he became visibly agitated, the Italian accent, hardly perceptible earlier, suddenly became stronger. He stood up and walked to the window. 'Rosa is basically a depressive. She suffers from what used to be called abulia – inhibition of will. She has a general sense of her own worthlessness. And when she sinks into one of her periodic depressions, she always reacts in the same way. She goes out looking for a man who will ill-treat her. The last time it happened, she was unconscious for two days with a fractured skull. You see what I am trying to say? She is the kind of girl who might end up strangled or battered to death. And I have never known a case of that type in which the patient inflicts violence on another. It would be completely out of character.'

Saltfleet tried to look reassuring. 'I understand that. But it's still necessary to speak to her. She may be able to help us.'

'Of course. But in fact, you have spoken to her already.'

Saltfleet looked at him in bewilderment. 'I have?'

'My secretary – the girl who showed you in.'

Saltfleet's immediate suspicion was that the doctor was lying to protect his patient.

'I think there must be some mistake. Your secretary doesn't fit the description.'

Moro said: 'Are you sure?'

'She certainly doesn't strike me as suffering from – whatever it was you said . . . a feeling of worthlessness.'

'You are right. She doesn't.' He looked almost apologetic. 'But Rosa does. And Rosa and Dorothy happen to share the same body.'

'Ah, I see. You mean she's a schizophrenic?'

'No, sir. Schizophrenia is a completely different illness. The word does not mean a split personality. It means simply a loss of contact with reality – a dissociation of the mind and feelings. Rosa is not a case of schizophrenia, but of what we call multiple personality. It is literally as if two people shared the same body, like two drivers of the same car.'

'Like Jekyll and Hyde?'

Moro looked dubious. 'Well, yes, I suppose so. That has rather substantial connotations. It might be better to speak of a Janus – the god with two faces.'

'Mmmm. I see.' Saltfleet had to think about that for a moment. 'And does your secretary realise she's two people?'

'Theoretically, yes.'

'What does that mean?'

Moro went to the mantelpiece, and took down two china figures of girls in crinolines. 'In most cases of dual personality, one of the personalities knows all about the other. It is as if one of them is up here' – he raised one of the figures in the air – 'and the other is down here. The one up here can see everything the other does. But the one down here is ignorant of the existence of the one up here. That, I say, is usual in such cases. But in this case it is different. Neither of them is able to watch the other. I am trying to find out why.'

'So if one of them committed a murder, the other wouldn't know about it?'

Moro shrugged. 'That is so.'

'That seems very convenient.'

'I see you find it hard to accept. But it is true. I could show you the history of dozens of similar cases.'

Saltfleet said: 'Dr Moro, when I rang your secretary half an hour ago and told her I wanted to see you, she did her best to prevent me from coming. She wouldn't even give me the address of this place.'

Moro said, with real concern: 'I am sorry. She had no right to do that.'

'Then why did she?'

'Not for the reason you think. Not because she has a guilty conscience. You see, another characteristic of these cases of dual personality is that they are opposites. If one is shy, the other is self-confident. If one is timid, the other is aggressive. Rosa is shy and timid, and Dorothy goes to the other extreme.'

Saltfleet said: 'So if Rosie is a masochist, Dorothy ought to be a sadist?'

Moro shook his head violently. 'No. no. That is taking it too far. Masochism and sadism are not personal qualities – they are abnormalities.'

Saltfleet said: 'I see.' But he was unconvinced.

'Perhaps it would be best if you spoke to Dorothy.'

'I'd like to.'

Moro leaned forward and pressed down a lever on the intercom. 'Dorothy, would you come in?' While they waited, he replaced the china ornaments on the shelf. The secretary came in, carrying a pencil and notebook. Moro said: 'Dorothy, this gentleman is a police officer. He would like to ask you a few questions.'

She raised her eyebrows. 'What about?'

Saltfleet said: 'Can you remember where you were at about eleven last night?'

She looked him direct in the eyes. 'I was in my room.'

'Are you quite sure?'

She glanced at Moro. 'Quite sure.'

Saltfleet said: 'Do you recall being in the George in Portobello Road last night?'

Her look of astonishment seemed genuine. 'Of course I don't.' She turned to Moro. 'Is he joking?'

Moro said: 'No, my dear. Answer his question.'

'I have.'

'Do you recall speaking to a man with a foreign accent outside the pub?'

She seemed puzzled, but interested. 'No, I don't. Who was he?'

'A Polish sailor on shore leave from Tilbury.'

She said: 'Ah, now I see.' She turned to Moro. 'He probably wants to talk to Rosa.'

Saltfleet said: 'Aren't you Rosa?'

'Good heavens no!' She asked Moro: 'Haven't you explained?'

'Yes. But he wanted to see for himself.'

She shrugged and turned to Saltfleet. 'I'm very sorry, but you can't. She's not in.'

He was puzzled. 'Not in?'

Moro said: 'Just a phrase we use.'

Saltfleet walked up to her, and raised his hand to her face. She tried to back away, but the desk was behind her. He said: 'Where did you get that bruise on your cheek?'

She flinched as he touched it. For the first time, her self-assurance wavered. Moro said: 'Tell him, my dear.'

'I don't know. I woke up with it this morning.' She asked Moro: 'Has Rosie been in trouble again?'

He said: 'Possibly. We don't know.'

Saltfleet was aware that she wanted to back away, but was unwilling to do it because it would have seemed like flight. It made her uncomfortable to have him so close. He said: 'The Polish sailor was murdered, and I'm investigating his death.'

She looked at Moro; it was her way of escaping Saltfleet's physical presence.

'While Rosie was with him?'

Saltfleet said: 'That's what I'm trying to find out.'

She looked up at him. 'Rosie wouldn't kill anyone. She's too much of a coward.'

'How do you know? I thought you didn't know her?'

Her eyes remained steady. 'I know enough about her to know she wouldn't kill anyone.'

He said: 'Would you?'

'I might.' It was said too coldly to be defiant. She placed

her notebook and pencil on the desk, then took the opportunity to move away.

Saltfleet said: 'You say Rosie's another person. But she's really an aspect of you, isn't she?'

She shrugged contemptuously. 'I hope not. She's an utter fool.' Secure in her personal space, she was again cool and confident.

Moro said: 'Pardon me if I interrupt you, Superintendent, but she is right. She is *not* the same person as Rosa. For practical purposes, they are two different people.'

'But they share the same body?'

'Yes.'

'Then they must also share the same brain. And she ought to know what happened last night.'

Moro said earnestly: 'They share the same brain, but not the same memories. In cases like this, the brain is divided into watertight compartments. It is Rosa you want to talk to.'

He said: 'When can I do that?'

Moro looked uncomfortable. 'I am afraid I cannot answer that.'

The girl said: 'May I go now?'

Moro looked enquiringly at Saltfleet. He shrugged. 'I suppose so.'

The girl went out, and closed the door quietly behind her. Her manner seemed perfectly controlled, but Saltfleet observed that she had left her notebook and pencil on the desk; it was an indication that she was rattled.

Saltfleet said: 'That young lady needs a spanking.'

'Alas, Superintendent, you cannot cure mental illness by spanking.'

Saltfleet said: 'I've got a feeling she's not telling me all she knows.'

Moro made a very Italian gesture with his hands and eyebrows. 'But I do not understand what you think she knows!' There was an openness and honesty about him that

48

made him very likeable.

Saltfleet said: 'Look, Doctor, I'll be frank with you. When I came here today, I didn't really expect to get much out of this girl Rosie. It was just a routine check. Now I've got a feeling – just a kind of instinct – that this girl is holding out on me. I suppose I could be wrong . . .'

Moro said: 'Pardon me, but you would only have to see Rosa to see that she would be incapable of hurting anyone.'

'I'd like to see her.'

Moro smiled suddenly. 'Ah. I can show you something.' He went to a filing cabinet in the corner. After a moment, he returned with a video-cassette. 'I can show you Rosa as she was two years ago.' He inserted the cassette into a video recorder underneath a television set. 'Please take a seat.' He switched on the television and drew the curtains. As a series of lines flickered across the screen, he said: 'I should tell you that this was shortly after Rosa tried to commit suicide. She had been living in a women's hostel.'

As he spoke, the screen cleared. There was a picture of a girl lying on a couch. She had blond shoulder-length hair. The camera came into close-up, and focused on her face. Saltfleet recognised the secretary, Dorothy; but the face was pale and washed-out, and there were dark shadows under the eyes. Saltfleet experienced a sudden contraction of the heart, a sense of unease that he found difficult to explain. The girl on the screen was obviously tense and nervous. Then Moro's voice said: 'You're not worried, are you, Rosa?'

She managed a faint smile. 'No, of course not.'

With a sudden shock, he understood his feeling of vague anxiety. The girl on the screen was like an older version of Geraldine. He stared with fascination, trying not to allow his face to show how deeply he was disturbed. Moro's voice was saying: 'Tell me your name.'

'Rosa Judd.'

'Your age.'

'Twenty-two.'

'Where you were born.'

'South Norwood.'

'That's right. Now I just want you to close your eyes and relax. Relax very deeply. Your eyes are heavy, very heavy, your whole body feels comfortable.' The girl was obviously very suggestible; her eyes closed immediately, and the lines of tension smoothed out from her face. 'Your whole body feels comfortable and heavy.' Moro said, from his chair behind the desk: 'She is an excellent hypnotic subject.' It was strange to hear his voice coming from two places at once. The voice on the screen was saying: 'When I count up to ten you will be deeply asleep. One, two, three, four . . .' The girl was breathing regularly; again, Saltfleet felt a twist of the heart as she reminded him of Geraldine asleep. He found it unbelievable that the girl on the screen was so unlike the secretary who had left the room a few minutes earlier, and so disturbingly like his own daughter.

A hand appeared on the screen, and raised the girl's eyelid; then it lifted her hand and allowed it to fall back again. Moro's voice said: 'Now I want to go back to what we were talking about yesterday. Do you remember?' The girl took some time to reply, then answered softly: 'Yes.'

'You were telling me about your cousin Joe – about how much you loved your cousin Joe.'

The girl smiled faintly. Then she said, in a clear, precise voice: 'I didn't love him.'

Moro said gently: 'But you told me yesterday he was your favourite person.'

The girl said, with calm conviction: 'I hated him.'

Moro said: 'Then why did you tell me yesterday that you loved him?'

She said: 'I didn't.'

Saltfleet leaned forward. He recognised the voice.

Moro said: 'Didn't you love your cousin?'

The girl said decisively: 'No. I thought he was a conceited

idiot.'

It was undoubtedly the voice of the secretary Dorothy. Moro himself seemed disconcerted.

'But didn't you . . . didn't you write in your diary: "Rosa is Joe's slave for life"?'

The girl said: 'She did.'

'Who is she?'

'Rosa.'

'Aren't you Rosa?'

'No.'

'Then who are you?'

The girl shook her head.

Moro said: 'Won't you tell me who you are?'

'Why do you want to know?'

'So I can help you.'

She said, with a coolness that Saltfleet recognised: 'Nobody asked for your help.'

There was a silence. Then Moro said: 'Won't you tell me your name? Just for politeness?'

She said: 'All right. You can call me Dorothy.'

'Good. Thank you. Do you mind talking to me?'

There was a long pause. 'No.'

'But you seem angry. Why are you angry?'

'Because you ask such stupid questions.' As if goaded beyond endurance, the girl opened her eyes and stared up at her questioner.

Moro switched off the video-recorder. Saltfleet was sorry; he wanted to hear more.

Moro said: 'That was Dorothy's first appearance. You can see that she is quite unlike Rosa.'

'Yes, I do see.'

Moro was pleased at the admission; he pressed his point: 'You agree that they are quite different people?'

Saltfleet felt the need to make amends for his earlier doubts. 'It's amazing, and I have to admit that I wouldn't have believed it unless I'd seen it.' He was still brooding on the resemblance to Geraldine. 'How on earth do you explain it?'

Moro made an expressive gesture. 'Psychologists have been trying to explain it for two centuries. So far, no one has succeeded. I have written a book about it myself. All we know for certain is that most of these people have experienced an unhappy childhood, and that some unpleasant experience of shock usually precipitates the split.'

Saltfleet shook his head. 'I can understand people changing from day to day, as their moods change. But she seemed to be two completely different people.'

'Quite. My own first suspicion was that her cousin Joe might be the key. I'd seen a photograph of Joe. He was handsome but *gòffo* – what do you say . . . loutish. Now Rosa is an intelligent girl – shy, but sensitive and intelligent. And even if she was fascinated by her cousin, she must have realised that he was stupid. Everyone has had the experience of being physically attracted by someone they don't really like. I believe that a part of Rosa adored Joe and wanted to be his slave, and another part thought: God forbid!'

Saltfleet frowned, shaking his head.

'But a part isn't another person.'

'Precisely. And that is what I realised as soon as I began to talk to Dorothy. She is, as you say, a completely different person. But perhaps even you do not realise how different. For example, Rosa is short-sighted, and has to wear glasses. Dorothy has perfectly normal sight. Do not ask me how that is possible – I can only tell you that it is so. This machine is an electro-encephalograph, for measuring brain rhythms. Everybody has his own individual pattern of brain rhythms, like his fingerprints. But Rosa and Dorothy have different brain rhythms. They are like two spirits sharing the same body.'

Saltfleet experienced a cold sensation in his spine, and had to make an effort not to show it.

'I will tell you something else. I have a patient who is a

subnormal youth. He worships Rosa, yet he cannot stand Dorothy. And he can tell the difference as soon as he walks into the room, even if she has her back to him.'

'Is that the boy who let me in – spiky hair and big shoulders?'

'Yes.'

'What's wrong with him?' Moro hesitated so long that he said: 'I'm sorry. Perhaps you're not allowed to talk about a patient?'

'Oh no. It is not that. In fact, you have a right to know, because he is here by permission of the local police. Do you know what a paedophile is?'

'A child molester?'

'That is putting it too strongly. He never harmed the girls. All he wants to do is tickle them.'

'Without their clothes.'

'Well, yes.'

'And the court placed him in your care?'

'Yes.'

Sensing that Moro was becoming defensive, Saltfleet changed the subject.

'You were saying about Rosie . . .'

'I was saying that he worships her and follows her round like a dog. Yet when Dorothy takes over, he can tell instantaneously, without even speaking to her. It is almost uncanny.'

The thought that suddenly struck Saltfleet made his hair prickle. He crossed to the window, in case his face betrayed his excitement. Controlling his voice, he said: 'Amazing.'

'It convinces me that two people can communicate directly – by a kind of sympathy.'

'And when shall I be able to see Rosie?'

'I'm afraid that is difficult to say. When Dorothy is in charge, she usually stays for several days.'

'And how long does Rosie stay?'

'Sometimes a day, sometimes only for hours. You see,

Dorothy is the stronger of the two.'

Saltfleet said, with mild irony: 'She won't let Rosie back into her own body?'

'You make her sound selfish. But you must remember that she has reason to be worried. Rosa tried to commit suicide. And if she kills herself, she kills Dorothy too.'

'But she's not suicidal any more?'

'I hope not. But she still likes to be beaten. It must be uncomfortable for Dorothy to wake up covered in bruises.'

'Isn't there any way of *making* Rosie come back?'

'There is no infallible method.'

'Are there any fallible ones?'

'Sometimes, under hypnosis, Rosa comes back again.'

'Could you try that?'

'Now?' Saltfleet nodded. 'That would be difficult. You see, we need Dorothy's cooperation. And she seems to be in a difficult mood today.' He snapped his fingers. 'But I have a suggestion. Every Sunday morning I give her an hour of hypnotherapy. Dorothy expects it then.'

'You want me to come back tomorrow?'

'If you would like to.'

'Very well. Could I – if necessary – bring someone else?'

'A police officer?' Saltfleet nodded. 'That might cause problems. Even with one stranger present, it could be difficult.'

'Then I shan't do it unless absolutely necessary.' Saltfleet wanted to reserve his right to bring Fitch. 'What time?'

'Eleven o'clock?'

'Good.' He held out his hand. 'Doctor, you've been very helpful, and I'm most grateful.'

'*Prego.* I hope you catch your criminal.'

'Incidentally, do you have anything I could read about split personality?'

'There is my own book.' He opened the glass-fronted bookcase and took out a volume in a torn dustwrapper; Saltfleet saw that there was a whole row of books with

54

Moro's name on them, mostly in German and Italian. 'I am afraid I cannot give it to you, but it is out of print.'

It was called *Researches into Mental Dissociation.* Saltfleet said: 'I'll return it tomorrow. By the way, there was one more thing . . .'

'Yes?'

'At the beginning of that video-tape, you asked her if she remembered what you were talking about the previous day, and she said yes. But it was Dorothy who was speaking. And you told me Dorothy didn't share Rosie's memories.'

Moro shrugged. 'Perhaps she said it because she sensed that was the answer I expected. Or perhaps it was still Rosa speaking, before Dorothy took over . . .'

'Ah yes, I see. Well, thanks again, Doctor. Please don't bother to come downstairs – I can find my own way out.'

He went slowly down the stairs, looking at the book. The style seemed simple and direct. At the bottom, he was startled when a hand touched his wrist. It was the dark-haired woman who had looked out of her room. She said in a whisper: 'Could I speak to you?'

'Of course.' He spoke in his normal voice, and she placed her finger on his lips, looking over her shoulder. She had put on a thin bed-jacket over the brassière, and was wearing a flowered cotton skirt; she was in her stockinged feet. She took his sleeve, and drew him along the corridor. Her door stood open. When they were inside, she closed it, and gave a sigh of relief.

'You're a policeman, aren't you?'

'That's right. How did you know?'

'I heard you say you were investigating a murder. I might be able to help you.'

She was a woman of about forty, and had obviously once been pretty; now her face looked pale and tired. But her eyes were very bright, and her teeth excellent. She made no attempt to sit down, or to offer him a seat, but stood looking at him intently.

He asked: 'How?'

'I think I may be able to give you a clue. There's a man who keeps frightening me with obscene phone calls.'

He looked round the room. 'Have you a telephone?'

'There's one outside, just opposite my door.'

'And what makes you think he might be a murderer?'

'The horrible things he says. He says' – she dropped her voice – 'that he wants to undress me, then bite my breasts and suck my blood. And he says he wants to make me lie on the bed and stick pins in me, all over me . . .'

Her manner convinced him that she was fantasising, or deliberately exaggerating. He said: 'Have other people had these calls?'

'Oh no, he rings off if anyone else answers the phone.'

'Have you reported it to the police?'

'Oh no. I'm not allowed out.'

'You could telephone them.'

She smiled pleadingly. 'But you're here now. I can report it to you.'

'It would be better if you reported it to your local police.'

She ignored him, grasping his hand. 'This man is a maniac. He said he wanted to cut off all my clothes with a knife, then bite me all over. And he knows about my strawberry mark.'

'Strawberry mark?'

'Below my navel.' Before he could prevent her, she had pulled up her skirt, and tucked the hem under her chin. She was wearing stockings and a suspender belt, but no panties. 'Look.' She pointed to the birthmark above the line of pubic hair. Saltfleet felt an involuntary stir of excitement, which he suppressed. Then he noticed the bruises.

'Where did you get those?' They covered her thighs and stomach.

She pouted. Her eyes were abnormally bright, and there was no mistaking her intense sexual excitement. She said: 'Someone tried to rape me.' She continued to hold up the skirt, and Saltfleet deliberately kept his eyes on her face.

'Who?'

'Frankie.'

'Did you report it to Dr Moro?'

'No.'

'Why not?'

'I didn't want to get him into trouble.'

'You didn't want to get him into trouble, but he tried to rape you?'

She smiled strangely, and came closer, so her body pressed against him. 'I don't tell half the things I know.'

'Such as?'

She took his hand, and tried to press it between her thighs. He gripped her hand to prevent it from moving. She said: 'I know Frankie isn't supposed to leave this house. But he follows Rosie every time she goes out.'

Suddenly he was alert. 'Are you sure?'

'Quite sure. They have to pass under my window to get to the side gate.'

She managed to pull his hand down so it was against her stomach.

'Did they go out last night?'

'I don't know. I can't remember . . .' She was moving gently against him, her eyes closed, trying to trap his hand between her thighs. At the same moment, he heard the creak of the floorboard on the other side of the door. When he pulled his hand away and took her by the shoulders, she opened her eyes like someone awakened from trance. He raised his finger to his lips, turned quietly, and wrenched the door open. He was in time to see someone disappearing into the next room.

'Who lives next door?'

'Rosie. Why, was she listening?'

'Somebody was.'

'The little bitch!' Her voice was suddenly normal.

He seized his opportunity. 'I'm afraid I have to go.' She

made no attempt to stop him as he went out and closed the door behind him.

He was back in Ladbroke Terrace Gardens a few minutes later. It was almost five o'clock. Miranda and Geraldine were sitting on the back lawn in the golden September sunlight. Miranda said: 'Come and have some tea?'

'I will in a moment. I've got a phone call to make first.'

He rang the Hammersmith police station, identified himself, and asked if they had heard from Inspector Fitch. A sergeant came to the telephone, and told him that Fitch had reported in half an hour before; he was now at the Tilbury police station. Saltfleet noted down the number. A few minutes later, he was speaking to Fitch.

'Hello, George. This is Greg Saltfleet.' He had decided that it was time for first names. 'I think I may have something for you.'

'Marvellous!' There was no mistaking his enthusiasm. 'What?'

'A suspect.'

'Who is he?'

'It's a long story. Any chance of calling in to see me when you get back from Tilbury?'

'I can, but it might not be today. I'm waiting to interview a couple of Choromansky's mates, and they might not be back until late. Could you give me a quick rundown over the phone?'

'All right. Briefly, I've discovered a kind of private mental hospital close to the scene of the murder. It's for people with sex problems. I've discovered that one of the last people to see this man alive – what's his name? – '

'Choromansky – Witold Choromansky.'

'One of the last people to see him alive was a girl called Rosie, who's a patient in this loony bin. She's a masochist – she likes being beaten up by sailors. And she's followed around by a kind of gorilla called Frankie – an over-developed teenager who looks like a zombie. I think it's possible he followed her last night, saw this sailor beating her up, and killed him. You've only got to check his shoes against the footprint in the flowerbed.'

'That's marvellous! But who is this Frankie? Do you know his other name?'

'No. But you can find out from the Notting Hill station – apparently they know all about him. He's been in trouble for molesting little girls.'

'I'll get on to them right away.'

'If you find anything interesting, would you ring me back?' He dictated the telephone number.

Miranda came in through the French windows as he was hanging up.

'Did you hear that?'

'Most of it. You sound as if you might have solved it.'

He smiled affectionately. 'I never count my chickens.'

'Will you get any credit?'

He shook his head. 'It's Scottie MacPhail's division. He tends to get pretty annoyed if people trespass on his patch.'

'Then why help him?'

'I'm not helping him. I'm doing it for my own satisfaction. My job can get pretty boring, you know. I've spent most of the past six months reading through thousands of witnesses' statements. And now, in a single afternoon, I've found an important witness and I may have found a murderer. It's more interesting than paperwork. Besides, I nearly got raped by a nymphomaniac.'

'What!'

He remembered that Geraldine was outside the window, and raised his finger to his lip. 'I'll tell you about that later.'

The telephone rang. It was George Fitch. He sounded excited.

'I've just talked to Bill Watts at Notting Hill. It sounds as if you could be right. This lad's called Frankie Jago, and he's a real troublemaker. If it hadn't been for this doctor, he'd be inside for a long time.'

'The doctor told me he was harmless – that he only wanted to tickle the girls.'

'I don't know about girls. Bill Watts says the trouble is knives. He's a knife freak. They fascinate him. He's been arrested twice for slicing up teenagers in quarrels.'

'My God!'

'That's what I said. He sounds as if he might be our man . . . Excuse me.' He spoke to someone in the office. 'Sorry about that. They've brought these sailors in for questioning. I'll call you back later.'

'Could you make it tomorrow morning? I'm taking my family out for dinner this evening.'

Geraldine came in as he replaced the phone.

'Did I hear you say we're going out to dinner?'

'Yes.'

'Hurrah!' She flung her arms round his neck and squeezed hard. Trying to see past the curtain of her hair, he thought: She's still ten years old underneath. Remembering the girl on the video-tape, he experienced a sudden overwhelming sadness.

FOUR

It was another golden September day, but with that distinct, chilly smell of autumn in the air, a compound of damp earth, dying flowers and leaves. He left the house at five minutes to eleven. Miranda and Geraldine had already gone out; Miranda had decided to go and see her parents, who had retired to St Albans. As he crossed Ladbroke Grove, he realised that he was experiencing an excitement that he had not felt since the Garrett case of 1976. Then it had been due to the battle of wits that had developed between himself and the crooked financier – a battle that ended abruptly when Sir Hugh Garrett fled the country for Sri Lanka. Now it was due to the fascination of the mystery of two women who shared the same body.

He was carrying *Researches into Mental Dissociation*. After spending half the night reading it, he was still no closer to understanding the problem. It began with the sentence: 'The unity of human consciousness is an illusion', and went on to talk about 'sub-systems' of personality, 'lowering of the mental threshold' and hysterical amnesia. Moro described one of his own cases, a patient who had been unconscious for a week after a road accident, and who had then developed into a dual personality, consisting of his former self, and a new personality that was hostile, suspicious and violent. Moro explained this as some kind of damage to the brain circuitry, and went on to apply the same explanation to a number of other cases. Twenty-four

61

hours ago, Saltfleet might have found it convincing; now, after watching Dorothy take over Rosa's body, he found it absurd. As he entered the green gate in the wall, his head was full of questions he wanted to put to Moro.

The front door stood wide open, but he decided to ring the bell; even off-duty, he had to obey the rules. Upstairs, a door slammed; a moment later, a man came down the stairs; although over six feet tall and heavily built, he moved with a cat-like delicacy. He gave Saltfleet a shy but friendly smile.

'You're the police inspector? Doctor Moro is expecting you.'

There was something odd about his face; it looked like a plastic bag that has been blown up, then allowed to deflate slightly; the shiny skin was covered with fine wrinkles. His eyes were a very pale blue. As they went up the stairs, he said over his shoulder: 'My name is Emil.' It was a very soft voice, a woman's voice. Saltfleet said: 'How do you do?'

The man took him to a room at the end of the corridor; it was a small office, and Moro sat behind the desk. Saltfleet observed the sandpaper nailfile on the desk, and the small handmirror, and inferred that it was Dorothy's office.

Moro said: 'Thank you, Emil. I'll see you at lunch.'

When they were alone, Saltfleet said: 'Another resident patient?'

'No. He comes at the weekend for treatment. He wants to have the sex change operation. He's an engine driver.' He picked up the book, which Saltfleet laid on the desk. 'Ah, thank you. Did you find it helpful?'

Saltfleet decided to be tactful. 'Very interesting. But there are dozens of questions I'd like to ask you.'

'Certainly. But perhaps we had better leave that until later? I've placed Dorothy in a light trance, so perhaps we'd better go and see her . . .'

Saltfleet said: 'First of all, there's something else I've got to talk to you about. Can Dorothy wait a few minutes?'

'Of course – all day if necessary. She is a deep hypnotic subject, and that is a rare phenomenon – only one in twenty of the population.'

'It's not about Dorothy. It's about Frankie.' Moro nodded. 'You told me yesterday that he was in here for tickling small girls.'

'That is true.'

'What you didn't mention is that he's a knife freak.' Moro met his eyes frankly.

'Because the question did not arise. Besides, I don't believe that has anything to do with his problems.'

'But you agree he *is* a knife freak?'

'He has an obsession with knives. But then, he is mentally no more than a child. When I was a child, I had an obsession with penknives.'

'But he's caused grievous bodily harm with a flick knife.'

'That was in a quarrel between rival gangs. I believe his opponents also had knives, as well as bicycle chains.'

'And you think that has nothing to do with his problems?'

Moro said firmly: 'I am certain of it. Frankie's problems are due to the brutality of his mother and his stepfather. They were both alcoholics. He is mentally retarded because his stepfather caused brain damage by beating him. The only person who loved Frankie was his younger sister, and he had to take care of her like a father. She used to enjoy being undressed and tickled – particularly in the genital region, because the whole family suffered from *Phthirius inguinalis*, the crab louse. That is why Frankie wants to tickle little girls. He wants to return to the happy days of childhood.'

Saltfleet said: 'I'll take your word for that. But I'd better be frank with you, and tell you that he's a suspect in the murder of this Polish sailor.'

Moro looked aghast.

'But . . . but why? Why Frankie? Why pick on him?'

63

Saltfleet said, gently but firmly: 'No, Doctor. We're not picking on him. You told me yourself that he follows Rosie around like a dog. And a strange lady on the ground floor told me that she's often seen him following her when she goes out in the evening.'

'Strange lady? Ah, you mean Harriet. But she is completely untrustworthy. If you had asked me, I could have told you that she fantasises all the time.'

'I didn't have a chance to ask you. She dragged me into her room as I was leaving yesterday. She started to tell me about how Frankie had tried to rape her.'

'Ah, you see!' Moro threw up his hands. 'Frankie would never try to rape an adult woman. They terrify him. That is why he is so fond of Rosa – because she is helpless and needs protection.'

'Well, I must admit, I didn't believe that part. But she had no reason to lie when she told me that Frankie follows Rosie when she goes out.'

'I am not saying it is impossible. I do not keep a twenty-four-hour watch on all my patients. But Frankie himself knows how dangerous it would be to leave this house. If the police saw him, he would go straight to prison. He is only here on condition that he remains indoors. As to Harriet, she is here because she cannot distinguish between truth and falsehood.'

'What does she do?'

'She makes obscene phone calls, preferably to police stations. She is fascinated by policemen.'

Saltfleet smiled. 'That explains a lot. She tried to undress in front of me.'

Moro raised his eyebrows with genuine astonishment.

'Then you are privileged. That is very interesting indeed. Usually she is content to do it over the phone. It is a sign that she is improving.'

Saltfleet said: 'I'm delighted to hear it.'

Moro sensed the irony. 'You find that amusing, but it is

profoundly true. You see, all sexually abnormal patients have the same problem – a failure to adjust to reality. They have a defective reality function – a term invented by Pierre Janet. They cannot distinguish properly between the real world and the world that is inside their heads . . .'

Saltfleet said: 'I think most people are like that.'

Moro looked delighted. 'Ah, sir, you are a philosopher. It is a privilege to meet a policeman who is also a philosopher.' For a moment Saltfleet suspected sarcasm; but Moro was obviously sincere. 'You are right, of course. A man with a perfect reality function would be a god. But in sexually abnormal patients – what used to be called sexual perverts – the lack of reality function is particularly obvious. If Harriet has graduated to exposing herself in reality instead of doing it over the telephone, it is a sign that her reality function is becoming stronger.' He leaned forward, and his eyes were mild and friendly. 'And now you will see why I feel worried when you tell me Frankie is a suspect. I am personally convinced – totally convinced – that he would not commit a murder, particularly a murder with sexual overtones, such as you describe. My task is to persuade him to come to terms with reality. And if you take him to a police station and accuse him of murder, you destroy the work of six months.'

Saltfleet said: 'Look, I'll tell you what. You say he's incapable of murder. So presumably you wouldn't mind helping to prove it one way or the other? How many pairs of shoes has he got?'

'Shoes? Only one pair, I imagine. Two at most.'

'Would it be possible for me to examine them?'

'Of course. Nothing could be simpler. Why?'

'We found a man's footprint in the flowerbed near the murdered sailor. If Frankie's shoes don't fit, then he's in the clear.'

'It shall be done. Could you tell simply by looking at the shoes on his feet?'

65

'No. I'd need to measure the sole and take an impression.'

'That is no problem. Emil is our odd-jobman, and he sometimes cleans shoes. If I told Frankie to take off his shoes to be cleaned, he would do it.'

'He wouldn't be suspicious?'

'He is like a child. He does what I tell him.'

'Fine. And if the shoe doesn't fit, I think I can promise you we shan't bother Frankie.'

Moro was obviously relieved; he held out his hand. 'It's a deal.' The words sounded quaint with the Italian accent, like one of the Marx Brothers. 'Now let us go to Dorothy.'

Saltfleet followed him down the corridor. Moro took a key from his pocket, and unlocked the door of his office. He explained to Saltfleet: 'I never leave a hypnotised patient in an unlocked room.'

The curtains had been drawn, cutting out the sunlight. Dorothy lay on the couch, her eyes closed.

Saltfleet asked, in a whisper: 'Am I allowed to speak?'

'Of course.' Moro spoke in his normal voice. 'She is asleep.'

He took a second chair and placed it by the head of the couch, inviting Saltfleet to sit down. He sat on the other side. Saltfleet noticed that she was wearing different clothes this morning: a smart grey suit, a blue silk blouse and grey shoes. She was still wearing red tights. He made a mental note to ask Moro whether Dorothy bought her own clothes, or shared Rosie's wardrobe.

Moro raised her eyelid and allowed it to close again. He said: 'Dorothy, can you hear me?' He repeated it slowly, his face close to hers. She nodded. He said: 'Who am I?''

'Doctor Moro.'

'That's right. Do you know where Rosa is?'

There was a long silence, then she said: 'Yes.'

'Is she there?'

'Yes.'

'Can you ask her to come?'

This time the silence was so long that Saltfleet thought she was not going to answer. She said finally: 'She won't.'

'Why not?'

There was another silence, then: 'She won't say.'

'Is she afraid?'

'Yes.'

'Afraid of what?'

'She won't say.'

Moro looked at Saltfleet and shook his head. 'I'm sorry.'

Saltfleet shrugged. 'It can't be helped. She'll be back some time.' He was surprised that he found it so easy to accept that Rosa was somewhere inside the sleeping girl, unwilling to come out, like someone refusing to answer the telephone.

Moro said: 'There *is* something we could try. Frankie might be able to persuade her. Will you excuse me?'

He went out, and Saltfleet was left staring at the girl on the couch. Even asleep, it was obvious that this was Dorothy. She lay with her knees and feet together, her arms by her sides, like a crusader on a tomb. He decided that it was the expression of the mouth that indicated Dorothy's presence: relaxed yet firm and controlled. Her breathing was soft and regular.

Moro came in, followed by Frankie. The youth was dressed in a blue T-shirt that showed his powerful biceps. Saltfleet glanced at his shoes; he was wearing frayed white plimsolls. He scowled when he saw Saltfleet, then transferred his attention to the sleeping girl.

Moro said: 'Ask her to come.'

Frankie sat down on the couch, by the girl's knees, and stared at her intently. He said hesitantly: 'Rosa . . . Rosie . . .'

When nothing happened, he moved closer to her face With surprising gentleness, he reached out and touched her cheek. He said: 'Rosie, the doctor wants to talk to you.' To

67

Saltfleet's surprise, he leaned forward, as if listening intently. Then he said to Moro: 'She won't come.'

'Why not?'

'She afraid.'

'Tell her she doesn't have to be afraid.'

Frankie said: 'Rosie. The doctor says you don't have to be afraid.' There was a silence, and again Saltfleet was astonished as Frankie seemed to listen intently. He was also touched at the way he had changed from an uncommunicative semi-imbecile into a protective human being. Suddenly he knew Moro was telling the truth when he said Frankie would never harm children.

Frankie said: 'She won't come.'

'All right. Thank you.' He said to Saltfleet: 'I'm afraid there's nothing more I can do.'

'Couldn't *I* try to speak to her?'

Moro shook his head. 'It wouldn't do any good.' Saltfleet noted the sarcastic smile that appeared briefly on Frankie's face.

'Can't *you* speak to her? They all seem to pay attention to you.' He was unwilling to accept defeat.

Moro was looking thoughtful. 'I suppose there *is* one more thing I could try?'

'What's that?'

'Deepening the hypnotic state. It sometimes works.' He took the girl's hand in both his own. He said softly: 'Can you hear me, Dorothy?' She nodded. 'I want you to go into a deep sleep, deeper than you've ever been in before. Deep sleep. Deep sleep. That's right. Breathe deeply. You're sinking deeper and deeper. Completely relaxed. Deeper and deeper . . .'

His voice was so soothing that Saltfleet began to feel drowsy. He noticed that Frankie was swaying slightly. Then, with a suddenness that startled them all, the sleeping girl stiffened convulsively; she flung up her right arm as if to ward off a blow.

Moro said: 'Dorothy, are you all right?' The arm remained raised. Moro touched it, then gripped the hand and tried to force it down. The arm seemed to be rigid. He said: 'Relax, Dorothy, I want you to relax. Everything is all right. You can relax now.' The arm suddenly fell. Saltfleet realised that the girl's face had become suddenly pale; she looked like a corpse. Her chest was no longer moving. He reached out for her wrist. Instantly, Frankie's hand had gripped his own wrist. The grip was so powerful that Saltfleet winced.

Moro snapped: 'Frankie, stop that! Let go.' He had to repeat it before Frankie released his grip. Saltfleet's wrist had become numb; it felt as if it had been trapped in a vice. Moro said reproachfully: 'He was only trying to help.'

He knelt down and placed his ear against the girl's breast.

'Her heart is beating.' He lifted her hand and released it; all the stiffness had gone. Saltfleet could see no movement of her breasts.

'She doesn't seem to be breathing.'

'I have seen this before. We call it the hypnotic syncope. I have taken her down to the level of zero consciousness.'

'Is she all right?'

Moro nodded. 'It should pass. I told you: she is a deep hypnotic subject.'

They all sat looking at the girl; Saltfleet would have said she was dead; the body had the total stillness of a corpse. He could tell that Moro, in spite of his assurance, was worried. After several minutes he asked: 'What happens now?'

'There is nothing to do but wait.'

'For what?'

'I don't know. The human personality is a strange interlocking system of tensions, of forces in counterbalance. In people like Rosa, most of that tension is negative – purely defensive. Even under hypnosis, some of these tensions remain. But she seems to have relaxed all her tensions . . .'

He was obviously speaking to reassure himself. Saltfleet sat there, gently massaging his bruised wrist. He felt no resentment about it; Frankie had reacted instinctively, like a dog snapping. Looking at the sleeping girl, he was suddenly overwhelmed by a sense of the mystery of the human soul. The body looked empty, a piece of abandoned machinery, like a rusting car on a dump. No one was inside it now, neither its original owner, nor the person who had forced her to share it. Then where were they now? The thought brought a shock that was like fear, a sudden recognition of an alien reality. He was in a solid, ordinary room, sustained by a sense of normality, of his own day-to-day existence; now he realised that the normality was a thin curtain, separating him from a universe in which everything was strange and mysterious. He wondered whether he ought to experience anxiety or terror in the face of this sudden recognition of his own ignorance, then realised that, deep down inside him, there was a curious certainty that he had nothing to be afraid of. At the same time, in a sudden flash of insight, he was aware of the unreality of his everyday self – of what Moro called the strange interlocking system of tensions that make up a personality. It was like a sudden glimpse into the engine room of a ship. He found himself wondering whether death would be a similar experience, an ability to move freely below the decks.

Moro said to Frankie: 'Try and talk to her.'

Frankie looked dubious; he obviously felt as Saltfleet did: that this was a corpse.

He reached out and placed his hand tenderly on her cheek, and bent forward so that, from where Saltfleet was sitting, he looked as though he was kissing her. He said in a whisper: 'Rosie. Rosie. Rosie. Listen to me, Rosie, can you hear me? Rosie . . . Rosie . . .' He sounded as if he was calling into some empty space.

Saltfleet observed him intently. He himself felt it was hopeless. But it was obvious that Frankie felt differently. He might have been a child trying to coax a kitten out of a tree. Moro had also observed it, and was leaning forward, watching the still face. Then, against the patterned wall-paper, Saltfleet noticed the slight movement of her breast. He said: 'She's breathing again.'

As he spoke, the girl shook her head, as if trying to shake off a fly. Suddenly, she was breathing normally. Moro patted Frankie lightly on the shoulder.

'Good work.'

Frankie blushed with embarrassment and pleasure. Moro took the girl's hand again, and said in her ear: 'Hello!'

'Hello!' Her response was so swift that it was as if she were awake. Her eyes still closed, she smiled into Moro's face. Then she struggled into a sitting position.

Moro said: 'How are you feeling?'

'Lovely!' The voice was normal and cheerful. Frankie had to move to make room for her on the edge of the couch.

Moro said: 'Do you know who I am?'

'I . . . think so.' She sounded doubtful.

Saltfleet was puzzled. The face was no longer that of Dorothy; it had become relaxed and trusting. Yet it was not that of the girl he had seen yesterday on the television screen, and who had identified herself as Rosa Judd. She no longer reminded him of Geraldine.

Moro said: 'Open your eyes.'

The girl made an obvious effort, contracting and stretching the muscles of her forehead. 'I can't.'

'Then I'll do it for you.' Moro gently raised her eyelids with his thumbs. The girl blinked, like someone suddenly exposed to the light. 'Now do you know me?' She shook her head vigorously; there was something child-like about the movement. 'But you know Frankie, don't you?' She stared at Frankie, then shook her head again. But when she noticed Saltfleet, her face broke into a delighted smile.

'I know *him*!'

'Who is he?'

'Uncle Greg, of course!' The childish intonation was again very obvious.

Saltfleet said: 'That's incredible!'

'What?'

'That *is* my name.'

The girl said: 'You see, he *is* Uncle Greg.'

Moro said: 'And who are you?'

She looked at the floor, pouting and smiling. Moro said: 'Come on, please tell me your name.' She obviously enjoyed being cajoled. 'Please?' She glanced sideways at Saltfleet.

'Ask him.'

Saltfleet made a guess. 'Rosie?'

She glanced triumphantly at Moro, 'You see, he knows.'

Moro said: 'And how old are you, Rosie?'

'Shan't tell.'

'Can you stand up?'

'Of *course* I can.' She flounced awkwardly to her feet, and almost fell; Saltfleet jumped up and steadied her. He said: 'Won't you tell us how old you are?'

She ignored him. Then, to his astonishment, she unbuttoned his jacket, and slipped her hand into his trouser pocket. Moro asked: 'What are you doing?' She smiled mischievously, trying the other pocket. Finding nothing of interest, she tried the pockets of his jacket. Her eyes lit up as she discovered a small plastic container of orange sweets. She asked coyly: 'Are these for me?'

'If you like.'

Moro asked: 'What are they?'

'Breath deodorants. They sell them at the tobacco kiosk.'

Rosie said: 'Can I have them all? Joe and Mary don't like sweets.'

Saltfleet smiled disbelievingly. 'Are you sure?'

72

She giggled. 'Well, not as much as I do.' She obviously found the plastic top baffling; Saltfleet had to open it for her. 'Can I?'

He said: 'If you're a good girl.'

'I am. I promise.' She put her arms round his neck and gave him a damp kiss on the ear. 'Are there any more?' She tried to dip her hand into his other pocket. Moro caught her wrist.

'Later, Rosie, not now.' She pouted, but accepted the authority in his voice. 'Now, come and sit down.' She sat in Saltfleet's chair, folding her hands in her lap, firmly clutching the sweets.

Moro said: 'How old are you, Rosie?'

'Seven years and seven months – no, eight months.'

'And where do you live?'

'Twenty-one Birchwood Road, Petts Wood, Orpington.' She said it as if repeating a lesson. Her eyes strayed to the severed hand in the case, and widened. 'What's that?' She ran over to the case and peered in. Saltfleet found it slightly uncanny to watch her; the movements and voice were those of a child, yet the body that of an adult. She asked breathlessly: 'Is it real?'

Moro said quietly to Frankie: 'Talk to her.'

Frankie obediently went over to the case, and said: 'No, it's not real. It's made of wax.'

She said with conviction: 'It looks *horrible*!' Her r's sounded like w's. As Frankie bent over the case, she noticed his hair. 'Why have you got such a funny haircut?'

He said cheerfully: 'You shouldn't make personal remarks. It's no funnier than yours.' Saltfleet observed that he was completely at home with her, and that she seemed to bring out a certain normality in him.

'It's *not* funny!' She reached up and felt her hair; her hand detected the elastic band that held the pony-tail in the nape of her neck. 'What's this?' She went to the mirror that hung in the corner, and tried to see the back of her head. Then, staring sideways, she noticed her own face. Her eyes widened with shock. She faced the mirror and stared at herself incredulously.

Moro said: 'What is it, Rosie?'

'I look different.' She sounded nervous and unsure of herself.

Moro said soothingly: 'No, you're just the same as always.'

'*He* says I look funny.' She pointed at Frankie.

He said conciliatingly: 'I didn't mean it. I was only pulling your leg.'

The mention of legs made her look down at her own; her nose wrinkled with distaste.

'Why am I wearing red stockings?'

With complete lack of self-consciousness, she pulled her skirt up to her waist. The tights seemed to astonish her.

'What are these?'

Frankie said: 'They're called tights.'

'I don't *like* red things.' She started to struggle out of them, pushing her knickers down with them. 'They're nasty.' She lost her balance, but Frankie caught her before she fell. She tried to free herself. 'Let me *go*.' Frankie obeyed, and she landed on the floor with a bump. She was sobbing with exasperation as she pulled off the tights and threw them across the room.

Moro said quietly in Saltfleet's ear: 'Try to get her to lie down on the couch.'

Saltfleet went behind her, saying gently: 'Come on. Up we get.' He helped her to her feet. 'Uncle Greg's here to look after you.'

Her reaction startled him. For a moment she stared blankly, as if he was a stranger; then her face contorted with rage and hatred. 'Get away from me!' She pushed him violently, so that he staggered. He looked at Moro, who was obviously as surprised as he was. He said: 'But why,

74

Rosie? What have I done?'

As he took a step towards her, she grabbed Frankie's hand and said tearfully: '*Please* don't let him touch me.'

This time Saltfleet was prepared; from Frankie's face he could see that her voice had touched some instinctive spring of protective obedience. As Frankie lunged at him, he automatically followed the procedure he had been taught in self-defence: stepping back, tripping Frankie with his right foot, then chopping at the back of his neck with the edge of his hand. Frankie collapsed and lay still. Rosie began to sob.

Moro came forward anxiously: 'Will he be all right?'

'Yes. He's just stunned.'

Moro put his arm round Rosie's shoulders, and said soothingly: 'Come and lie down. Come on now.' She permitted herself to be led to the couch. 'It's time you went to sleep.' She shook her head violently. 'Yes, yes, you've had a lot of excitement for a little girl.' He waved Saltfleet out of her line of sight. 'Come along now, lie down.' She allowed him to press her shoulders down on the couch; he prevented her from twisting her head to look at Frankie. 'That's right. Now close your eyes. Now I'm going to count up to ten, and when I finish counting, you'll be fast asleep . . .'

A few minutes later she was breathing peacefully. Frankie stirred, and Saltfleet watched him cautiously as he sat up. But he seemed bewildered and subdued, massaging the back of his neck. Moro asked him with concern: 'Do you feel all right?'

'Got a headache.'

'Well, sit there with your head on your knees and it will go away.'

Saltfleet wondered whether he ought to say something apologetic and decided against it; Frankie had obviously been intent on doing him grievous bodily harm.

Moro picked up the tights from where they had landed

on the desk. 'I think we'd better put these back on. I wouldn't like her to wake up without them.' Saltfleet helped him to put them on the sleeping girl, raising her buttocks clear of the couch. He said: 'It was the tights that seemed to cause it.'

From where he was sitting on the floor, Frankie said: 'They're the colour of blood.'

Both looked at him curiously, Moro said: 'What difference does that make?'

Frankie only grunted. Moro asked him: 'How do you feel now?'

'Bit better.'

'Then perhaps you'd better go and lie down in your room.'

Frankie dragged himself wearily to his feet. Saltfleet caught Moro's eye and pointed at his shoes. Moro understood immediately.

'Where are your shoes, Frankie?'

'Don't know.'

'Aren't they in your room?'

'They've gone.'

'Have you searched for them?'

He nodded sullenly.

'You mean someone's taken them?'

'S'pose so.'

Moro and Saltfleet exchanged glances. Moro said: 'Go and look again. I'm going to tell Emil to clean them. See if you can find them and bring them to me.'

Frankie said with exasperation: 'I tell you they've gone!' Saltfleet could see the annoyance was genuine; no actor could have simulated that mixture of respect for Moro and indignation at being asked to do the impossible.

When Frankie had gone, Moro said: 'That is strange. I cannot imagine what has happened to them.'

'Is there a stove or a furnace in this house?'

'There is a furnace in the basement.'

76

'Is it lit?'

'Yes.'

'Then I'd like to bet those shoes have been burned in it.'

'But why should Frankie burn his shoes?'

'Not Frankie. Dorothy.' He glanced down at the sleeping girl; her breathing was light and regular. 'She was listening outside the door when I was talking to your patient downstairs – Harriet.'

'But why should Dorothy try to protect Frankie? She doesn't like him and he doesn't like her.'

'But she'd want to protect Rosie. Because they share the same body. And if Rosie was involved in this murder, then she's an accessory.'

Moro smiled patiently. 'But I must tell you frankly that I do not believe for one moment that Rosa could be involved in this murder.'

'Frankie could. Frankie could have followed her when she went out on Saturday, and watched her being picked up by this sailor. And when he saw the sailor beating her up, he could have intervened and murdered him. Can you give me one good reason why that shouldn't be true?'

Moro said: 'Yes, I can give you one very good reason. You say this was a sex crime – that the victim was mutilated. Frankie would never do that. I agree that he might kill a man in a rage. But he has no cruelty in him, no malice. You must have seen that today, when he was talking to Rosie. He is like a child.'

'But he might have been in a rage when he mutilated him.'

'No. Think of it. If you are in a rage, and you kill somebody with a knife, this releases your anger. I am speaking now as a doctor. In Berlin, and again in Algiers, I worked with the police as a medical expert. I have seen six cases in which there was mutilation of the genitals. In one, it was done by a woman whose husband was unfaithful. The other five cases were all sadistic homosexuals.'

'So you think we ought to be looking for a sadistic homosexual?'

'I think it is probable. I know of at least two men in this area who would be capable of such a crime.'

'Would you be willing to give us their names?'

'If necessary. But I think they are probably already known to the local police. And I am not saying I think that either of them is a murderer. I am only saying that I think they are more likely than Frankie. Let me point out that we do not know that Frankie left this house on Saturday.'

Saltfleet looked down at the girl. 'She's the only person who could tell us.'

'And she *will* tell us, believe me. I cannot tell you when that will be. Now this child has appeared, it forms an extra complication.'

'The child has never appeared before?'

'Never. She is a personality fragment that remained dormant until I placed her in deep hypnosis. I did not even suspect her existence. Now I have to find out why she split off from the rest of the personality.'

'Does there have to be a reason?'

'Of course, there is always a reason. Usually some tragedy or violent shock. When the child comes back again, I shall try to find out.'

'Would it be possible for me to be present when that happens?'

'Of course. With pleasure. You find the case interesting?' Moro was obviously pleased.

'Fascinating. But I'd also like to be around when Rosie – the later Rosie – reappears.'

'That could be at any time – even now. Would you like me to wake her up and see what happens?'

'If that's possible.'

'Very well.' He placed his hand on the girl's forehead. 'When I count up to ten you are going to wake up. You will feel completely relaxed and refreshed. I'm going to count now. One, two . . .'

Saltfleet watched her curiously. She showed no sign of life until Moro reached eight; then her lips moved. At nine, her eyelids stirred; at ten, they opened. He felt a wave of disappointment; the look in the eyes and the set of the mouth made it obvious that Dorothy was back. She smiled at Moro; then she saw Saltfleet, and the smile vanished. She raised her wrist and looked at her watch.

'It's late.'

'Yes, my dear, we've taken longer than usual today.'

'May I go?'

'Yes.'

She sat up and swung her legs on to the floor. She noticed a crooked seam in the tights and frowned, pulling it straight. Then she stood up and walked out of the room, without looking back.

Moro said apologetically: 'I'm afraid she doesn't like you.'

Saltfleet said: 'I know. What I'd love to know is why.'

FIVE

The house in Ladbroke Terrace Gardens was still empty. His regret that they had not returned – even a few hours' absence from his family made him miss them – was mixed with a certain relief. The past two hours had disturbed him deeply; he felt the need to understand why. Murder cases often touched his sense of pity or outrage; but there was always a basic sense of detachment, the recognition that it was his job to solve them, not to brood on the problem of evil. Yet sometimes, in the evening, as he smoked his pipe and drank a glass of beer or wine, he thought about the problem of why human beings are driven to rob and kill. He always reached the same conclusion: that crime springs out of a certain mistrust of life. It was a mistrust he had never shared; even as a child, he had never felt the need to push to the front of a queue, or cheat at exams; there was an underlying certainty that it was unnecessary. And now the sight of a child's voice issuing from an adult body had produced a twinge of mistrust, a sense of vulnerability. He wanted to drag it into the light of understanding.

He took a can of cold lager from the refrigerator, poured it into a tumbler, and drank most of it down without lowering the glass. His body relaxed with gratitude; but the underlying sense of unease remained. He now regretted returning Moro's book so promptly; it might contain a sentence – even a phrase – that would provide the key to what disturbed him. If a person was not a person, if an individual was not undividable ... A fly walking across the tabletop distracted him, and made him aware how difficult it was to pin down an unformulated insight.

The doorbell rang. It was 2.30 P.M., the time Miranda said she would be home; she must have forgotten her key. But when he opened the door, he found himself looking into the round, perspiring face of Detective Inspector Fitch. The squad car was parked on the double yellow line in front of the door.

'Hello, George. Come in.'

'Thanks. Not disturbing you, I hope?'

'No. I'm on my own. Miranda's gone to see her mother.'

'Good. I wanted a word with you alone.'

Saltfleet led him into the kitchen. 'Take off your coat. You look hot.' He saw Fitch looking at the lager can. 'Like a beer?'

'Oof! What a good idea.' He removed the well-worn raincoat and placed it, folded neatly, on the draining-board. 'Ah, thanks. Cheers.' Saltfleet opened another can for himself, not because he wanted it, but to make Fitch feel at ease.

'Had a busy morning?'

Fitch said: 'There's been an interesting development.' Saltfleet waited. 'This bloke Choromansky might be more than he seems.'

Saltfleet nodded sympathetically; he understood Fitch's need to talk to someone, to get things clear in his mind. 'That's interesting. In what way?'

'You know I went down to Tilbury yesterday? I talked to the captain of this ship – chap with an unpronounceable name like Crackovsky. I'd got this interpreter with me, but the captain spoke English anyway – pretty poor, but I could understand him.' If Saltfleet had been Fitch's superior, he would have warned him that this was a mistake. Speaking English might provide an illusion of direct communication, but the captain would be more forthcoming in his own language, and might add some vital fragment of information. 'He told me Choromansky was the second engineer, and that he didn't know him very well – he told me to talk to the first engineer and the steward, because they often went drinking with him. Now when he said the steward, my ears pricked up. I've known one or two stewards when I was in the merchant navy, and half of 'em were queers. They weren't back, so I asked him to contact me at the station if they came. That's when I rang you. Then these two sailors turned up at the station – they'd arrived back just after I left the ship. Well, as soon as I saw this steward, I knew he wasn't a homo – he'd got naked girls tattooed all over his arms. And the first engineer was a big ape with broken teeth. Neither spoke English, so I had to use the interpreter. But they couldn't tell me much – they both said Choromansky was a loner who didn't talk much about himself. The engineer thought he'd got a wife in Poland. He said he'd sailed with him several times, but still didn't know much about him. When I asked them if he was homosexual, they both said "Nie" – I didn't need that translating – but I got a feeling there was more to it than that.'

'Why?'

'Oh, just the way they glanced at one another. So I'm keeping that one open. Anyway, they didn't seem to know much either. Said he'd been drinking with them the night before, and that he'd told them he'd be away for the weekend. So that meant he must have had somewhere to stay the night in London. I decided I'd better check that one out. So this morning, I rang the Polish Embassy to see if they knew of any place where a Polish sailor might stay . . .'

'Hadn't you contacted the embassy before?'

'Only to report his death and promise to keep in touch. They didn't seem very interested. But when I rang this morning, there was a message to phone this attaché at his home. And what do you think he tells me? That Choromansky has only just joined the ship!'

'Only just joined it?' Saltfleet was puzzled.

'That's right. He'd been in London nearly a month, at the London Hospital in Whitechapel Road. He arrived on August the twenty-eighth from North Africa on a ship called the *Pilsudski*, suffering from jaundice. At least, that's what they thought it was. His eyes and his skin had gone yellow. So he went into the London Hospital, and after a few days they decided that it wasn't jaundice after all – just some obstruction of the liver. But Choromansky stayed on in London until there was another ship he could join as second engineer. Apparently that's quite normal – they go into what's called a pool until they can join a ship. During that time, he stays in an annexe of the hospital, and he can wander off all day, so long as he's back at night.'

Saltfleet said: 'Why didn't the captain tell you that?'

'That's what I wanted to know. So I managed to talk to him on the telephone – sent a man down from the Tilbury station. He said he didn't think it was important, and anyway, I hadn't asked him about it. I pointed out that Choromansky could have been killed by someone he'd met that month in London. He said he was very sorry, and that was that. I couldn't prove he was withholding information.'

Saltfleet again thought of explaining the importance of interviewing a foreign witness through an interpreter, but decided against it; it might sound officious.

Fitch said: 'The next thing to do was to check at the London Hospital in Whitechapel. I drove over there, and managed to talk to the doctor who'd examined Choromansky when he came in. He said it *was* jaundice – but he called it something else . . .'

'Hepatitis.'

'That's it. But it wasn't the infectious kind. Apparently the infectious kind makes your shit turn white and your pee turn brown. He said he thought it was due to a gallstone in the . . .' Fitch took out his notebook: 'A gallstone in the bile duct. But it cleared up in a few days. So Choromansky was allowed out.' Fitch sat back in his chair and drank his beer. 'So it looks as if he could have met his killer while he was wandering around London.'

'Any idea what he did during that time?'

'I talked to the porter. He said Choromansky was interested in English history. He left this behind in the hospital.' He took a small book from his jacket pocket. It was called *Norman Britain*. Saltfleet took it from him; it was well-thumbed, and some passages had been underlined in pencil. 'There was another Polish sailor there in the annexe with him, and the porter said they used to go out together. This other man – called Zapolski – sailed ten days ago. So I'm going to try to track him down.'

'The Polish embassy can help you there.'

'I know.' Fitch smiled triumphantly. 'I've already talked to the attaché. He says they should be able to contact him in a couple of days.'

'In the meantime, it might be worth checking on the pubs in Whitechapel – particularly the ones where prostitutes hang out.'

Fitch nodded. 'That's next on my list. And of course, there's this lad you found out about – Frankie Jago. We've got to try and check that footprint.'

'That may not be too easy. I've been there this morning. He says his shoes have disappeared.'

Fitch looked at him sharply over his beer. 'That sounds suspicious.'

'Not necessarily. Don't forget he's in a kind of loony bin. That kind of thing happens all the time.' Saltfleet was surprised to find that he was feeling vaguely protective about Frankie.

'Yes, I suppose you're right. Still, we'd better pull him in for questioning.'

Saltfleet deliberately changed the subject.

'Incidentally, did you ask the doctor if he X-rayed Choromansky for gallstones?'

'No, why?' Fitch looked slightly defensive.

'I just wondered. If the symptoms vanished so quickly, it's just possible he was faking.'

'I suppose so.' Fitch was obviously doubtful. 'How would he turn his skin yellow?'

'That wouldn't be difficult. I seem to recollect that chewing cordite has that effect. Soldiers used to use it during the war to fake sickness.'

'Would it turn the eyes yellow?'

'I'm not sure of that.'

'One of his eyes was so bad he had to wear a patch over it.'

Saltfleet said: 'There's an easy way to find out. Let's ring Aspinal.'

Fitch followed him into the next room. His address book was lying by the telephone; he looked under 'D' for doctors. Aspinal might be away – he often spent weekends at his country cottage – in which case he would try Leo Jackson of the London Hospital Medical College. The phone rang half-a-dozen times; he was about to hang up when Aspinal's voice answered.

'Francis, I'm sorry to bother you on a Sunday. It's Greg.'

'Don't apologise. I was dozing in my armchair after a self-indulgent lunch.' Saltfleet thought he heard a girl's laugh in the background. 'What can I do for you?'

'Can you tell me if there's any way to fake the symptoms of hepatitis – for example, by chewing cordite?'

'Cordite wouldn't do it. It makes you look sick, but it

turns you grey. But there are plenty of other drugs that would work. Mepacrine hydrochloride's about the most obvious – it's used for the treatment of malaria, and produces much the same symptoms.'

'Yellow skin and eyeballs?'

'That's right. I seem to remember that several of the anti-malaria drugs have the same effect – paludrine, amadiaquine, chloroquine phosphate. Do you want to hang on while I look it up?'

'Don't bother. It's not important. But that first one you mentioned . . .'

'Mepacrine.'

'Would that inflame the eyes so that an eye-patch was necessary?'

'Well, no. It might make them sensitive to light, but it would have the same effect on both. You'd need dark glasses.'

'One more question. How would you tell if the jaundice was caused by a gallstone in the bile duct?'

'By the symptoms. It causes muscular spasms, so he'd have had quite a lot of pain.'

'Would you have him X-rayed?'

'Not necessarily. The jaundice usually comes on *after* the stone has passed through to the bowel. So it would probably have been excreted. Are we talking about this Polish sailor?'

'Yes. Did you notice any sign of jaundice?'

'No. But I wouldn't if it took place more than a few days ago.'

'Anything else you noticed during the PM?'

Aspinal chuckled. 'I thought you weren't interested?'

'I'm not really. But I've got George Fitch here with me.'

'Ah, I see. No, it was much as I expected. Death was due to a knife wound in the left ventricle, caused by a blade about half-an-inch wide – I'd guess a switch blade. It must have happened very quickly – no defensive wounds on the hands.'

'Thanks a lot, Francis. That's been a tremendous help.'

'There was one thing that might interest Fitch. He had a tattoo on his chest. And the inscription was in Russian.'

'I'll pass that on to him. Thanks again.'

As he hung up, Fitch asked: 'What was that?'

'He said the sailor had a tattoo with an inscription in Russian.'

Fitch thought for a moment, then shrugged. 'I don't see that means much. He might have served in the Russian navy or merchant fleet.'

'Still, that business of the eyepatch makes me wonder.'

'Why?'

'Aspinal says that if his eyes were inflamed, he'd need dark glasses – not just one eyepatch.' He could see that Fitch still failed to understand. 'Look, suppose for a moment that he was faking the jaundice. Why should he do that?'

Fitch grinned. 'Because he wants a couple of weeks in London with free board and lodging.'

'Yes, but doesn't it strike you as a bit odd that an ordinary second engineer should speak Russian and English – as he must have done to read that book – as well as his own language? And he's interested in English history, and he leaves a book behind to prove it? And he leaves the ship with an eyepatch which he probably doesn't need?'

'Why would he wear an eyepatch?'

'You can hide a lot under an eyepatch – for example, a microfilm. Some microfilms are so tiny you could even hide them under an eyelid – which would produce inflammation of the eye.'

'Aha!' Fitch suddenly understood. 'You think he could have been a Russian agent?'

'In the light of the other facts, I'd say it's a possibility.'

Fitch was obviously unhappy about it. 'A Russian spy

who spends his time looking at old churches?'

'Who told you that? The porter?' Fitch nodded. Saltfleet experienced a rising tingle of excitement. 'Everything you say makes it sound more suspicious. He even goes out of his way to tell the porter he's interested in old churches.'

Fitch shook his head. 'But why churches?'

'Because they're the perfect cover. He could meet other agents and exchange information without anyone suspecting. "Excuse me, sir, but could I look at your guide book?" And he can go anywhere he likes and claim he's looking at historical monuments.' With his forefinger, Saltfleet flipped open the book on Norman Britain; it fell open at a page with several pencil markings. He read aloud: '"There was an early settlement in Cheltenham, and a church existed there in AD 803. The manor belonged to the crown and was granted to Henry de Bohun, Earl of Hereford, in the twelfth century. In AD 1252 it was bought by the abbey of Fécamp in Normandy"... I'd like to bet Choromansky paid a visit to Cheltenham.'

Fitch said with excitement: 'You're dead right! He went there on a day excursion – the porter told me.' Saltfleet sighed, shaking his head. 'But what's at Cheltenham?'

'Well, to begin with, the General Communications Headquarters.' He could see this meant nothing to Fitch. 'The place that all Foreign Office traffic has to go through. The place they arrested that spy two years ago.'

Fitch said: 'Oh Christ.'

Saltfleet shrugged. 'I could be wrong. That's just a guess. But it's interesting that the book falls open at that point.'

Fitch said gloomily: 'I suppose I'd better tell MacPhail.'

'And the Special Branch.'

Fitch pulled a wry face. 'Do you think that's necessary?'

'If spying's involved they've *got* to be told.'

'You know what they're like. They'll probably take over the whole case.' A prejudice against the Special Branch is not uncommon in the police force.

'Come on and finish your beer.'

Fitch looked thoroughly crestfallen as he followed Saltfleet back to the kitchen. But he brightened when Saltfleet offered him another can of lager. '*Are* we certain of the facts? Suppose the jaundice was genuine? Suppose he really was interested in English history? That book looks genuine to me – it's obviously been read from cover to cover.'

Saltfleet said patiently: 'That's a spy's job – to look genuine. He'll go to endless trouble to cover up his tracks. Of course, it's your decision. But my advice would be: tell them right away. It doesn't matter if you're wrong – you'll get credit for being on the alert.'

'Yes, I suppose you're right.' Fitch was visibly relieved. They sat in silence, while both drank. Saltfleet glanced at his watch and wondered what was keeping Miranda.

Fitch said: 'Even if he *was* a spy, I can't see why anybody should want to kill him?'

'Perhaps his own people. He could have been a double agent and they found out.'

Fitch chuckled sardonically. 'Could even have been MI5.'

'No. They'd have simply arrested him.'

Fitch glanced at his watch, and drained his beer. 'Thanks again for the drink. That was badly needed. You must have a few with me some time.'

'Any time.'

As he escorted Fitch to the door Fitch said: 'By the way, what about this girl you mentioned – the one who talked to Choromansky before he died?'

Saltfleet said: 'I've seen her. I don't think she knows anything. But I'll give you her address.'

'I'll see what MacPhail says. Thanks again.'

Watching him climb into his car, Saltfleet thought: A decent man, but too easily discouraged. Because he was discouraged by the spy development, he hadn't bothered to take down Moro's address. Somehow, he lacked the instinct that made a good detective.

He went upstairs to the bathroom. It was twice the size of his bathroom at home, and had a circular tub made of green imitation marble. On the edge of the tub there was a small, battered teddy bear with a blue ribbon tied round its neck. It made him smile. Although Geraldine had brought only a few toilet articles and a nightdress, she had still found room for the teddy bear in her overnight case. When she was a child, she used to talk to the teddy bear in her bath. Now, although she no longer slept with it tucked in bed beside her, she still liked to see it on the edge of the bath.

It brought a glimpse of innocence and vulnerability, of a naked small girl with wet hair clutching a damp teddy bear as her mother wrapped her in a bathtowel. Suddenly, he understood clearly what disturbed him about Rosa Judd. She had also been innocent and vulnerable. But the adult world had somehow failed to give her the protection that Geraldine had always taken for granted. The result was this nightmare of confusion, of a mind lost in some shadowland between two realities.

He also understood why Geraldine's sexual explorations caused him so much distress. She was moving into a realm of experience where he could no longer protect her. Yet the teddy bear revealed that she was still a child. She was not yet ready for love affairs, and the exploitation of males who wanted to prove their virility . . . He made a determined effort to put the subject out of his mind, to think instead of the Polish sailor and whether he could have been an agent of the KGB. But before he had reached the bottom of the stairs it had come back again. It would have been so much nicer if Geraldine had been like her mother at the same age, confiding her heartaches to her diary, and dreaming about stolen kisses at Christmas parties. Why did modern girls have to dispose of their virginity so early? Again, the gross physical image made him wince: of Geraldine naked on a rug, her legs parted and her eyes closed. A month ago the image would have filled him with rage; now it brought a sense of weary resignation.

He looked at the time, and realised that he had not eaten since breakfast. In the refrigerator he found a pork pie, still wrapped in cellophane, and a bowl of spring onions. By the time he had eaten half the pie, washed down with the remainder of the lager, he felt better. The depression had vanished, and given way to intense curiosity. He could understand a child being broken by ill-treatment; but he found it impossible to imagine how this could turn into guilt and a desire to be beaten and humiliated. What had gone wrong? How had a normal seven-year-old – who sounded very much like Geraldine at the same age – lost all her confidence and certainty?

His training made it impossible to sit still and brood on it. He needed facts, not speculations. He looked up Moro's telephone number in the telephone book, and dialled the Institute of Sexual Science. A voice he recognised as Emil's answered.

'Could I speak to Dr Moro? It's Chief Superintendent Saltfleet.'

A moment later, Moro was on the line.

'What can I do for you, Superintendent?'

'Any luck finding Frankie's shoes?'

'I'm afraid not. I think you must be right about them.'

'I'm afraid it's possible the police may want to talk to him. You can see that it looks very suspicious.'

Moro sighed. 'Yes, I see.'

'Would it be possible to find out what size shoes Frankie takes?'

'Now?'

'No. But some time before they question him. If his shoe size is different from that footprint, he'll be eliminated as a suspect.'

'Yes, of course. That should be no problem.'

'Good. There's one more thing, doctor. What happened

to Rosie's parents?'

'They died a long time ago.'

'And her aunt and uncle?'

'Her uncle is also dead. The aunt is still alive, as far as I know.'

'Does she realise what's happened to Rosie?'

'I believe so. I wrote to tell her, but she never replied.'

'Could you give me her address?'

'Yes. Just one moment.' After a pause he read aloud: 'Seven Park View Drive, Orpington.'

'Is there a phone number?'

'I'm afraid not.'

'What's her name?'

'Mrs Violet Jarvis.'

'Would you object if I went to see her?'

'Of course not. Please try to persuade her to take some interest in her niece. And I would very much like to speak with her myself.'

'All right, doctor, I promise I'll do what I can. Let me give you this phone number, so you can let me know about the shoes.'

Miranda and Geraldine came in as he hung up. Miranda said: 'I'm sorry we're so late. You know what they're like. They insisted that we stay to lunch. I tried to ring but got no reply.'

'Do you still want to go to the zoo?'

'Oh no.' She dropped on to the settee with a sigh of relief. 'We're both worn out.'

'In that case, would you mind if I went out for a couple of hours?'

'All right.' Miranda never asked questions. 'Will you be back in time for dinner?'

'Yes, I promise.' He kissed her on top of the head. 'We'll go to that Greek place off Queensway.'

* * *

92

The drive to Orpington took less time than he expected. Towards the end of a warm Sunday afternoon, most of the traffic was flowing in the opposite direction, returning from the south coast. He drove to the end of the Old Kent Road, then to Bromley via Lewisham. In Petts Wood Road he stopped to consult his London atlas; this was an area with which he was unacquainted. His eye fell on Birchwood Road, and for a moment he tried to recall why it sounded familiar. Then he remembered: Rosie had mentioned it that morning when she gave her address. He drove out of his way to look at it, and was struck by its pleasant suburban anonymity; fifty yards away, on the other side of the railway line, was the green expanse of Petts Wood. It seemed an agreeable place for a child to grow up in.

Ten minutes later, he drew up in front of the house in Park View Drive; the park seemed to be a small recreation ground, and boys were enthusiastically playing football. In the heatless golden sunlight, the tidy gardens and neatly trimmed hedgerows looked like an illustration from a gardening catalogue. Number seven had a dark brown front door. When he rang the bell, there was silence; the house seemed to be empty. But after the third ring, he heard a movement inside. The curtain of the front window twitched, and a face looked out; he pretended not to notice. A moment later, the front door opened. A bespectacled woman with a broad red face looked out suspiciously.

'Mrs Jarvis?'

'Yes.' The manner had a touch of hostility.

He smiled reassuringly: 'I'm Chief Superintendent Saltfleet of the CID. I wanted to speak to you about your niece Rosa Judd.'

At the mention of the CID, a look of alarm crossed her face; she glanced quickly up and down the street, as if to see whether anyone had overheard. She said: 'You'd better come in.'

He followed her into the sitting-room. The house had a smell of furniture polish. The velvet armchairs had protective covers on the arms and the place where a head would rest. A cage by the window contained a budgerigar. She said: 'You'll have to excuse the untidiness.' Saltfleet looked around the room, but could see no sign of untidiness except the sewing basket on the table, and a *News of the World* on the settee. She said: 'What's Rosie been doing?'

Saltfleet chose his words carefully: 'I suppose you can say she's in trouble.'

'Yes.' The tone of her voice implied: I'm not surprised. 'Won't you sit down?'

It was not often that Saltfleet found himself disliking someone at first sight; but there was something about the broad face, and its contrast with the prim, tight mouth that he found distasteful. At the same time, he sensed that she was accustomed to being disliked, and that this made her defensive. He set out to make her feel at ease.

'What a pleasant little house you've got.' He watched her take a cushion cover out of the basket, and slip a thimble on her finger. 'Have you lived here long?'

'Forty-three years, since I was first married.'

'You're lucky.'

She said guardedly: 'Sometimes I think so.' He decided not to pursue that one.

The shelf over the fireplace contained several photographs. The one in the centre showed a good-looking young woman whose hair was set in a neat permanent wave; with surprise, he recognised a younger version of the woman sitting opposite. The chin was a little too determined, and the smile lacked spontaneity; but the mouth had not yet acquired the slightly sullen twist. Next to it was a photograph of the same woman standing beside a man, with a boy of about ten in front of them. He started to ask: 'Is that your husband?', but before he could complete the sentence she had interrupted: 'What's Rosa been doing?'

He cleared his throat, wondering how much to say. 'I'm investigating a murder – of a sailor. Your niece was one of the last persons to see him alive.'

'Ah?' Her alertness showed she was interested; but she went on sewing without looking up.

'Now the problem is that I haven't been able to question your niece. You know she's . . . mentally ill?'

'So I've heard.'

'And I wonder if you can . . . tell me something about her.'

She looked up. 'You mean you want to know if she's shamming?' There was a gleam of satisfaction in her eyes.

'Well . . . yes, to some extent.' He could see that was what she wanted to hear.

She looked back at her needlework. 'I can't help you much. I haven't seen her in ten years.'

'No? He tried to sound interested and curious. 'Why is that?'

'She lived in this house for nigh on three years, and we treated her like a daughter. So when she ran away from home I washed my hands of her.' The control in her voice could not disguise a grim satisfaction.

Saltfleet took out his notebook, to introduce a formal note into the conversation.

'What age was she when she came to live here?'

After a pause: 'Twelve-and-a-half.'

'And why was that?'

'Because my brother Fred died. I was the nearest relative.'

'What did he die of?'

'Heart attack.'

'What was your brother's profession?'

'He ran a firm that made vacuum cleaners. F. and H. Smythe.'

'And your brother's wife?'

'She died of Goodpasture's Syndrome.'

Saltfleet said conversationally: 'That's one I've never heard of. What is it?'

'A rare disease of the nerves.' As Saltfleet wrote it down she added: 'She was never very stable.'

'Mentally?'

'That's right.'

'And when did she die?'

'In 1963. When Rosie was five.'

'Poor child. It must have been a bad shock.' She said nothing, but he noticed that her mouth tightened. 'Did your brother marry again?'

'No.'

He said sympathetically: 'He must have been very upset.'

She looked up at him; her stare was hard and unwavering. 'If you want to know, it was a blessing.'

'Why?'

'Because she was a . . .' She stopped herself, then said more calmly: 'She behaved like a slut.'

'She was unfaithful to him?'

'Yes.' She snapped it out.

'With anyone in particular?'

'With anybody who'd have her.' The contempt was savage.

'And did your brother know about this?'

'He soon found out.' She stared at him sombrely; he could see that he had tapped a powerful spring of emotion. 'He came back one afternoon to collect some papers, and found her on the settee in the front room. The man was one of his own salesmen. Fred ordered him out and asked her how she could do such a thing. She said:

"Because I need a man, and I'm not married to one."' It was evidently something that she had brooded about a great deal.

'What did she mean by that?'

She shrugged. '*I* don't know.' Her tone implied: Don't ask stupid questions. He suddenly realised that she reminded him of someone; but the memory eluded him.

'Who looked after Rosie after her mother died?'

'I did, mostly.' He let the silence lengthen. She went on finally: 'She used to come here out of school, and her father would pick her up when he came home from work.'

'Who did their cooking?'

'He did.'

'It must have been a lonely life for a child.'

'She did all right.'

The doorbell rang; she started and looked at the clock. Saltfleet also checked the time; it was nearly six o'clock. He said: 'You've got visitors. I'll leave you now.'

As she stood up, he remembered: she reminded him of Elvira Sams, the Watford poisoner. Mrs Sams had that same air of irritable taciturnity, implying that the world had subjected her to endless provocation and annoyance. She had been sentenced to death in 1953 for the murder of three husbands with arsenic, and Saltfleet, then a Detective Constable, had been present at her arrest. She would never have been suspected if she had not poisoned a neighbour's dog.

While Violet Jarvis was out of the room, Saltfleet looked more closely at the photographs on the shelf. In the picture with the man and the small boy, she was still an attractive woman, but was already becoming over-weight. The boy, who wore a school cap and blazer, was also too plump for his age; the woman's hand was resting on his shoulder, and he was looking at the camera with a complacent and self-conscious smile. The man, obviously her husband, had a moustache and wore a trilby hat; he was handsome, but there was something weak about his face. This was confirmed by a photograph at the end of the shelf; he was wearing a military uniform with a bandsman's cap, and the moustache looked almost rakish; underneath it, the chin was weak and the mouth indecisive. But the mild eyes were humorous and good-natured.

He turned away from the shelf as she came back into the room. She was followed by a man in his mid-twenties; Saltfleet immediately recognised the boy of the photograph. He was still too fat, and the hair was already receding; but the face was oddly unchanged, as if it had been simply enlarged. He looked curiously at Saltfleet. Saltfleet said: 'How do you do?'

'How do.' He asked his mother: 'Have I come at a bad time?'

'No. He's just leaving.' It was plainly intended as a hint.

Saltfleet said: 'You must be Rosie's cousin Joey?'

He looked astonished. 'That's right.'

'I've come to talk to your mother about Rosie.'

She interrupted: 'I don't think there's any more I can tell you.'

Joey ignored her. 'What's a matter with Rosie?' He spoke with a broader London accent than his mother.

Saltfleet said: 'I'm investigating a murder.'

Joey's eyes gleamed. 'A murder!' His voice tended to be pitched too loud, as if he used it for asserting his authority. Saltfleet observed that he had his father's weak mouth.

Saltfleet turned to Mrs Jarvis, smiling urbanely. 'Would you mind if I had a word with your son?'

Before she could answer, Joey said: 'Of course she wouldn't.' He dropped heavily into the armchair. 'How about a cup of tea, Ma?'

She said: 'All right.' It was obvious that Joey was accustomed to giving her orders, and that she enjoyed it.

She went out.

Joey said: 'What's going on?'

Saltfleet said: 'Well, as you know, your cousin Rosie is in a mental home in Notting Hill.'

He shook his head. 'I didn't know. Nobody told me.'

His mother's voice said from the kitchen: 'Yes you did. *I* told you.'

'You did not!' His voice was so loud that Saltfleet winced.

'I told you she was ill.'

'You didn't tell me she'd gone bonkers.' He turned to Saltfleet. 'What's this about a murder?'

'I'm investigating the death of a sailor. Your cousin was one of the last persons seen speaking to him.'

'Rosie wouldn't kill anyone.' It was obviously a spontaneous reaction.

'I'm sure she wouldn't.'

'Anyway, who is this sailor?'

'He was a Pole on shore leave. He was trying to pick her up.'

'And did he?'

'We don't know. It's possible.'

'Are you trying to tell me she's on the game?' He had evidently decided that, as a policeman, Saltfleet could be treated as an inferior. Saltfleet was not offended; he knew that someone who was unafraid of him might tell him more than someone who was nervous in the presence of the law. He said: 'She *has* been known to pick up men.'

Joey whistled slowly; his eyes were bright with curiosity and excitement. 'Well, well, well.' As his mother came into the room with a tea-tray he said: 'Another one of 'em in the family.' He explained to Saltfleet: 'Rosie's mother was the same.'

Mrs Jarvis said drily: 'He already knows that.'

'Still,' Joey said, 'she didn't used to do it for money. Did she, Ma?'

'I wouldn't know.' She went out again.

Aware that the sound of the kettle would drown their voices, Saltfleet said: "Why does your mother hate Rosie so much?"

Joey shrugged: "Ma doesn't need a reason to hate somebody.' He added, after a moment, 'If she had a reason, she never told me.'

Saltfleet said: 'I gather that your cousin was in love with you?'

Joey said complacently: 'I suppose so.'

'And how did you feel about her?'

'Oh, I suppose she was all right. She wasn't exactly a beauty.' He gave a snort of laughter. 'You know she lost all her hair at one point?'

'No. Why was that?'

'Oh, some skin disease.' He pulled open a drawer in the table beside him, and took out an album. 'Look, that's her.'

Saltfleet took the album on his knees. It was a picture of two children on a beach, building a sandcastle. They looked about eight years old. Joey was smiling confidently; Rosie was staring up at the camera with wide eyes, totally serious. Her face was covered with a rash, and the hair was sparse and stringy. Saltfleet felt his throat contract; the resemblance to Geraldine was unmistakable. It was something in the expression of the eyes and the set of the mouth rather than in the physical features.

He turned the page, and saw another picture of the two children. They were on a fairground, looking through a hole in a canvas which turned their faces into Mickey Mouse and Donald Duck. Both were grinning with delight. The girl's face was rounder, and the hair looked shiny and normal.

Saltfleet asked: 'When was this one taken?'

'I dunno.' Joey looked over his shoulder, then removed the photograph and looked at the back. 'Oh, that was in

August 1965. We took her to Southend for the day.'

'Before this one?' He pointed to the other picture.

'Yes. Her hair fell out later.'

'What caused it?'

'They said it was brain fever.'

'How did she get that?'

Joey glanced slyly at the kitchen; replacing the photograph, he spoke in Saltfleet's ear.

'Her dad caught us in the cupboard. He nearly went crackers. I thought he was going to kill her.'

'When was that?'

'It was at her birthday party – her eighth birthday.'

'What were you doing in the cupboard?'

'Sshh!' Joey looked up nervously. 'Usual things kids get up to. You know.' He winked.

'Was her father very strict?'

Joey resumed his seat as his mother came into the room with the teapot.

'Oh yes. One of those hellfire Baptists, always reading the Bible.'

Mrs Jarvis said, with a touch of reproof: 'He was a very good man.'

'I'm not saying he wasn't. But he made Rosie's life a misery, didn't he?'

'She usually deserved it.'

Saltfleet turned the pages of the album. There were several photographs of Joey and Rosie together; as children they had obviously been inseparable. He could see at a glance which photographs had been taken after the illness, even after the skin complaint had vanished and the hair grown back to normal: she had become pale and withdrawn. Joey, on the other hand, became visibly chubbier and more self-confident. One picture showed him wearing a sailor collar and cap, and waving a stick of rock at the camera; in the background, Rosie looked at him adoringly.

Mrs Jarvis handed him his tea; she placed her finger on the page. 'That was taken at Fred's funeral service.' It showed a group of people outside a crematorium; Rosie looked skinny and gawky, as unattractive as a plucked chicken. Joey was already six inches taller than she was, and looked cheerful and self-confident.

'That was when she came to live with you?'

'That's right.'

Later photographs showed Joey with a well-developed blonde girl. Saltfleet said: 'Who's that?'

She said: 'Oh, that was Joey's first girlfriend – I've forgotten her name.'

'Diane.'

There were only two more photographs of Rosie, one with her uncle, one with a group of girls. In these, the resemblance to Geraldine was striking. She had become pretty, and the breasts were small but round. In the group photograph with the girls, she was wearing a mini-skirt, and her legs were disturbingly shapely. In the other picture, she was wearing jeans; her uncle had his arm round her waist, and she had her head on his shoulder.

Saltfleet said: 'Why did she run away from home?'

Joey shook his head. 'She went a bit funny.'

Mrs Jarvis, he noticed, said nothing; she behaved as if the question had nothing to do with her.

'Could it have been because you started having girlfriends?'

'I s'pose so.' He glanced at his mother for confirmation, but she kept her eyes on her plate.

Saltfleet tasted his tea; it was almost unbearably sweet. She noticed his grimace.

'Is something wrong with it?'

'Er . . . just a little too sweet for me.'

'Oh, I'm sorry. Joey likes a lot of sugar.' She held out a plate piled high with slices of plum cake and apple pie. He refused politely. She placed it beside Joey, who examined

102

it with interest, and finally selected a large slice of cake.

Saltfleet glanced at his watch; it was a quarter past six. If he was to be home by eight, he had to leave soon.

'One more question. Where did Rosie go when she left home?'

Joey tried to answer, but had to shake his head apologetically; the words were muffled by the cake.

Mrs Jarvis said: 'She went to work at a holiday camp in Filey. As a kitchen maid.' Without undue emphasis, the words managed to express boundless contempt.

Joey said: 'She used to be a good little cook. She cooked for her dad, even when she was seven.'

'Did she write from the holiday camp?'

Mrs Jarvis said: 'Once or twice.'

Joey said: 'Oh, she wrote quite a lot!'

'Did you ever try to persuade her to come back?'

Mrs Jarvis said decisively: 'I wouldn't have her back.'

'Was there a quarrel before she left?'

The woman shook her head. Joey said: 'Well, there were quite a few rows at one time and another. Rosie and Ma just didn't see eye to eye. Ma didn't like it because Dad always took Rosie's part.'

'That had nothing to do with it!' she glowered at her son. 'I didn't like her because she was sly.'

Joey shrugged, and selected a piece of apple pie. It was evidently a subject on which he was prepared to allow his mother the last word.

Saltfleet stood up. 'Thank you for your help. It's all been very useful.'

Joey said: 'What'll happen to Rose . . . if she's guilty?'

'Nothing. Nothing *can* happen to her, since she's in a mental home.'

'And what about the bloke?'

'He's in the same place.'

Joey said: 'God! They can't half get away with it, can't they!'

Saltfleet said: 'Don't bother to see me out.' Mrs Jarvis nodded without looking up from her tea; it was plain she felt the visit had gone on too long. Joey said: 'I'll see you to the door.'

'That's kind of you.'

Joey glanced nervously at his mother. 'And perhaps I'd better give you my phone number . . . in case Rosie needs help . . .'

Mrs Jarvis bridled. 'We're *not* getting involved with her again.'

Joey sighed. 'No. I didn't say we were.'

'I know what Alice would say about it!'

'All right, all right!' He almost shouted the words at her. She dropped her eyes submissively, but the mouth remained tight and sullen.

Joey was muttering under his breath as he showed Saltfleet to the door. His face was red and angry. To relieve the tension, Saltfleet said: 'Is Alice your wife?'

'Yes.'

'Any children?'

'Three.'

Saltfleet lowered his voice. 'If you want to give me your telephone number, I'll let you know what happens.'

Joey looked over his shoulder to make sure the sitting-room door was closed, then pulled a card out of his top pocket. It said: 'Joseph B. Jarvis. Haulage Contractor', with an address in Orpington. Joey raised his finger to his lips; Saltfleet smiled understandingly, and slipped the card into his own pocket.

He had to back away from the large green Datsun that was parked in front of his Rover. As he was pulling out into the road, there was a tap on the windscreen; Joey was standing there. Saltfleet wound down the window.

Joey said: 'Tell Rosie . . .' He fumbled for words. 'Tell Rosie I hope it works out all right.'

He turned and hurried guiltily into the house.

SIX

When he woke up the next morning, Saltfleet was suffering from a mild hangover; he had allowed the proprietor of the Greek restaurant to persuade him to drink two glasses of a powerful spirit called raki with his coffee. There was no headache; only a curious feeling of sluggishness, as if he was dragging a ball-and-chain on each ankle.

At 7.30, Miranda drove Geraldine to Waterloo to catch the 8.10 for Thames Ditton. As she kissed him goodbye, Geraldine had kept her arms round him longer than usual; he sensed that it was an attempt to reassure him. Oddly enough, it was no longer necessary. On the previous evening, as he had watched Geraldine eating stuffed vineleaves and aubergine moussaka, and washing them down with retsina, he had been overwhelmed by the contrast between his own daughter and the girl who had grown up in a motherless home in Orpington. It was as if some inner kaleidoscope had been shaken; quite suddenly it was a matter of absurd indifference whether Geraldine was a virgin when compared with the central fact that she was safe and confident and emotionally unscarred. The idea of her returning to Charlie's urgent embraces still disturbed him, but it no longer produced the same sense of helpless outrage.

He sat at the kitchen table, and drank three cups of strong coffee. It felt strange not to be working. At about this time, his assistant would be arriving at the office and looking through the crime reports from his divisions, and the Criminal Record sheets compiled by the Divisional Collator. And his colleague Scottie MacPhail would find on his own desk the report on the murder of Witold Choromansky.

At nine o'clock precisely he rang Dr Moro. Dorothy's voice answered the phone. It sounded as cool and detached as ever. He said: 'This is Superintendent Saltfleet. Could I have a word with Dr Moro?'

'I'm afraid he's busy. Could I take a message?'

'No, you couldn't. I need to speak to him personally.'

'Could you tell me what it's about?'

'Yes. It's about you.'

There was a silence; then she said: 'Hold on a moment, please.'

He chuckled to himself, his hand over the mouthpiece. If she had continued to refuse to let him speak to Moro, it would have looked as if she was motivated by self-interest.

Moro's voice said: 'Good morning, Superintendent.'

'Good morning, doctor.'

'You want to know about the shoes?'

'That was one of the things I wanted to talk about.'

'I had to wait until Frankie was asleep. Unfortunately, they had no size marked in them. But I measured them. They were exactly twelve-and-a-half inches long.'

'Thank you. The other thing I want to talk to you about is Rosie. Could you spare me half an hour later today?'

'Of course. What time would suit you?'

'Ten o'clock?'

'I will make sure that I am free.'

Miranda came in, carrying an armful of groceries. She said: 'Scottie's over there in the gardens.'

He went into the front room, and peered out of the window. Scottie MacPhail drove a brown Ford Zodiac, and it was parked in front of the gate. Without bothering

106

to put on his jacket, he strolled across the road. The gate was open. MacPhail was standing by the flowerbed, accompanied by Constable Evans, the Scene of Crimes officer from Notting Hill. He called: 'Hello, Scottie!'

MacPhail said: 'Good God, Greg! What are you doing here?'

He was a tall, thin man, with the bony face of a Highlander. It was typical of him to be at the scene of the crime by nine in the morning; he was known as one of the most efficient officers in the CID. Unfortunately, his imagination sometimes failed to match his efficiency.

'I'm on holiday. And I'm staying in the house right across the road.'

'Which makes you suspect number one.' MacPhail's attempts at humour often fell flat. Evans laughed politely.

'Feel like a cup of coffee?'

'No thanks. I don't have time. The Constable was just showing me the footprint he discovered.'

Evans said awkwardly: 'In fact, Mr Saltfleet found it.'

'Did he indeed.' Saltfleet wished that Evans had kept quiet; he had no objection to someone else taking the credit. He leaned forward, and looked at the footprint, which still showed clearly on the damp earth.

'How long would you say that was?'

Evans said: 'It's exactly twelve-and-three-quarter inches. I measured it.'

'That's a large shoe.'

Evans said: 'Size eleven, same as mine.'

MacPhail looked keenly at Saltfleet. 'Reached any conclusions?'

'Oh no. I was only here for a couple of minutes. I'd guess it's just an ordinary sex crime – a sadistic queer.'

MacPhail grunted. He said after a pause: 'That may be what they intended us to think.'

'They?'

MacPhail lowered his voice, glancing at Evans, who was

on the other side of the flowerbed. 'It may be a five hundred.' Dossiers for the Special Branch were marked 'Box 500'.

'Spying?'

'Could be. That's something Fitch sniffed out. He's better than I thought.'

'He struck me as being on the ball.'

MacPhail grunted noncommittally. Saltfleet looked at his watch.

'Oh well, I'd better get my breakfast. See you back at the office.'

The telephone was ringing as he entered the house; from the kitchen came the sound of frying. Miranda called: 'Would you get that, Greg?'

It was Fitch.

'I've been talking to Dr Roberts, the man who examined Choromansky when he went into hospital. He says he's certain it *was* jaundice.'

'How could he be so sure?'

'He says he's often seen the effect of antimalaria drugs, and they're not at all the same.'

'Did you ask him to explain the difference?'

'Well . . . no. I took his word for it.'

Saltfleet shook his head with exasperation. He said: 'So you've decided Choromansky wasn't a spy?'

Fitch sounded worried. 'Wouldn't you say so?'

'I wouldn't say anything until I'd made further investigations.'

'What would you suggest?'

'Well, to begin with, I'd ring Aspinal at University College Hospital and find out if there's any other drug that induces the symptoms of hepatitis.'

Fitch sounded disappointed. 'Do you really think it's worth it?'

'It's always worth it.' Saltfleet had to keep the irritation out of his voice. 'Aspinal's had a day to give it some thought – he may have another idea. And then I'd send a photograph of Choromansky to Special Branch, together with his fingerprints. They may be able to identify him. The Polish Secret Service can't have all that many agents in the KGB.'

Fitch said, without enthusiasm: 'No, I daresay you're right.' That 'daresay' exasperated him; it implied that Fitch was less than half-convinced. When he hung up he rammed the phone back on to its cradle.

His temper improved at the sight of the egg and bacon. This was the first time since Saturday that he had been able to speak to Miranda alone; he took the opportunity to describe what he had been doing. Under normal circumstances he seldom spoke to her about investigations in progress; this was not due to professional reticence so much as to an almost superstitious desire to keep his hunches to himself until they had been tried and tested. The present case was different; not only because he was on somebody else's 'patch', but because he wanted her to share his fascination with the mystery. Her total absorption made him aware that he had succeeded.

When he had described his first interview with Moro she interrupted to ask: 'How can you be sure she's not pretending?'

He shook his head. 'You'd have to see her for yourself. She's genuinely ill.'

'That's not what I mean. Are you sure this girl Dorothy isn't pretending? This doctor says that one personality usually knows what the other is doing and thinking. Why not in this case?'

'I just don't know. That's the problem. I have to take Moro's word for these clinical matters, and I've no way of knowing whether he's right. It's completely beyond my experience.'

The clock struck the hour. He jumped to his feet. 'I must go. I promised to see Moro at ten. I'll try to be back soon.'

'Don't worry. I've a lot of shopping to do.' She helped him on with his jacket. 'But you don't think this girl Rosie had anything to do with the murder?'

'I think it's unlikely. What really baffles me is what turned her into a masochist . . .'

'Oh, I can tell you that.'

He stared at her. 'What?'

'Guilt.'

'What about?'

'I don't know. But about something.'

'Yes, I suppose you're right.' He thought it over for a moment. 'Yes, of course you're right. But what on earth could she feel guilty about?'

The gate of the Institute of Sexual Science stood open. As he started to mount the steps, the front door opened. A tall, gaunt woman came out; her face was beautiful, but ravaged and tired. Moro, dressed in a white smock, stood behind her. She stared at Saltfleet with a frightened, guilty expression, then hurried past him.

Moro said: 'Good morning.'

Saltfleet looked round at the woman; she looked back at him suspiciously as she went out of the gate.

'She looks as if she knows me.'

Moro said: 'No. She is like that with everyone.' He led Saltfleet up the stairs. 'Poor woman, she has a strange problem.'

Saltfleet wanted to ask what it was, but decided it would be tactless.

They went into the office. Some of the cases had been covered with black velvet to protect them from the sunlight. He asked: 'Where's Dorothy?'

'She has gone to her room with a headache. That may be a good sign.'

'Why?'

110

'She often gets a headache before Rosa takes over.'

'Does that mean that Dorothy's getting weaker while Rosa's getting stronger?'

'No. In many cases, you would be quite correct. But not in this. Dorothy is far stronger than Rosa. But I suspect that Dorothy vanishes when it suits her. Besides, today we have our games therapy session, and Dorothy hates that.'

'What is it?'

'If you stay around you will see.' He opened the cupboard, and took out a white smock. 'I wonder if you would mind putting this on? I think it should fit.'

'Of course. But why?'

'So the patients will assume you are a doctor. Most of them have strong guilt feelings – like the woman you passed at the door. She prefers her Alsatian dog to her husband. When her husband caught them in a compromising situation, he insisted that she should have treatment.'

Saltfleet said: 'My God!'

In fact, the smock was rather tight; but when he removed his jacket, it fitted perfectly. Moro helped him to button it.

Saltfleet said: 'I feel rather a fraud in this.'

'That is better than driving my patients away – which is what would happen if they knew you were a policeman. Now, before we talk, I have just one more patient to see.'

Saltfleet was worried. 'Hadn't I better leave?'

'That is unnecessary. Just sit there, beside my desk.'

'Are you sure it's . . . legal?'

'Perfectly. All my records are open to the police. In exchange, I am allowed to keep patients here when they are awaiting trial for sex crimes. Would you mind telling me your Christian name?'

'Gregory.'

'Ah yes, of course. Then I shall call you Doctor Gregory. Would you excuse me one moment?'

He returned a few seconds later, followed by a small,

grey-haired man, who regarded Saltfleet with anxiety.

Moro said: 'This is Doctor Gregory. What can I do for you today, Mr Trimble?'

The little man glanced nervously at Saltfleet.

'It's a bit delicate.'

'Are you in trouble with the police again?'

'Oh no! Nothing like that. I mean it's in a delicate place . . .'

'Show me.'

Without hesitation, the little man unbuckled his belt, and pushed down his trousers. 'It's down here.'

'Oh dear, the same as before. Lie down.'

The man kicked off his trousers, then lay down on the couch. He bent his knees, opening his legs; the skin inside his thighs had a red, chapped appearance. Moro bent down and peered at him. He delicately pressed a point beneath the scrotum; the little man winced.

'Is it a needle?'

'Yes.' His voice was hoarse.

Without a word, Moro went to his desk, and took from a drawer a white enamel dish containing surgical instruments; from this he took a pair of tweezers. He knelt at the end of the couch, and carefully prodded with one hand, using the tweezers with the other. The man suddenly whined with pain; then his face relaxed into a beatific smile. With a jerk, Moro pulled out a small needle. He dropped it into the wastepaper basket. The man sighed and started to sit up. Moro said sharply: 'Lie still.'

'But it's all right now.'

'No it isn't. It could turn septic.' Moro took a disinfectant spray from his desk, and directed it between the man's legs. Then he strapped on a large pad of cottonwool with an inch-wide piece of sticking plaster. 'All right. Now you can go.'

The man scrambled awkwardly into his trousers, tripping over in his haste. Then, walking with bow legs, like a jockey, he went out.

Saltfleet asked: 'What's the matter with him?'

'He gets sexual stimulation from sticking needles into his genitals. Sometimes he sticks them in too far, and then he comes to me to get them out.'

'Doesn't he make himself ill?'

'No. He has been doing it all his life – he seems to have built up a resistance.'

Moro washed his hands at a sink in the corner.

'Now, you came to me to talk about Rosa.'

'I went down to Orpington to see her Aunt Violet yesterday. I also met her cousin Joey.'

'Ah!' Moro became deeply attentive. 'Please tell me.' He sat down behind his desk.

'This Aunt Violet doesn't strike me as a very sympathetic character. She obviously hates Rosie. When I told her I was investigating a murder, I got the feeling she rather hoped Rosie was guilty.'

'Did you find out why?'

'Her version is that they treated Rosie like a daughter, and Rosie behaved liked an ungrateful little slut.'

Moro shook his head. 'A girl of fourteen does not run away from home unless she is very unhappy – particularly if she already comes from a broken home.'

'That's what I thought. The aunt also told me some things about Rosie's childhood. Her father seems to have been a religious fanatic, a hellfire Baptist – I didn't learn that from the aunt but from her cousin Joey, Rosie's father caught his wife being unfaithful with one of his travelling salesmen – did you know that?' Moro shook his head. Saltfleet took out his notebook. 'She used an interesting phrase. When he asked her how she could do such a thing, she said: "Because I need a man, and I'm not married to one."'

'From which you infer . . ?'

'That she may have been something of a nympho-

113

maniac, and he thought sex was filthy.'

'That is interesting, very interesting. Rosa mentioned that her father was a regular churchgoer. But she didn't say he was a religious fanatic. That shows she still feels loyal to his memory.'

'Joey told me something else. At her eighth birthday party, her father caught her in a cupboard with Joey. Joey said: "He almost went crackers. I thought he was going to kill her."'

'Crackers – that is insane?' Saltfleet nodded. 'That is a very important discovery.' Moro went to the filing cabinet, and came back a moment later with a buff-coloured file. 'This is her medical record. It shows that at the time of her eighth birthday, she spent three days in a state diagnosed as encephalitis lethargica – that is a viral infection of the brain. But it could not have been a virus because she recovered within a week. I guessed that it was ordinary brain fever due to emotional stress. After that, she lost all her hair and developed a skin complaint, a kind of psoriasis. But when I talk to her about it, she pretends she cannot remember. And when I tried asking her about it under hypnosis, she had hysterics and woke up. I am very grateful to you for telling me these things.'

Saltfleet shrugged; praise always embarrassed him.

'If her father thought sex was filthy, he must have made her life hell after the cupboard episode. He probably told her that losing her hair was a judgement from God.' A thought struck him. 'My wife says it was guilt that turned her into a masochist. *That* could be the answer. Her father made her feel that sex was filthy . . .'

Moro said with excitement: 'But perhaps she has inherited some of her mother's sensuality. So when she experiences sexual desire, she feels the need to punish herself by finding someone who will beat her. That *must* be the answer.' He rubbed his hands with pleasure. Then the smile faded. 'Except for one thing. If he was such a puritan, why did he allow her to go on seeing her cousin?'

'Because he had no choice. He was at work all day, and his sister looked after Rosie when she came home from school. Besides, I've seen photographs of Rosie after she lost her hair. She was so thin and ugly she'd have been safe with a sex maniac.'

'Yes. You are obviously right.' He smiled wryly. 'You have discovered more about Rosa in a few hours than I found out in six months.'

Saltfleet smiled and shrugged; his unspoken thought was that if Moro had taken the trouble to drive to Orpington, he could have found it out for himself. He said: 'The problem is: does it help?'

'Of course it helps. It helps me to understand what Rosa is trying to suppress.' He looked at his watch. 'Let me go and see what is happening to her. If I can, I'll bring her back here.'

Saltfleet said uneasily: 'Is that a good idea, after what happened last time?'

'It is a risk I am willing to take. You have a right to see what happens. Excuse me.'

Left alone, Saltfleet looked into the glass cases, and tried to decipher the typed notices with the aid of his half-forgotten school German. Then he moved to the glass-fronted bookcase. He had been intrigued by a pile of leather-bound photograph albums on the bottom shelf; now he picked up one of these and read the neatly typed label: *Transvestitismus und Tödliche Unglücksfälle bei Autoerotischer Betätigung*; he translated this: transvestism and deadly accident through autoerotic activity. The photographs inside were of males dressed in women's underwear and hanging from nooses, mostly in sitting positions. One man was dressed in oversize baby clothes, including a diaper held in position with a huge safety-pin.

He had encountered many such cases, particularly in his days on the Vice Squad. As a young Constable he had found it impossible to believe that strangulation can produce sexual excitement. But within a month of leaving training school, he had been summoned by a hysterical prostitute who wanted him to try to revive a customer. The man had hired her to stimulate him as he hanged himself, with instructions to cut him down as he lost consciousness. She had left it too late, and he had strangled to death – but not before he had achieved orgasm. In all later cases he had encountered, the individual was alone at the time of death; the devices for releasing the pressure were often ingenious.

The album seemed to cover more than half a century; he found it interesting to observe the changes in styles of underwear over the years, from the knee-length bloomers of the 1920s, through the camiknicks and French knickers of the thirties and forties, to the inadequate bikini briefs of the eighties. On the point of closing it, his attention was arrested by one of the later photographs; something about the swollen face seemed familiar. Then he recognised it; the little man called Trimble, whom he had watched having a needle removed from his genitals. He was seated in a device made of black leather straps, which seemed to be suspended from the ceiling. The head had fallen sideways, supported by a noose. The genitals seemed to be tied up in black plastic.

On the opposite page there was another photograph showing the black leather device; but the man suspended in it seemed to be in his twenties. The black suspender belt and stockings had been pulled down so they were around his knees. On the same page there was a close-up photograph of his thighs and genitals. This showed unmistakable bite marks, and a number of red spots that looked like cigarette burns.

When Moro came back, five minutes later, Saltfleet was seated at the desk, the album open in front of him. Moro said: 'I am sorry to keep you so long. I have put her to

116

sleep. Would you like to come down?'

Saltfleet pointed to the album. 'Can you tell me who took these photographs?'

Moro moved behind his chair. 'Ah yes.' He hesitated. 'They were given to me by the man you saw this morning, Albert Trimble.'

'But who took them?'

'A certain . . . homosexual voyeur. I will tell you his name if necessary.'

Saltfleet noted the hesitation, and made an instant decision.

'No, it's not necessary.' He closed the album. 'But I'd like to speak to Mr Trimble some time.'

'Of course.' Saltfleet thought he detected a note of relief. 'But I would prefer that you did it in the character of Dr Gregory. Most of my patients are terrified of the police.'

'Yes. I understand perfectly.' He stood up, and replaced the album on the bookshelf. 'What's happening with Dorothy?'

'She was suffering from a severe headache.'

'Did it come on after I telephoned you this morning?'

'Yes.'

'Then I'm probably responsible. I told her I wanted to talk to you about her.'

'Why?'

'To try and stop her being so damned obstructive.'

Moro smiled wryly. 'It seems to have worked. But I had great difficulty placing her under hypnosis.'

'Do you think you might persuade Rosie to reappear?'

'I am going to try. Would you like to come down?'

Saltfleet followed him to the ground floor. He already knew which was Dorothy's room; he had glimpsed her disappearing into it two days earlier. It was large and pleasantly decorated, with the walls distempered a light pastel shade. The girl lay asleep on the bed, her hands

117

folded on her stomach; she was breathing peacefully and regularly. The room had many personal touches: matching Victorian ornaments on the shelf, a silver horseshoe on the wall over the bed, a chart of the zodiac. He was also interested to observe, on the mantelpiece, a number of photographs, including one of cousin Joey as an adult; it indicated that they had been in touch in recent years.

Moro pointed to a chair by the window; Saltfleet sat down quietly. He wanted to comment on the photograph, but felt instinctively that Moro would prefer him to remain silent.

Moro seated himself on the bed, beside the sleeping girl, and raised her eyelids one after the other; then he raised her wrist, and allowed it to fall back. He leaned over her, saying softly: 'Dorothy, can you hear me?'

Her lips moved silently, forming the word, 'Yes.'

Moro placed his hand on her forehead.

'I want you to go into a deep sleep, deeper than you've ever been in before . . . deep relaxation, like sinking down to the bottom of the sea. Down, down, down. It's so peaceful and comfortable . . .'

For a few moments the girl's breathing became deeper; then she sighed and gave a slight shudder. After that the breathing became gentle and shallow. Five minutes later, as Moro continued to talk in a whisper, the movement of her chest had become almost undetectable.

Moro took her pulse and was apparently satisfied. He took a miniature tape-recorder from the desk, switched it on, and placed it on the pillow by her head. He leaned forward, and spoke with his mouth close to her ear:

'Is Rosie there? I want to speak to Rosie. Are you there, Rosie?' For almost a minute nothing happened. Then the breathing became perceptible again, and a faint smile made her lips curve. Moro said: 'Rosie, are you there?' Suddenly the smile changed into a grin; instantly, Saltfleet recognised that the child was back.

Moro also saw it. 'Say hello, Rosie.'

The smile became impish and mocking. After a moment she said: 'Hello!' It was the voice of a mischievous child.

Moro said: 'And how do you feel today, Rosie?'

'I'm all right.'

'No headache?'

'Of *course* not! I never get headaches!' It sounded so pert and natural that it seemed absurd that she should be lying with her eyes closed.

'How old are you, Rosie?'

The answer came promptly: 'Seven.'

She tried to sit up. Moro pressed her shoulders down on the bed.

'No, dear, I want you to lie still like a good girl.'

'I can't see!' She raised her hands to her face; Moro grasped the wrists and forced them down. She struggled for a moment, then gave way.

Moro said soothingly: 'That's right. It's not time to wake up yet. I want you to go back to sleep again. Go right back to sleep.' There was a note of command in his voice. After a moment, her breathing again became shallow and regular.

Moro said: 'Can you still hear me, Rosie?' After a pause, she smiled and nodded. 'Now I want you to go back to your seventh birthday. You're seven years old today. You're just waking up in the morning, and it's your seventh birthday. Are you going to have a party?'

'No.' The voice was sad.

'Why not?'

'Because I broke the goldfish bowl.'

'You broke the goldfish bowl? How did you do that?'

'It wasn't me. Joey did it. But I said I did because I didn't want Joey to get into trouble.'

'And Joey let you take the blame?'

She said defensively: 'Joey doesn't know.'

'And what did your daddy give you for your birthday?'

'A book called *The Children's Bible*.' Her lack of enthusiasm was obvious.

'Does your daddy make you read the Bible?'

'Yes.'

'Why?'

'He wants me to get to heaven.'

'And do you want to get to heaven?' She nodded. 'Why?'

'I want to see Mummy again . . .' Her mouth trembled; it was obvious she was on the point of tears.

Moro said quickly: 'All right. Go back to sleep now. Back to sleep. That's right.' He placed his hand on her forehead. 'Now I want you to come forward to your eighth birthday. It's the morning of your eighth birthday. You're eight years old today. You'll soon be a big girl, won't you?' She nodded, smiling happily. 'Did Joey give you a present?'

'Yes.'

'What was it?'

'A hairslide with a green butterfly.'

'And what did Daddy give you?'

'A dolly with golden hair and a lovely blue dress.'

'And are you going to have a birthday party?' She nodded. 'And who's coming to it?'

'Joey. And Sidney Pepper. And Mary Franklin. And Merryl and her sister Jessica. And their brother Bill. And Minny. And Minny's going to bring her little dog Scatterbrain. That's all.'

'Now I want you to come forward to half-past four in the afternoon. Have all your guests arrived?'

'Yes, except Mary Franklin. She fell over some milk bottles and cut her leg.'

'What have you had for tea?'

'Chocolate cake, and lime jelly and raspberry jelly and a trifle with cherries. Aunty Vi made that.'

'Have you played any games yet?'

'Yes, musical chairs and I spy and hunt the thimble. And now we're playing hide-and-seek.'

'Where are you now?'

She smiled mischievously. 'In the cupboard.'

'Are you alone?'

'No. Joey's in here with me.'

'What are you doing?'

She smiled secretively. 'Shan't tell.'

'Oh do. You can tell me.'

She shook her head firmly.

Moro said: 'Is he kissing you?'

'No!' She sounded impatient.

'Aren't you afraid someone might come and find you?'

'No.'

'Why not?'

'They don't know we're in the playroom.'

There was a silence. To Saltfleet's surprise, the girl on the bed suddenly blushed. Her hands went down defensively to her thighs.

Moro said: 'Tell me what is happening?'

'He's . . . being naughty.' Her hands pressed down fiercely on her dress.

'How?'

She gave a gasp, then giggled. 'I can't tell you . . . Joey . . . Please stop it.' Her voice became breathless. 'You're hurting me. Oh Joey, don't.' But it seemed clear that Joey was ignoring her. Suddenly she became tense, and made a movement as if to push her dress down. 'There's somebody . . .' Although they were expecting it, her piercing scream shocked them both. Moro tried to place his hand over her mouth; she pushed it aside and screamed again and again. The door burst open; it was Harriet, the woman from next door. As she called 'What's happening?', the girl's screams suddenly turned to hysterical sobs. She twisted sideways on the bed, raising her hands as if to defend her head. Her shoulders were

121

shaking violently, and tears ran from under the closed eyelids. Saltfleet went to the bed, and tried stroking her hair. He was able to distinguish the words she kept repeating: 'Don't hit him, please don't hit him. It was all my fault . . .'

As Moro pushed her shoulders back on to the bed, the convulsions gradually stopped. Moro said: 'It's all right now, there's nothing to worry about.' She continued to whimper, then began to breathe quietly. Even when she seemed to have fallen asleep, her breathing continued to be racked with periodic convulsions.

Moro turned to Harriet and gestured imperiously; she went out, closing the door softly.

Saltfleet looked at the tear-stained face and experienced a surge of pity. He said: 'That didn't seem to do much good.'

Moro smiled, and stood up. 'On the contrary, it did a great deal of good. Look how calm she looks now.' It was true; it was the face of a sleeping baby. 'What I have done is to make her relive a painful experience, to try and get it out of her system. We call it abreaction therapy. The next time I make her relive it, she won't be nearly so upset. She'll be able to describe exactly what happened.'

Saltfleet looked doubtfully at the sleeping girl, whose breathing was soft and regular. 'What happens now?'

'Now we leave her to sleep, and see what happens when she wakes up. If she feels well enough, she can take part in the games therapy session this afternoon. Would you like to stay here to lunch?'

Saltfleet said: 'It's very kind of you. But there are some things I have to do.'

SEVEN

From the Institute of Sexual Science in Lansdowne Gardens to the Notting Hill police station was a walk of precisely three minutes.

He showed his warrant card to the pretty policewoman on duty and asked: 'Is Police Constable Evans available?'

'Yes, sir. He's in the CID room with Chief Superintendent MacPhail. Would you like to go up?'

This was a setback; he had no wish to let MacPhail know he was working on the case: He said: 'No, I won't interrupt him now – I'll telephone him this afternoon.'

'Right you are, sir.'

A burly man with a black moustache came into the station, scowled at the girl, and went into the office of the duty sergeant. There was something familiar about the baggy, yellow face, with dark rings under the eyes.

He leaned forward and asked the girl quietly: 'Who's that?'

She also kept her voice down. 'A man called Joe Lefkowich.'

'Of course. South American Joe.' Elfie's husband had changed greatly since he had last seen him, almost twenty years ago. 'What's he doing?'

'He has to sign the bail register twice a day.'

'What did he do?'

'Slashed someone with a knife. I think they found an

unlicensed shotgun too.'

Saltfleet said: 'Well, well.' He smiled at her. 'Thanks very much.'

He hurried out; it would take Joe only a few moments to sign, and watch the sergeant countersign.

Seconds later, Joe came out. Saltfleet said: 'How's it going, Joe?'

He received a glance of sour hostility, which changed into a broken-toothed grin.

'Well, if it ain't Inspector Pepperpot.' It was an old joke, dating back to their first acquaintance, at the time of the Thames Nude murders; another variant was 'Saltcellar'.

They shook hands. Saltfleet said: 'It's nice to see you. It's been a long time.'

'Yes. Elfie said she'd seen you.'

'I thought I'd look her up, for old times' sake.' He would not mention that Elfie had helped him with information, even to her husband.

He realised why he had failed to recognise South American Joe. Twenty years ago he had the figure of an athlete, and the swarthy good looks of a Mexican villain in a cheap cowboy movie. Now he was fat, his skin had turned yellow, his teeth were stained, and the good looks had disintegrated into an air of flabby self-indulgence. His nickname came from a popular song of the 1930s, which contained the lines:

'Every home he puts a sandal in
He makes women play the mandoline,
Si, si, si, si, South American Joe.'

Joe's women had always been willing to do a great deal more than play the mandoline; one of them had committed suicide when he threw her out, and on several occasions their alibis had saved him from prison. This helped to explain why, although known to be a formidable man with a knife – rumour said he had been trained by a

Paris apache – he had never been convicted of any offence.

Saltfleet said: 'Mind if I walk along with you?'

'That's all right. I'm not proud.'

It made Saltfleet aware that the old underlying aggressiveness was still there, a sneering air of defiance of authority, covered with an insolent pretence of humour.

Saltfleet said: 'Sorry to hear about your trouble.'

Joe said quickly: 'It was self-defence.'

'I meant your back trouble.'

'Oh, that.' He grinned wryly, acknowledging his mistake. 'Yes, that's what you get for clean living.'

'And what's the problem with the law?' Saltfleet decided it would be best to ask openly; Joe was obviously oversensitive, and tactful avoidance of the subject would only make things worse.

He scowled. 'Some bastard of a magistrate who thinks he's funny.'

'What happened?'

'This bloody nigger in All Saint's Road says: Fuck off whitey. Well I don't take that from anybody. So I kicked him in the balls. Then he pulls a knife, and I get mine out for self-defence. Then these coppers come and grab us – it was the carnival – and the wog manages to get rid of his knife – slips it to one of his pals.'

'Did you cut him?'

Joe said with satisfaction: 'Just a scratch.' Saltfleet knew about Joe's scratches; one rival pimp had needed thirty stitches, from the knee to the groin.

'You're lucky they didn't throw the book at you.'

Joe said bitterly: 'That's what they'll do. But they're taking their time. They've been out to get me for years. This is their first chance, so they're making the best of it. Reporting twice a bloody day.' He spat. 'As if I'm a fucking juvenile delinquent.'

He could understand Joe's fury. There had been a time

125

when a Sunday newspaper had denounced Joe as 'the vice king of Notting Hill', and called him 'one of the most dangerous men in London'. Yet no one had ever succeeded in convicting him. Now he was charged with what he regarded as a minor offence; depending on the seriousness of the wound he had inflicted, he might have been given a stiff fine or suspended sentence. To make him report twice a day – as if he might otherwise abscond – sounded like a deliberate humiliation, an attempt to teach him that he was now a toothless lion. Saltfleet did not particularly like Joe, and, under normal circumstances, would have regarded his downfall with satisfaction. But speaking to him like this, seeing things temporarily from Joe's viewpoint, he could sympathise with his sense of outrage, and agree that it looked like flagrant injustice.

'That doesn't sound fair.'

'Fair! It's bloody rotten!' It was impossible not to be amused by Joe's capacity for self-pity; this man who had spent his life intimidating women sounded on the verge of tears. Saltfleet pretended not to notice.

'But what's the delay about?'

'They found an old shotgun under the floorboards. It hasn't been fired in twenty years, but they still say it sounds like one used in that East End mail van robbery.'

'And I suppose that's impossible?' He tried not to sound too curious.

'Of *course* it's bloody impossible!' But he said it without indignation; it was a sign of how far his morale had been undermined.

Saltfleet said: 'Leave it with me. I'll see what can be done.'

Joe shot him a startled and suspicious glance. 'That's nice of you.' He was obviously taken off-balance. But he knew Saltfleet well enough to know he was a man of his word.

To cover the embarrassed pause, Saltfleet changed the subject. 'Is Elfie at home?'

'She was when I left.'

'I wouldn't mind a word with her. I want to ask her about homo prostitutes.'

'What, around here?'

'Yes.'

'There's not many. Since they made it legal, they use clubs instead of cottages.' (A cottage was a public toilet.)

'Are there any clubs in this area?'

Joe thought for a moment. 'Not as far as I know. There's Mick's Café near the tube station – a lot of 'em get in there. But they'd just be poofters – I mean they wouldn't be on the game.'

They stopped outside a house in Kensington Park Road. Joe said: 'Do you want to come up and have a word with her?'

'Thanks, I'd like to.'

As they climbed the stairs, Joe gave a gasp and placed his hand on his spine. 'God, my bloody back's killing me today.' He mounted slowly, one hand on the banister.

The door opened before they reached it; Elfie, wearing an apron and a scarf tied around her head in a turban, looked surprised and pleased to see him.

'Hello, Greg! What you doing here?'

'I met Joe in the street.' He tactfully avoided mention of the police station.

'Come on in.' She looked at Joe with concern. 'You look rotten.'

'I am. I'm bloody awful.' A film of sweat had formed on his face.

'Go and lie down, and I'll bring you a cup of tea.'

Joe allowed her to help him into the bedroom, and Saltfleet noted the tenderness in her manner; he found it mildly surprising that a man like Joe could inspire so much affection. She came out, closing the door gently behind her.

He said: 'I'm sorry to see Joe like this.'

'This shotgun business is getting him down.'

'I know. I'll see if I can find out what it's all about. If there's anything I can do . . .'

'Thanks.' She sounded brusque, but he knew this was only her manner; she found it hard to accept favours.

He followed her into the kitchen and watched her fill the kettle. In her apron and turban she looked like any other housewife interrupted in her cleaning. She said: 'Like a drink?'

'That'd be nice.'

'I know you CID blokes like Bell's, but there's only Irish.'

'That's fine.'

He watched her pour a large measure for him, and a smaller one for herself. They said cheers.

'Wouldn't Joe rather have whisky than tea?'

'No. He's not allowed to drink since this jaundice.'

'He's had jaundice?'

'Can't you tell by his skin?'

'I'm sorry. He's certainly had his problems.'

She sighed. 'He's not growing old gracefully.' The kettle began to simmer. 'Why don't you go and sit down while I make the tea? I'll be with you in a moment.'

The flat was well-furnished and very tidy; it might have belonged to a retired bank manager. There was a video-recorder under the television set, and a glass-fronted bookcase with book club editions and Reader's Digest Condensed Books. The book that lay open by the side of the armchair was called *Desert Lover*.

Elfie went into the bedroom, and a moment later tiptoed out again. 'He's asleep.' She might have been talking about a baby. She put the tray on the table.

'Would you like a sandwich?'

The whisky had made him aware that he was hungry. 'I don't want to eat Joe's lunch ...'

'That's all right. He'll be asleep for the rest of the afternoon.' She placed the ham sandwiches on the arm of his chair. 'How's the case getting on?'

'Not too bad. We've found that the sailor had been in London longer than we thought. Now it's a matter of trying to find out what he did and where he went.'

She removed her apron and sat down. 'What about this girl – Rosie?'

'I've seen her. I don't think she had anything to do with it.' With his mouth full of ham sandwich he was disinclined to go into detail.

'Neither do I. Unless she had a man with her.'

Saltfleet nodded. 'What puzzles me is the mutilation. It makes me think we could be looking for a sadistic queer. Do you know of any in this area?'

She stared at the carpet frowning. 'No ... There's Eric Page – he goes in for whipping schoolboys. But he'd never kill anybody.'

'Do the police know him?'

'Oh yes. He's been inside a couple of times for corruption of minors.' She poured him more whisky. The silence lengthened as he ate. She said: 'Ever seen a snuff movie?'

He nodded. 'The Dirty Squad seized one the other day.'

'Are they genuine – I mean do people really get killed?'

'Oh yes, this girl got killed all right. And disembowelled.'

'Christ! What kind of people enjoy that type of thing?'

'People like this bloke we're looking for.'

She said: 'Sid Warris – who runs the video library on the corner – said some bloke had been asking about snuff movies.'

'If he wanted to see a girl killed, he probably wasn't

129

queer.'

'He didn't. He was only interested in boys.'

'That sounds promising. Did he tell you anything about the man?'

'No.'

'Did he know him?'

'I don't know. You could ask him.'

'Thanks. I will. Is he a friend of yours – Sid Warris?'

'I suppose so.'

'Would you mind introducing me to him? It's always better if a friend introduces you.'

'Of course.'

'Thanks. And I'll ring Roy Coates and try and find out about Joe.' Superintendent Coates, of Notting Hill, had known Saltfleet since they both joined the force.

'I'd be glad if you would.'

'You say this shotgun hadn't been used?'

'No! It'd been under the floorboards for years – it was all covered in dust. You know what Joe's like – he thinks everybody's after him. They used to be, back in the old days. But he doesn't need a shotgun now. I kept telling him to get rid of it.'

'What about this brawl he got into? Did he hurt the man badly?'

'He needed a few stitches. But the other bloke pulled a knife first.'

Saltfleet said: 'I can't understand Joe. He used to be more careful.'

She chuckled suddenly. 'Do you really want to know what caused it?'

'Yes.'

She went to the bedroom door, and listened with her ear against it. She took a stool from under the table, and sat down close to Saltfleet.

'Joe's been having trouble with his old man.' She

gestured in the direction of her pubis. 'That dose of clap did him no good. And it really seems to upset a bloke when he can't get it up any more. So he went to see the doctor, and got some pills – big golden things, I've forgotten what they were called. Well, they made things a bit better, but not much. He tried taking a double dose, but that made him feel sleepy. So he went to the doctor and asked if there was anything stronger. And the doc recommends this stuff called – Christ, what the hell was it called . . . testo something.'

'Testosterone?'

'That's it. Methyl testosterone, that's what it was called. Bloody expensive it was, too.' She gurgled with laughter. 'Anyway, that did the trick all right. One dose of that and he was screwing like a rattlesnake. Turned him into a sex maniac. He'd never been like that, even in his young days. But it also turned him very nasty – aggressive, you know what I mean? I didn't mind, of course. I'm used to it. Some of the other girls didn't like it much when he started slapping 'em around. So that's why he got into this fight with this nignog – he'd been taking this methyl testosterone stuff . . .'

'Did the magistrate know this?'

'Christ no!' She shot an alarmed glance towards the bedroom. 'And for God's sake don't tell anybody. Joe'd rather go to jail than let anyone know his old man wouldn't stand up.'

'Nobody has to know. It needn't come out in open court. If his doctor was willing to write a letter to the magistrate . . .'

She was obviously worried. 'He'd kill me if he found out I'd told you.'

'Don't worry. You know me.'

She nodded doubtfully. 'He'd hate to feel people were laughing behind his back.'

'That won't happen. What about this doctor? Do you think he'd do it?'

'Oh yes. It wasn't his fault. He warned Joe about the stuff.'

'You mean he warned Joe it might make him violent?'

'Oh no. He warned him it might give him jaundice.'

About to finish his whisky, Saltfleet lowered the glass. 'What?'

'It gives some people jaundice, this stuff.'

'Real jaundice, or just a yellow skin?'

'No, real jaundice. That's what Joe's had.'

Saltfleet finished his whisky thoughtfully. 'Do you think this video shop will be open?'

'I should think so.'

'Would you mind coming down with me?'

'Sure.' She went to the bedroom door, opened it, and peeped in. She closed it quietly. 'Fast asleep.' Saltfleet helped her on with her coat. She said: 'By the way . . . I know I don't really have to ask you this . . . but can I tell Sid that you don't give a damn if he's renting porno films?'

'Of course.'

The video library had replaced a workman's café in which Saltfleet had often eaten egg and chips. There were two customers in the shop; they waited outside until they left, then Elfie went in alone. Saltfleet watched her talking to the man behind the counter. A moment later she beckoned him in.

'This is Sid Warris. Sid, this is Greg Saltfleet.'

They shook hands; Warris was a short, powerful man with a bald head and a forehead corrugated into deep lines. His manner was friendly without being ingratiating.

'What can I do for you?'

'Elfie told me you had a customer who was enquiring about snuff movies. Could you give me his name?'

'Gordon.'

'Is that his Christian name or surname?'

'Surname.' He went to a small filing cabinet at the end of the counter, and extracted a card, which he handed to Saltfleet. It read: 'Gordon, G, 9 Colville Place, W11.'

'No telephone number?'

'He said he wasn't on the phone.'

'Do you ask for a deposit?'

'Only on the adult movies.'

'What kind of films does he like?'

'Anything violent – the more sickening the better.'

'Such as?'

Warris reached under the counter, and handed Saltfleet a pamphlet. The cover said: 'Adult Film Corporation'; the address was in Copenhagen. The list of titles included *The Castrator*, *Spike in the Guts*, *Tits, Bums and Razors* and *The Monster from Hell*. A section on the last page was headed 'For younger viewers', and included *Choir Practice* and *Rape in the Changing Room*.

Saltfleet said: 'Do they really make porn for children?'

'No. That's really paedophile stuff, but I don't carry it.' His smile was just a little too open and frank.

'You've never checked up on this address?'

'No need to. He's a regular customer, always returns the tapes on time.'

'You know there's no Colville Place in this area? There's Colville Square, Colville Road and Colville Terrace, but no Colville Place.' Saltfleet knew his West Eleven by heart.

'Blimey, I didn't know that.' But he said it without surprise.

'Could you describe him for me?'

'Well, let's see. Little chap – shorter than me, with black curly hair – my guess is it's a toupee. Mid-thirties, round face with a snub nose. Always well-dressed – must have an

133

office job of some kind because he wears a suit on weekdays and a sweater and corduroys at weekends. Oh, and he's got a scar across his knuckles, as if somebody cut him.'

A customer came into the shop; Saltfleet decided not to wait.

'Thanks a lot, Sid.'

'You're welcome.'

Outside, Elfie asked: 'Was that any use?'

'A lot.'

'In spite of the false address?'

'If he gave a false address he must have had a reason. People with nothing to hide don't give false addresses.'

It was half-past-one when he let himself into the house in Ladbroke Terrace Gardens. He was glad to find no one at home; it relieved his guilt about Miranda. A note on the kitchen table read: 'Josie rang up and I'm taking her to lunch. Your meal is in the fridge.' Josie Barlow was Miranda's best friend in Thames Ditton; they shared a curious passion for jumble sales.

In the refrigerator he found a cold beef salad and a slice of blackcurrant cheesecake; but he was not hungry; instead he poured himself a beer. Then he rang the Notting Hill police station and asked for Roy Coates; it was only on the offchance, and he was not surprised when the switchboard operator told him Coates was out at lunch. Next he dialled Scotland Yard and asked for the Vice Squad.

'Is Inspector Rice there?'

'Who's calling, please?'

'Chief Superintendent Saltfleet.'

Barney Rice had been Saltfleet's sergeant when he was on the Vice Squad. He had a photographic memory, and the promotion was well-deserved.

'Hello, Greg.' He had a pleasant Yorkshire voice whose homely intonation had lulled many a criminal into a sense of false security. 'What can I do for you?'

'Barney, I've got a tricky one here because I don't know if he's got a criminal record and I don't know his real name. I'm wondering if you'll recognise his description.'

'Go ahead.'

'He's calling himself Gordon, initial G, but I suspect that's a pun on the Gay Gordons. He's a sadistic queer, has black curly hair, probably a toupee, and a snub nose . . .'

Rice interrupted with a chuckle. 'He doesn't have scars across his right knuckles, by any chance?'

'Yes, that's the one.'

'His name's Tony Spraggs and I don't know a more vicious little bastard. It'd be a real pleasure to get him behind bars.'

'Can you tell me about him?'

'He's a sado-masochist – doesn't care if he beats or gets beaten. He likes black boys if he can get 'em, but he's not particular. He spends a lot of his time looking for rough trade in Hell's Kitchen, down by Charing Cross.'

'I haven't come across that one. Is it new?'

'Been open about six months. It caters for queers and these lads in leather jackets who go around on motorbikes and wear Nazi gear. You get the real roughnecks there – skinheads and bovver boots and the lot. Up to a year ago, they used to hang around the meat market.' Rice was referring to the vicinity of the gentlemen's toilet in the Piccadilly Underground. 'Too many queers were getting beaten up and robbed, and after that fellow Sykes got killed we decided to make 'em move on. Now you'll find them around Hell's Kitchen.'

'They're mostly prostitutes?'

'Depends what you mean by prostitute. Most of them

135

aren't homosexual, and of course that attracts the queers. They'll flog somebody for money, or even screw him, but they won't allow anybody to do it to them. They usually charge about twenty quid a time.'

'How did you come across this Spraggs character?'

'About a year ago we got a complaint from a black woman living in North Finchley. Her son had joined the International Motor Cycle Club, and he met Spraggs and got invited to a party in Notting Hill – that's where Spraggs lives. When he woke up he was coughing blood and he realised he'd been beaten and raped. The lad's doctor said he had liver damage from heavy doses of some anaesthetic. We got the lad to swear out a complaint, and the local police picked up Spraggs. But he got some trick cyclist to swear that he was under treatment for his sexual problems and he got bail. Then the lad suddenly withdrew his complaint – I'm pretty sure Spraggs got a few strong-arm boys to pay him a visit. So we had to let it drop.'

'Do you happen to know the name of the trick cyclist?'

'Can you hold on while I get the file?' A moment later he came back on the line. 'It was Dr Roberto Moro. Do you want his address?'

'No thanks. I've got it. What does Spraggs do for a living?'

'You won't believe this, but he works for the Church Commissioners.'

'Couldn't you drop a hint to his boss about his activities?'

'I've done more than that – I've told him the lot. And he as good as told me that if I didn't stop persecuting this poor innocent homo, he'd get questions asked in Parliament. These people wear blinkers and earplugs.' It was evident that he was still smarting from the recollection. 'How did you get interested in Spraggs?'

'I've seen some photographs that I think he took.'

'Aha.' There was no mistaking the interest in Rice's voice. 'What of?'

'People in a kind of leather cradle with a rope round the neck.'

'That's him all right. Have you got the photos?'

'Unfortunately, no. I saw them at Moro's.'

'Any chance of getting hold of them?'

'It might be difficult. But a man who takes photographs like that probably has a whole collection in his flat. If you could find some reason to get a search warrant . . .'

Rice grunted. 'That's the problem.'

'I might be able to help you there. You remember that sailor found murdered in Ladbroke Grove at the weekend? I think Spraggs could be the man we want.'

'I didn't realise there was a sexual angle.'

'Mutilation of the genitals.'

There was a pause while Rice digested this. Then he said: 'My God!' Saltfleet could almost see the gleam in his eyes. 'Yes, that sounds promising.' Rice did not believe in superlatives.

'When I saw these photos, it struck me that the man who took them could be the killer.'

'Who was the pathologist?'

'Aspinal.'

'And who's in charge of the case?'

'A Detective Inspector from Hammersmith called Fitch.'

'Yes, I know him. Where do you come in?'

'I don't. I'm supposed to be on holiday. So I'd rather you didn't mention me – especially to Scottie MacPhail.'

'No, of course not. Where can I reach you if I need to?'

After giving him the number, Saltfleet said goodbye and hung up. He tried to ring Aspinal but found, as he expected, that he was still out at lunch. After that, he rang

137

the Hammersmith station and asked for Fitch; he was told that Fitch had been out all day. He left a message, asking Fitch to ring him, or call in if he came past – it was likely that Fitch was making routine enquiries in the area at that moment.

The sun had come out, and was shining on the back garden. He took his beer outside, and sat in the rocking-seat. He was feeling tired, but pleased with himself. Swinging gently back and forth, with the sunlight warm on his skin, and the scent of damp earth and autumn flowers, he experienced a sense of total contentment. In moments like this, he felt at one with himself and with the world. Saltfleet had joined the police force because he was interested in people, fascinated by the oddities of human psychology. What he had not anticipated was the frustration: the endless routine enquiries, hours spent searching through voters' lists and talking to the rating department of the local council, sitting in Q cars for hours, sometimes days, watching a doorway or a window; above all, the knowledge that much of this effort would be wasted. But then there was the occasional case that made it all worthwhile, when everything seemed to fall into place. This seemed to be one of them, and it made no difference that he was only indirectly involved. He rocked gently in the sunshine, and allowed his mind to toy with the possibilities as if it were a problem in chess.

The telephone startled him, and made him realise that he had allowed himself to doze. He hurried in through the French windows.

'Is that you, Greg? It's Francis.'

'Hello Francis. It's kind of you to ring back.'

'No trouble. What can I do for you?'

'Ever heard of a drug called methyl testosterone?'

'Not offhand. Hang on while I look it up.'

He was away for some time. When he came back he said: 'This is rather interesting.'

'Yes, I thought you'd think so.'

'Used in small quantities in various potency drugs . . . Liable to cause jaundice in its more concentrated form. Do you think Choromansky used it?'

'It seems possible. The doctor who examined Choromansky says it was definitely jaundice, not some antimalarial drug.'

'According to this, it might turn him into a sex maniac.'

'Does it say that?'

'Pretty well – it says "has been known to induce various degrees of satyriasis". I only knew one man with satyriasis – a Hungarian intern – and he once told me he'd had eight women in twelve hours. He was a kind of one-man stud farm.'

'Incidentally, did you get any photographs of the man's genital region, with the mutilations?'

'I didn't, but the police photographer did. The Exhibits Officer probably has them.'

'Good, that's marvellous. Thanks a lot.'

'Any time.'

He was writing a note to Miranda when he heard her key in the lock. She was accompanied by Josie Barlow, a pretty woman in her early forties. He said: 'I'm glad you came back. I'm just on my way back to Moro's. Do you mind?'

'Of course not. I'm going to show Josie how to make Boeuf Stroganoff.'

Saltfleet kissed Josie on the cheek. He felt warm and protective about her; her husband, a psychiatrist, had recently deserted her for his eighteen-year-old secretary.

'Why doesn't Josie stay to dinner?'

She said: 'How nice. I'd love to.'

That eased his conscience. He felt a positive elation as he hurried back towards the Institute of Sexual Science; it was like anticipating the next episode of a serial.

EIGHT

The door stood open; he placed his finger on the doorbell, then changed his mind. In the hallway, he stood and listened; from somewhere along the corridor there was the sound of a radio. He went quietly up the stairs, and rapped lightly on the door of Moro's office. When there was no reply, he opened it. Emil was in the room, arranging chairs.

'Hello, Emil. Is the doctor in?'

'I think he's in the other office. I'll go and get him.'

'Don't bother. I don't want to disturb him. I'll wait.' He sat down on the couch, which had been moved into a corner. All the chairs in the room had been arranged in two rows along the rear wall; the desk had been pushed into a corner.

As soon as Emil had left the room, Saltfleet went to the bookcase and took out the photograph album labelled *Transvestitismus*. He turned to the end pages, and quickly removed the photograph of the close-up of male thighs and genitals. He was slipping it into his back pocket when the door opened. It was Dorothy. She said: 'What are you doing?'

As she spoke he experienced a wave of relief; it was the voice of the seven-year-old child. He smiled at her.

'Looking at pictures.' He replaced the album.

'May I see?'

'No. They're not suitable for little girls.'

'Oh, *please*!' To his surprise, she placed her mouth against his ear, then whispered again: '*Please*!' And, as he shook his head, she took it in her hands to hold it still, and he felt the warm tip of her tongue explore his ear. It produced a shock of sexual pleasure. She giggled, and he felt one of her hands slip into his trouser pocket. He stood still and allowed her to explore the other pocket; then she plunged both hands simultaneously into the pockets of his jacket. She found what she was looking for: the small container of orange sweets.

'Are these for me?'

'Yes.'

'Thank you, Uncle Greg.' She used the flat, expressionless voice of a child who has been told to be polite; but he was aware that this was a game, an attempt to imply that their relations were strictly formal. In effect, she was denying the intimacies of a few moments ago.

'Will you tell me a story?'

'Yes, all right, dear.'

'Thank you.' Again the flat, polite voice.

He allowed her to take his hand and lead him across to the couch. He sat down, and tried to pull her down beside him; instead, she waited until he was comfortable, then sat on his knee, placing her arms round his neck. He said: 'Don't you think you're getting too big to sit on my knee?'

He regretted it immediately; she looked as if he had slapped her face. She said: 'Don't you want me?'

To forestall tears he said quickly: 'Yes, of course I do. It's just that you're getting to be a big girl . . .'

'I'm not very big.' It was true; she seemed to weigh scarcely more than a child.

'No, not *very* big.' He squeezed her reassuringly.

She buried her face in his neck. 'Go on, then.' He had a sudden sense that he had been manipulated.

'All right. Once upon a time . . .'

The door opened; Moro came in, followed by a tall man with a blond moustache. If he was surprised to see Rosie sitting on Saltfleet's knee, he concealed it well. He only smiled and said: 'Good afternoon.'

Saltfleet said awkwardly: 'Good afternoon.' He whispered to Rosie: 'I'll tell you the story later.'

She said imperiously: 'No, now!'

Moro came to the rescue.

'Rosie, do you want to play games this afternoon?'

'Yes please!'

'Then why don't you go and change into your pretty dress – the one with the yellow stripes?'

She sighed. 'Oh, all right.' She kissed Saltfleet on the cheek. ''Bye, Uncle Greg.' She was play-acting again.

'Goodbye Rosie.' He noticed that as she went out she smiled flirtatiously at the man with the blond moustache.

Moro said: 'This is Rick Henderson. Rick, this is . . . Dr Gregory.'

Saltfleet was not entirely happy about the deception, but he tried not to let it show as he shook hands; Henderson was in his mid-twenties, and had piercing blue eyes. His head was half-bald, and the high forehead gave him an appearance of intellectuality.

'Rick will also be in our therapy group. Would you like to go and get changed, Rick?'

The young man said 'OK' and went out; he had an American accent.

Moro said: 'Would you mind putting on your white coat now?'

Saltfleet grimaced. 'If you really think it's necessary.'

Moro placed his hand on Saltfleet's arm. 'Please, you must not think of it as some kind of deception. In games therapy, we play many different roles. While you are here you must forget you are a policeman and become a doctor. Because it *is* pure chance that you are a policeman and not a doctor. Under different circumstances, you might have become a doctor and I might have become a policeman.' He handed Saltfleet the laboratory coat.

'You mean we're all playing roles all the time?'

'Precisely. But we are not aware of it because we have identified with our roles. Think what would happen if a film actor lost his memory every time he played a part, and believed he had really *become* the person he was playing. Suppose, for example, that you had to play the part of a criminal. You would have a vague feeling that there was something wrong. You would feel that this was not "really you". You would feel that you had been forced into this role by some accident of fate, but that it did not correspond to your true self. That conflict would produce the state we call neurosis. And you can also see that the way to cure the neurosis would be to make you aware that you are not a criminal but a policeman.'

Saltfleet said: 'And that might not be my true self either.'

'Only you can decide that. Do *you* think that your true self is a policeman?'

Saltfleet thought about it. 'Sometimes I think it's closer to a farmer. But I'm too interested in people to be a farmer.'

He finished buttoning the white coat. Moro took his jacket from the chair and hung it in the cupboard.

'There, now you are a doctor. I want you to think of yourself as a doctor. For this afternoon you *are* a doctor.'

As he spoke, the woman called Harriet came into the room; she was wearing a pink two-piece suit that was far too young for her. She had mascara-ed her eyes, and was wearing bright lipstick. She gave Saltfleet a vague, charming smile, then recognised him. She said: 'Why, it's the nice policeman!'

Moro said firmly: 'No, it is not, Harriet. This is Doctor Gregory.'

She peered into Saltfleet's face; she had put something in her eyes that made them look bright and very large.

'But I recognise him . . .'

Moro interrupted: 'For this afternoon he is Doctor Gregory. You know the rules.'

She looked downcast. 'Yes, of course. I'm sorry.' She held out her hand. 'How do you do, Doctor?' Saltfleet shook her hand. She tilted her face close to his and whispered: 'But I prefer you as a policeman.'

Moro said sternly: 'That's enough, Harriet.'

The door opened; Emil came in, carrying one handle of a large trunk; a blonde woman was holding the other. It was evidently heavy. As they put it down, Saltfleet realised that the blonde woman had a moustache; it was the American called Rick. He was wearing a red dress, a short fur coat, and high-heeled shoes. They placed the trunk with some care, parallel to the desk and about ten feet from it; evidently its position was important. Both went out again.

Saltfleet asked: 'Who is Rick?'

'He is a new patient. He suffers from extremely aggressive feelings towards women.'

'A sadist?'

'Not precisely. A sadist enjoys inflicting pain. Rick has no desire to cause pain for its own sake. But when he makes love to a woman, he is suddenly overwhelmed by a feeling of anger. In Los Angeles he almost killed a girl with whom he was spending the night. That – between ourselves – is why he left America.'

Saltfleet observed that Moro made no attempt to lower his voice, and that Harriet was listening with fascination.

'And does he *want* to be cured?'

'Of course. He is terrified that if he starts to make love

to a girl, he might lose control and kill her.'

'A sort of Rosie in reverse?'

Moro seemed to be struck by this. He said thoughtfully: 'Yes, a Rosie in reverse . . .'

Rosie came into the room with Frankie; she was wearing a bright summer dress with stripes of green and yellow. Saltfleet noticed that Frankie was holding her hand as they came in, but that he seemed embarrassed, and let go when he saw Moro.

Moro stood up and gazed admiringly at Rosie: 'What a pretty girl.' She blushed with pleasure. 'Won't you come and sit down?'

'I'll sit next to Uncle Greg.' She sat beside Saltfleet, and allowed her bare shoulder to rub against his coat.

Emil and Rick came in, carrying Chinese screens. These were set up carefully between the desk and the trunk, forming an enclosed area like a stage. Emil opened the trunk, and propped its lid upright with a broom handle. Finally, Emil carried the tall mirror from the corner of the room, and propped it against the desk, placing a pile of books at its base to prevent it from slipping. Saltfleet watched with curiosity as Emil rummaged in the trunk, and took from it a morning coat and a waistcoat. Standing in front of the mirror, he put on the waistcoat, then took an enormous watch from the trunk, and arranged it so that the gold chain arced across his stomach.

Saltfleet placed his mouth close to Moro's ear. 'Wouldn't it be more appropriate if Emil dressed as a woman?'

Moro shook his head. 'No. Because, you see, Emil is already a woman. He is a woman in a male body.'

Emil had donned the morning coat, then took a collapsible top hat from the trunk, punched it upright, and placed it on his head. A white bow tie, a monocle and a large black cigar completed the transformation. As he surveyed himself in the mirror and clipped the end off the cigar, there was a spontaneous burst of laughter and applause from the audience. Emil turned and frowned at them with mock indignation; glaring haughtily through the monocle, he looked like the Capitalist Pig of left-wing cartoonists.

They seemed to be in no hurry to get started; during the next ten minutes, a number of people drifted in and sat down. It was clear that they all knew one another well. Without exception, they looked at Saltfleet with intense curiosity. Under cover of the general conversation, Moro whispered brief accounts of their case histories. A smartly dressed middle-aged woman with shoulder-length dark hair and a sensual mouth had an obsession about under-age boys, and tried to pick them up in cinemas. A nervous young man with thin lips and a prominent Adam's apple had made three attempts to murder his father. A nondescript little man who looked like a bank manager – and who was, in fact, an insurance representative – had an obsession with excrement, and paid prostitutes to evacuate their bowels on a sheet of glass over his face. Saltfleet observed that none of them cast a second glance at Rick, although Moro had mentioned that this was his first group therapy session. Only Rosie kept stealing glances at him, evidently fascinated.

As the clock struck three, Moro said: 'It is time to begin.' He signalled to Emil, who went and drew all the curtains, and turned a spotlight on the stage area. Moro went to the trunk, took from it a long, grey wig, which he carefully adjusted on his head, spreading the hair over his shoulders. He placed on his nose an enormous pair of green spectacles with no glass in them, then clamped the wig firmly in place by putting on a dunce's cap with signs of the zodiac. From the trunk he took a clown's mask on a stick, and a staff that had evidently been cut recently from a hedgerow. When he banged the staff on the floor, all the chatter ceased instantly.

'Ladies and gentlemen, welcome to our games therapy session.' He spoke quietly and seriously, with no attempt at showmanship. Saltfleet was interested to observe that the wig and glasses, far from making him look absurd, seemed somehow perfectly natural. 'Today we have three guests with us. Dr Gregory is an expert on antisocial behaviour.' Saltfleet restrained himself from smiling. 'Rick Henderson is an architect by profession, and he is from America. You may feel that you have seen Rosie before, but you haven't. She is only seven years old, and she is with us for the first time.' Rosie turned round and beamed at the people behind her.

'For the benefit of the newcomers, I will summarise the principles of games therapy. Your personality is basically your way of seeing yourself.' Moro went and stood in front of the mirror. 'But it is not necessarily the real you.' He placed the clown's mask over his face, and turned to the audience. 'It is merely a mask that you have created by thinking about yourself in a certain way. And thinking about yourself in a certain way makes you act in a certain way. So your thinking reinforces your actions and your actions reinforce your thinking.' Rosie looked puzzled, and began to suck her thumb. 'And the result may be the creation of a personality that bears no relation to your true self. Yet because it has set hard, like a mask, it is almost impossible to take off your face.

'Now you all know that you feel like a different person in different situations. When you talk to a very forceful personality, you feel weak. When you talk to a weak personality, you feel strong. When you are confronted by an interesting challenge, you respond by feeling more alive, and that is because the challenge makes you develop a new personality. Now the aim of games therapy is to allow you to try on different personalities, in the way a woman might try on new hats.' He reached into the trunk, and took out two masks, which he tried on in quick succession, one of Mickey Mouse, the other of a fair-haired child with pink cheeks. He ended by holding all three masks by their sticks in one hand, like a deck of cards, and peering over the top of them. 'Every time you change your mask, you have a glimpse of your true self. And when you learn the nature of your true self, you begin acting and thinking differently, and your problems disappear.' He looked at Saltfleet. 'Any questions, Dr Gregory?' Saltfleet shook his head.

Moro tossed the masks on the desk. 'Very well, who would like to begin today? Frankie, how about you? I think it must be your turn...' Frankie pulled a face. 'How about the policeman and the burglar? That's one we haven't done for a long time. Come along.' Frankie stood up unwillingly, and slouched into the stage area. Moro bent over the trunk, and produced a policeman's helmet, and a toy truncheon, apparently made of black plastic. Frankie accepted the helmet and put it on reluctantly. 'Now, Frankie, you have to choose a burglar.'

Moro sat down again. Frankie looked carefully around the audience, evidently enjoying his position of authority. He pointed with his truncheon: 'You.' He indicated the middle-aged woman with shoulder-length hair. She said: 'Oh no, please!' Frankie darted his forefinger at her with a commanding gesture. She sighed and stood up. 'Oh, all right. But I don't want to be a burglar. Could I be a Peeping Tom?' She was addressing Moro. He said: 'You must ask Frankie.'

Frankie said: 'Yes, OK.' He spoke with casual self-confidence.

The woman sighed. 'In that case, I'll have to change.'

She stripped off her fur wrap, and tossed it on to the desk with a dramatic gesture. Then, taking her time, she rummaged in the trunk, and finally selected a blue boiler suit, a trilby hat, and a Fu Manchu moustache. Then she went behind the Chinese screen; a moment later, her skirt appeared on top of it, then her underslip. By leaning back slightly, Saltfleet could see her taking off her blouse; it was evident that she had no real desire to conceal herself.

Frankie, meanwhile, was strolling importantly up and down the stage, swinging the truncheon. His performance resembled a Nazi storm-trooper more than a policeman. He strutted arrogantly, twisted his face into a ruthless grimace, and seemed to be looking around for somebody to hit. Then he stopped to admire himself in the mirror, fingered an imaginary moustache, and smacked the truncheon into the palm of the other hand.

The woman came out from behind the screen, now dressed in the boiler suit; it looked absurd, since her shoulders were bare, and the strap of her brassière showed. The hat was too large for her, and the moustache was lopsided. While Frankie continued to admire himself, she tiptoed across the stage with exaggerated caution, peering to right and left. As the policeman turned, slowly and ponderously, Rosie giggled and gripped Saltfleet's hand.

After a poor beginning, the woman began to warm to her part. She saw something that fascinated her, and watched with sudden absorption. Then she crouched down, opened an imaginary garden gate, and tiptoed forward, apparently gaining the shelter of a bush. Frankie strolled up and down, pretending not to see her. On the second occasion, she heard him, and seemed to shrink into the shadow of the bush. To his surprise, Saltfleet found he was becoming involved: he could imagine the lighted window, the girl taking off her clothes, unaware of the prowler, the Peeping Tom torn between his fear of the law and his compulsion to spy on the girl.

As the prowler straightened up, his joints made a cracking noise. Instantly, the policeman was alert, trying to peer into the darkness of the garden. He dropped on all fours, and crawled behind the desk, cautiously pushing aside the fur wrap as if parting a privet hedge. The prowler tiptoed across the stage and hid behind the trunk. Both peeped out simultaneously, and quickly ducked again. Rosie burst into hoots of laughter, and the rest of the audience chuckled. The two principals ignored this, and continued the game with concentrated attention. Moro placed his hand on Rosie's shoulder, and raised his finger to his lips.

The policeman gently pulled out the top drawer of the desk, and propped his truncheon in it; then he placed the helmet on top of the truncheon, so that it looked as if he was still behind the desk. Rosie stuck her thumb in her mouth, and began to suck furiously, holding the lobe of her ear in the other hand. The policeman had slipped off his plimsolls, and was crawling behind the screen to try to take the prowler in the rear. Everyone laughed; the prowler, puzzled by the immobility of the helmet, peered round the edge of the trunk to see what was happening. At that moment, Frankie leapt to his feet behind her, shouting: 'I arrest you in the name of the law!' There was a burst of applause, with Rosie clapping frantically. The woman was heard to say: 'That wasn't fair!', but Frankie ignored her, beaming at the audience as he held his prisoner by the back of the boiler suit.

Moro stood up, and placed a hand on each of their shoulders. 'You were both excellent.' He told the woman: 'You had me totally convinced that you were watching someone undressing.' She smiled with gratification. 'And you were brilliant, Frankie. You would make a marvellous policeman.' Frankie grinned proudly, and shot a triumphant glance at Saltfleet.

Moro said: 'Now, Rick, do you feel you are ready to join in the game?'

'I think so.'

'Good. Then let me give you your subject. You are a married woman who is bored with her husband. So she decides to go and earn a little money as a prostitute. Do you think you can do that?'

'I guess so.' Rick posed in front of the mirror and patted his hair with a typically feminine gesture.

The woman who had played the prowler had retired behind the screen to change again; Saltfleet observed with interest that this time she moved out of view of the audience.

Moro said: 'Usually you are allowed to choose your own cast, but since you don't know most of us, I'll do it for you. David, would you take the part of the husband?' He pointed to the nervous young man. 'Emil, perhaps you could be a customer? Would anyone like to volunteer to be the other customer?' The insurance representative raised his hand shyly. 'Thank you Mr Maudesley.'

It was soon clear that Rick was a talented actor. With the young man called David, he improvised a scene at the breakfast table, with the two of them sitting in facing chairs. The husband read his newspaper and made boring remarks about the weather and the stock market; the wife replied with totally irrelevant comments about her neighbours, her mother-in-law, and the health of their dog and cat. Rick's acting was almost professional; to imitate a woman so well, he must have observed them closely. It was also easy to guess that Moro had chosen the nervous young man because he wanted to see how he handled the part of a husband and father; in fact, the performance bore all the signs of being modelled on someone he knew well.

When the husband had left for the office – and returned to his seat – the wife put on make-up, brushed her hair, and left the house. Emil, who acted as sceneshifter, came and removed the chairs. In the next scene, the wife stood on a corner, and made subtly inviting gestures to passing males. Her first customer – Mr Maudesley – emerged from behind the screen, wearing a bowler hat and carrying an umbrella. What followed was a brilliant piece of mime. When the girl caught his eye, he was clearly unable to decide whether it had been an accident. He pretended to remember something he had left behind, and went back again. She caught his eye again and raised her eyebrow. Still unable to believe it, he hesitated, then went back. This time, she helped him out by asking him the time. Evidently paralysed with nervousness, he took out his watch, then cringed as she took his arm. Suddenly terrified at what he was letting himself in for, he allowed himself to be led away. The audience clapped.

Now Emil, who had been watching from the wings, sauntered forward; he smiled at the girl, and peered at her through his monocle with just the right touch of casual arrogance. The girl smiled back and stopped. The little man suddenly became aware that he was about to lose his prize, and tried to drag her on; the girl resisted. Saltfleet was surprised by his sense of the human reality of the situation; these people had become so absorbed in their drama that they had ceased to be actors. Emil was determined to get the girl; but the little man was so indignant that he had lost his usual timidity. For a moment the situation hung in the balance as the two men glared at one another; then, as Emil tried to take the girl's arm, the little man raised his umbrella threateningly, and brushed the hand aside. Out of the corner of his eye, Saltfleet saw Moro nod approvingly. It looked as if the two men might come to blows; then Emil shrugged and turned away. The audience burst into spontaneous applause.

The scene that followed was evidently in the girl's bedroom. She came in, followed by the little man, who seemed to have acquired a new self-confidence. He watched her hungrily as she removed her hat and coat, then let her take his bowler hat and umbrella. As she turned to face him, he reached out to touch her cheek; the gesture had genuine tenderness. His hand travelled hesitantly down from her shoulder, caressing her arm. Then, with a suddenness that startled them all, she grabbed him in her arms and began to kiss him hungrily. It was like a boa constrictor suddenly wrapping itself round its prey. The little man struggled frantically, then broke free, his face red with humiliation.

Moro was on his feet instantly. 'Good! Very good, both of you!' His tone restored a sense of normality. He placed his hands on their shoulders. 'That was a brilliant example of the reversal of a situation.' It gave the little man time to recover; he smiled shamefacedly, and went back to his seat. Moro said: 'Thank you, Rick. We are delighted to welcome you to our group.' Rick grinned self-consciously, and sat down. Saltfleet had to admire the smooth way in which Moro had defused the situation.

Rosie removed her thumb from her mouth to say plaintively: 'When are we going to play *real* games?'

Moro smiled at her. 'What would you like to play? Hide-and-seek? Musical chairs?' She nodded solemnly. 'I don't see why not.' He smiled at the others, tacitly inviting their cooperation. 'Shall we do that? Let's arrange the chairs for a game of musical chairs.'

Rosie said: 'But we haven't got any music!'

Rick said: 'Yes we have. I've got a tape-recorder. I'll go

154

and fetch it.' He evidently felt the need to redeem himself.

They all carried their chairs into the centre of the room, and placed them in two rows, back to back.

Moro said: 'I know. I've got an idea.' He took Rosie's hand, and led her to the desk. 'Let's pretend it's your birthday. Sit down, so we can all see you. How old are you?'

'Seven years and eight months.'

'Let's pretend it's your eighth birthday, and you're going to have a party. Is there anyone you'd like to invite?'

She nodded eagerly. 'Yes. Joey.'

'All right. Frankie can be cousin Joey. Come over here, Frankie. Would you like to sit down beside Rosie? Move over, Rosie.' She smiled brightly at Frankie. 'What did Frankie give you for your birthday?'

'I don't know.'

Frankie said: 'Yes you do. I gave you a hairslide with a green butterfly.'

A look of perplexity crossed her face; then she smiled: 'Oh yes, I remember.'

Moro said: 'And what did your daddy give you?' She shook her head. 'He gave you a dolly with golden hair and a lovely blue dress, didn't he?'

She frowned, and looked at him with an expression of sudden mistrust. He smiled reassuringly: 'And who's coming to the party beside Joey? How about Merryl and her sister Jessica and their brother Bill?'

She looked at him in astonishment. 'How do you know them?'

'Ah, I know a lot of things. Shall we ask Sidney Pepper? And how about Minny and her little dog Scatterbrain?' She nodded, her face still puzzled. 'And shall we ask Mary Franklin? Oh no, I forgot – she fell over some milk bottles and cut her leg. Did you know that?' Rosie was obviously worried; her face had the expression of someone trying hard to recall something that eluded her.

Rick came back with an expensive radio cassette recorder. When he pressed the control button, the room filled with the sound of rock-and-roll music. Rosie grabbed Frankie's hand.

'Oh, come on.' Her doubts seemed to vanish instantly.

Eight chairs had been placed in the centre of the room, so Saltfleet was obliged to join in. Moro sat on the desk and controlled the music. They all trooped around the chairs; Rosie moved with a hopping, skipping movement. Moro allowed the music to play for several minutes before he stopped it for the first time; Saltfleet made sure he was the one who was unable to find a chair. Rosie said sympathetically: 'Poor Uncle Greg!'

Saltfleet stood beside Moro as the music started again. He said in Moro's ear: 'I hope you know what you're doing.'

Moro shrugged ironically.

After ten more minutes, there was only one chair left, and Rosie and Frankie were marching around it. The music stopped. Both tried to sit down simultaneously. Shrieking with laughter, Rosie pushed Frankie off. Frankie fell on the floor, and everyone applauded. As Frankie looked up ruefully, Rosie flung her arms round his neck and kissed him on the cheek.

Moro clapped his hands for silence. 'What shall we play now?'

Rosie said: 'Hunt the thimble?'

Frankie said: 'How about hide-and-seek?'

'All right, hide-and-seek. Anywhere in the house. I'll count up to a hundred, then I'll come and look for you. Off you go.'

Within moments, the room was empty except for Saltfleet and Moro. Saltfleet said: 'Does Frankie know about this?'

'Yes. I explained to him before we started.'

'Any idea where they'll hide?'

'Yes. In the cupboard in Dorothy's office.'

'What are you going to do?'

Moro said: 'I'm afraid I am going to eavesdrop. Are you coming?'

Emil was sitting on the top step of the stairs, reading a newspaper. Moro said: 'Take the others down to the kitchen and make some tea. We'll resume the session in twenty minutes.'

Saltfleet asked: 'Do they all understand what's going on?'

'Not exactly. But they'll all try to be helpful. That is why games therapy is so useful. People stop thinking about their own problems and try to help other people.'

. The door of Dorothy's office stood slightly ajar. They both listened carefully, then Moro pushed it open. Saltfleet observed that the hinges had been oiled recently; Moro obviously thought of everything.

The large green cupboard in the corner looked as if it had been an airing-cupboard. As they tiptoed into the room, they heard a giggle from inside. Then there was silence. Saltfleet was glad he was wearing rubber-soled shoes. Moro caused a floorboard to creak, and he heard Rosie's voice say: 'Sshh!'

Frankie's voice said: 'What is it?'

'I heard something.'

There was a silence, then: 'No, there's nobody there.'

Saltfleet and Moro took their places on either side of the cupboard. Circular airholes had been drilled into the side panels to allow the escape of moisture, so every movement inside could be heard quite clearly.

Rosie said: 'Do you think they'll look for us?'

'Not in here they won't. They'll never find us.' There

was a creak, then Rosie said: 'Are you comfortable?'

'Yes, I'm all right.'

There was a long silence, broken by creaks and rustling noises. Then Rosie's voice said: 'Don't you like kissing me?'

'Course I do.' But Frankie's voice sounded insincere; no doubt the knowledge that he was being overheard exercised a restraining influence.

'Why have you stopped then?'

Saltfleet and Moro exchanged glances; there was no mistaking the imperious note in her voice.

There was another long silence, broken only by rustling noises. Then Rosie's voice said: 'They come undone.'

Frankie said: 'What's in there?'

'Me.'

Saltfleet began to feel uncomfortable; the sighs that followed made him feel like a Peeping Tom. It also brought back memories of Geraldine and the boatshed. Yet he no longer experienced the curious mixture of anger, jealousy and erotic excitement. Because he was identifying with Rosie and her miserable childhood, the thought of interrupting them saddened him; but to identify with Rosie was to identify with Geraldine.

Rosie said with sudden urgency: 'Ooh . . . Joey.' She gave a gasp, then a giggle. 'Joey, please stop it.'

'All right.' He sounded almost relieved.

'No, don't stop it. Go on.'

Moro caught Saltfleet's eye and nodded; unwillingly, Saltfleet nodded back. Moro tiptoed across the room, opened the door, then closed it with a slam. There was immediate silence from the cupboard; Saltfleet could imagine the hasty rearrangement of clothing. Moro walked across the room with normal footsteps, and yanked open the cupboard door. Saltfleet caught a glimpse of Frankie and Rosie, both semi-recumbent on a pile of blue-striped pillows and bolsters.

Moro shouted furiously: 'What's going on there?'

He grabbed Frankie by the collar and dragged him out of the cupboard, still shouting angrily. Rosie, like Frankie, was fully clothed; but a pair of white knickers were around her knees. Moro was striking Frankie on the head and shoulders.

Rosie shouted: 'Please don't hurt him. It was my fault.'

Saltfleet was glad Frankie's face was turned away from her; he was grinning.

Rosie came out of the cupboard, sobbing quietly, and hitching up her knickers. Saltfleet noticed that the buttons at the back of her dress were undone down to the waist. He caught a glimpse of bruising.

Moro said sternly: 'Get back to your room, miss. I'll deal with you later.'

Still sobbing, she went out. Frankie took the opportunity to pull up the zip of his fly; Moro pretended not to notice. Then Frankie saw Saltfleet, and his face flushed.

Moro placed an arm round his shoulders. 'Thank you, Frankie. You were a great help.'

Frankie said awkwardly: 'That's OK.' He was avoiding Saltfleet's eyes. 'Do you want me any more?'

'No, thank you.' Frankie hurried to the door. 'Oh, there is one more thing. If I may ask an indiscreet question . . . Did Rosie need much . . . er . . . , encouragement?'

Frankie said: 'Gawd, no!' It was obvious that he was telling the truth.

'Thank you.' Frankie went out.

Saltfleet said: 'Shouldn't we go to her?'

Moro shook his head. 'Oh no. She'll be fast asleep as soon as she lies down.'

'How can you be sure?'

Moro smiled. 'Experience. It always happens after

159

abreaction therapy. She has exhausted her emotions. Now she needs to sleep.'

'Are you *sure* she's exhausted her emotions?'

'Ah, you mean that she didn't react as violently as she did this morning. That is natural . . .'

'That's not quite what I meant. This morning she was reliving the experience under hypnosis. This afternoon, she knows she's playing a game. She knows Frankie isn't cousin Joey. So why should it exhaust her emotions?'

Moro nodded. 'Of course I understand your objection. I can only tell you that it is so. The first time I saw abreaction therapy, I felt the same. It was at a psychological conference in New York. The patient was a woman who had an emotional breakdown after her lover told her he was leaving her for another woman. It happened in a new car, and she was wearing a mink coat. The doctor told us he was going to make her relive the entire experience for our benefit, while she was fully awake. Of course, none of us really believed him. He made the woman sit in a chair, placed a mink coat around her shoulders, and used a spray that smelt like fresh leather on the back of her hand. And we all watched her go through the whole experience again. It would have been quite impossible to fake it. That was when I suddenly got the idea of games therapy . . .'

Saltfleet said: 'But it *would* also be possible to fake it. How can you know for certain?'

Moro shook his head vigorously. 'You saw what happened in the session with Rick and Arthur Maudesley. Rick thought he was playing a game, but in fact, he showed us exactly why he becomes violent with women.'

Saltfleet said curiously: 'Why?'

'To begin with, Rick obviously has a strong female component in himself. But he comes from a background that places great emphasis on masculinity and virility, so he rejects the idea. When he gets into bed with a girl, he suddenly gets the feeling that she has lured him there – that she is like an octopus waiting to seize its prey. So he has a desire to make her suffer.'

Saltfleet said: 'What about the little man – did he reveal anything?'

'He revealed everything. He cannot believe that he is attractive to women. Yet he adores women. I happen to know that he had sexual feelings towards his mother and elder sister, and that they were both very beautiful. Now he wants to be punished and humiliated by prostitutes, and the uglier they are, the better he likes it. What interested me this afternoon was when he got angry because Emil tried to take the girl away, and stood up for himself. If he would learn to do that all the time, his problems would vanish. Unfortunately, Rick spoiled everything by grabbing him like that . . .'

'And did you learn anything about Rosie?'

'A great deal. Until this afternoon, I believed that she was a poor, innocent little girl who let her cousin do whatever he liked . . .'

Saltfleet grunted. 'I knew that wasn't true this morning.'

'Did you? Then you are more observant than I am.'

Saltfleet shook his head. 'When you asked her what she was doing in the cupboard, she said: Shan't tell. She knew exactly what was going to happen. And when she said: Joey, stop it, she didn't mean it. She'd have been disappointed if he'd stopped. She's a little sensualist. Shall I tell you something else? Before you came into the room this afternoon, she put her mouth close to my ear, as though she was going to whisper, then she tickled my ear with her tongue. You know the effect that has on males? I think you may be right when you said she was a sensualist like her mother.' The insights were flooding into his mind as he talked. 'And that trick she has of pushing her hands into a man's trouser pockets – she did *that* before you came into the room. Yet she knows perfectly well that I keep the sweets in my jacket pocket.'

Moro looked doubtful. 'For a seven-year-old girl, that may not have been deliberate.'

'I'm not saying it was. I think it was instinctive. And I think she probably did the same kind of thing with her father.' Moro shook his head. 'I know you think of him as a kind of mad puritan. But if he was a mad puritan, why did he marry her mother in the first place?' Now he was drawing on the insights that had come to him outside the cupboard, and everything suddenly seemed clear. 'I think there was a kind of unconscious sexual relation between father and daughter. He wouldn't have dreamed of acknowledging it, but he probably thought of her as a second wife – a wife who wouldn't be unfaithful to him, as his real wife had been. Then he caught her in the cupboard with Joey, and he was furious and jealous. He wouldn't acknowledge that he was jealous, but that's what he was. What's more, he probably knew instinctively that she started it. Boys of Joey's age – respectable middle-class boys – are shy and sexually backward. I think it was Rosie who led Joey on.'

Moro said slowly: 'You could be right. I must think about it.' He stared thoughtfully at the cupboard, with its disarranged pillows. 'If you are right, then Rosie must have sensed the real nature of her father's anger. She must have known that it was based on sexual jealousy. Yet he told her that sex was wicked and that she would go to hell. It must have created terrifying strains in her mind . . .'

Someone knocked on the door, and they both started. Rick looked in.

'The group is back in your office, sir.'

'Thank you. I'll be there in just a moment.' He asked Saltfleet: 'Are you going to join us?'

162

'No. I have some things to do, if you don't mind.' As they went along the corridor he said: 'Shouldn't we check that Rosie's all right?'

'Yes, of course.'

The door of Rosie's room was closed; Moro opened it gently and looked in. Rosie was in bed, covered up; Frankie sat on the chair near her head. He looked sullenly at Saltfleet.

Moro asked: 'Is she all right?' He placed his hand on the girl's forehead; she breathed more deeply, and stirred. Moro smiled at Saltfleet. 'You see, she is sleeping peacefully.'

Saltfleet looked down at the pale face, and his heart contracted. He said: 'It looks like Rosa.'

He leaned across the bed and pulled back the bedclothes. On the exposed flesh of her back there was a yellow fading bruise. He took hold of the material of the dress, and tugged it down; another bruise was revealed on the shoulder. Then, with a violence that startled him, Frankie snatched the bedclothes and pulled them back.

'Why can't you leave her alone?'

Saltfleet looked down gravely. 'You know why I can't leave her alone.' Frankie dropped his eyes. 'A man was murdered two days ago. She was with him shortly before he died.'

Moro smiled at Frankie. 'You don't believe she had anything to do with it, and neither do I. But she's got to tell us herself.'

Frankie said: 'She can't tell you nothing.'

Saltfleet said: 'Why?'

Frankie shrugged, avoiding his eyes.

Moro said: 'I must get back to the group.'

Saltfleet said: 'Will it be all right if I come in the morning?'

'Of course. Whenever you like.' He rearranged the

bedclothes round the girl's neck. 'Perhaps you will be able to talk to Rosa.'

Frankie went out, slamming the door. The sleeping girl sighed and stirred, but did not awaken.

Saltfleet said: 'I'd like to know why Frankie's so sure she can't tell me anything.'

NINE

There was a brown official envelope lying on the doormat; it was addressed to Detective Inspector Fitch.

Miranda and Josie were in the sitting-room, with the French windows wide open; the sun had moved round from the garden, but the air was still soft and warm. They were drinking dry sherry.

'Sherry, darling?'

'No thanks, I need something stronger.' He poured himself a generous measure of Gerald's malt whisky. It was a peaty variety from northern Skye, darker in colour than normal blended whisky and less fiery to the palate; he drank it neat. Gerald knew that his brother-in-law was something of an expert on whisky, and that a well-stocked drinks cupboard, with at least a dozen varieties of malt, was a major inducement in persuading him to stay.

'Any calls for me?'

'No.'

'I think we can expect a visit from Fitch – I found an envelope for him on the doormat.'

'In that case, I hope he makes it soon. Dinner should be ready by seven.'

It was pleasant to relax into the deep leather armchair, with his feet on an upholstered stool, and the whisky bottle within reach on the side table.

Miranda said: 'I hope you don't mind, but I've been

telling Josie about this girl Rosie.'

'Of course I don't. It's not a secret.'

Josie said: 'Douglas had a similar case once.'

Saltfleet was instantly alert. 'Can you recall the details?'

'Yes. There was this girl Joanna . . . Joanna Fitton –
about fifteen, and she lived in Croydon with her mother –
a broken home. It started when she began sleepwalking.
Of course, they didn't bother much about that – a lot of
teenagers sleepwalk. But one night, this girl Joanna fell
over a broom handle in the dark, and woke up. And she
didn't seem to know her mother. She was just sitting there
in the dark, and talking about a car accident. Her mother
thought she was still dreaming, and got her back to bed.
But it kept on happening – I don't know how many times
– until they began to realise it wasn't just a dream. When
she woke up in the middle of the night, she claimed to be a
French girl called Michelle, who claimed she'd been killed
in a car accident after a drunken party. The odd thing was
that she didn't speak with a French accent, and didn't
seem to speak much French either – just school O-level
French. I can't remember a lot of the details now. But
Douglas was consultant to the local education authority at
the time, and they called him in when this girl Jennifer –
did I say Joanna? it was Jennifer actually – failed her
exams for the sixth-form college. Her mother claimed that
the other girl – Michelle – kept taking over when Jennifer
was supposed to be working, and she'd wake up the next
morning and find she hadn't done her homework. Well,
Douglas's first reaction was that it was a try-on. Then one
evening, just as we'd finished dinner, we got a call from the
mother saying the French girl had taken over. So he
rushed to the house right away. And I've never seen
anyone so shaken as he was when he came back. He'd
interviewed Jennifer several times, and he knew her pretty
well. And he said that Michelle simply wasn't the same

person.'

Saltfleet nodded. 'That's the baffling thing. They really *are* different people.'

'Anyway, they let her take the exam again – on Douglas's recommendation – and she got to sixth-form college. But it didn't do much good, because the same thing started all over again. So after a while she left, and got a job as a waitress. And then the odd thing happened. The proprietor's wife was a spiritualist, and she got the girl along to a seance. And while they were all sitting, holding hands in the dark, she went into a trance, and this girl Michelle came through. Of course, Douglas was furious when he heard – he said it was all a lot of nonsense. But it seemed to work.'

'What do you mean, it seemed to work?'

'She stopped having problems. Apparently she became a – what d'you call them – a medium. I think Douglas said she had a Red Indian spirit guide. But after that, we didn't hear from her any more.'

Miranda asked: 'Did you ever meet her?'

'I saw her on a few occasions – that was in the days when I acted as Douglas's receptionist.' Saltfleet observed the shadow that crossed her face. 'She seemed to be a perfectly ordinary girl.'

Partly to distract her he asked: 'What was Douglas's theory about it all?'

'Well, at first, as I've said, he thought she was shamming. He thought it was just an excuse for not working hard enough. Then when he got to know her he changed his mind, and decided it was all unconscious. He still thought she was shamming, but not consciously. He talked about the shadow – that's Jung's term – apparently it means the repressed part of the personality, the part that hasn't had a chance to express itself. That's why he was so shaken the first time he met the French girl. He did his best to prove she was just a part of Jennifer's personality. For example, he got Jennifer to write a list of every book she'd ever read. He was hoping to discover that she'd read about this French girl somewhere. But he couldn't.'

Miranda asked: 'Did anyone ever try to check up whether the French girl really existed?'

'Well, not really. The girl said she'd lived in some fairly large town – Lyon, I think, and she had a rather common name . . .'

Saltfleet thought: Typical. Too bloody lazy to follow up an obvious lead.

Josie said: 'In any case, he totally lost interest when the girl got mixed up with spiritualists. And he suddenly switched back to his original opinion – that she'd been faking all the time.'

'Faking?' Saltfleet was incredulous.

'Well, in a manner of speaking. He thought she wanted attention. She was a rather plain girl – in fact, downright ugly. The only person who'd ever cared about her was her father, and he walked out when she was a child. So Douglas's theory was that she just craved attention, and her unconscious mind hit on this method of getting it.'

'But I thought you said he'd been deeply shaken when he confronted the French girl for the first time – that he realised she was a completely different person?'

'Well, yes, but then . . . well, I can understand what he felt. We don't really know anything about the unconscious mind, do we? Even a good actor can make you think he's a different person, or a ventriloquist with his dummy. Anyway, I think it was the spiritualism bit that did it. He simply couldn't take it seriously any more.'

Saltfleet repressed the comment that sprang to his lips. He had never liked Douglas Barlow, finding him complacent and irritating; now it struck him with utter conviction that the man was a fool. But Josie remained

168

oddly loyal, and it would be better to keep his conviction to himself.

Miranda asked: 'What did this French girl do when she took over?'

'Nothing much, as far as I know, except listen to pop records. And she had a taste for strong peppermint. Jennifer could always tell when Michelle had been around because of the smell of peppermint. She used to raid Jennifer's moneybox and go and buy peppermint. Jennifer tried hiding it in the most obscure places – she even tried burying it in the garden – but it made no difference. Michelle always seemed to know exactly where it was.'

Saltfleet said: 'Christ.' Miranda looked at him in surprise.

Josie also looked momentarily surprised – Saltfleet seldom used strong language at home – but took it as a compliment to her storytelling. She said: 'Yes, it *was* rather extraordinary. I wish Douglas had tried to go into it more than he did – I thought he might have a best-selling book there. But he didn't seem to *want* to take it seriously . . .'

Miranda had observed his thoughtfulness; she said: 'What is it, darling?'

'Nothing. Just a sudden thought. Would you excuse me a moment?'

He went upstairs to the bedroom extension, and dialled Moro's number. After several rings, a woman's voice said: 'Hello?' It told him what he wanted to know. It was Dorothy's voice.

He heard the doorbell ring, and replaced the telephone without speaking.

Fitch was in the sitting-room; he was just saying; 'No thanks, I won't take my coat off. I'll only be staying a minute. I hope I'm not interrupting . . .'

Miranda said: 'Not at all. We were just going to start

169

the dinner. Could I offer you some smoked salmon?'

'Oh no, really, thank you, ma'am. It's very kind of you . . .' Fitch became self-conscious in the presence of women.

When Miranda and Josie had gone out Saltfleet said: 'What can I offer you to drink?'

'A spot of that would go down very nice.'

Saltfleet poured him some of the malt. 'Sit down.'

'Oof, thanks! That's better. It's been one of those days. I've only just got back from Tilbury, and then I got a call from your friend Barney Rice on the Vice Squad . . . Oh, this is nice.'

Saltfleet refilled his own glass, and sat down.

'What's happening?'

'A lot. I thought I'd pop in and bring you up-to-date. It's the least I can do after all your help.'

Saltfleet took the brown official envelope out of his jacket pocket.

'That came for you.'

Fitch looked bewildered. 'What, here?' He tore it open. It contained a photograph wrapped in a sheet of white paper. Fitch's face wrinkled with disgust. 'Ugh!'

Saltfleet felt in his back pocket, and took out the photograph he had removed from Moro's album; it had assumed a slight concavity from being pressed against his buttock. He tossed it on to Fitch's lap.

'Try comparing it with that.'

Fitch stared at the photographs, then at Saltfleet.

'They can't be the same man?'

'No. To begin with, this one wasn't dead when it was taken. Could I see?'

Fitch handed him both photographs. The one that had arrived in the envelope – with the compliments of the Exhibits Officer – was a close-up of Choromansky's genitals. It showed clearly that the penis had been partly severed. A number of small but ugly knife wounds had penetrated the skin above the penis and in the immediate region of the thighs. The pubic hairs had been shaved off to show the wounds more clearly.

The photograph from Moro's album resembled the other only superficially. The genitals protruded from black leather straps, which formed a kind of harness; Saltfleet recognised the raw red blotches on the penis and thighs as cigarette burns. The pubic hairs showed traces of blood, which ran from a cut just above them, and there was a bite mark, showing a distinct imprint of teeth, on the inside of the thigh. In detail, the photographs were basically unlike; yet what emerged, as they lay side by side, was an overwhelming similarity; it lay in the air of violence, of deliberate cruelty, that emanated from both.

Saltfleet handed them back to Fitch.

'I reckon that any magistrate would give you a search warrant on the strength of those.'

'But you say there's no connection?'

'I don't know. To me, they look as if they could be the work of the same man.'

'This Tony Spraggs character?'

'That's right.'

'Rice has been telling me about him. He seems to think the boy's mother might give evidence, if we could get Spraggs behind bars. Apparently the boy has been bleeding internally since it happened, and it's done him a lot of damage – mental, I mean. So his mother's feeling pretty vengeful.'

'I can imagine.'

'Where did you get this photograph?'

'From this Sexual Institute I told you about. The doctor in charge has a collection of them.'

'Any idea of the man's identity?'

'No, but it couldn't be too difficult to establish – there's another photograph that shows his face.'

'What makes you think Spraggs is our man?'

'Something Moro said. When I was talking about the murder, he said: I can think of at least two people in this area who'd be capable of it. I was pretty sure that the man who took that photograph lives in this area – because I saw another photograph with another one of Moro's patients in it. And they were obviously taken in the same place.'

'Are you sure this man Spraggs took this photo?'

'No, I'm not. I could easily find out from Moro – he offered to tell me the name if it was important. But I didn't want to let him know I was interested in Spraggs.'

Fitch glanced up sharply. 'You think he might warn him?'

'No. I don't think he'd do that. But policemen and psychiatrists tend to be on opposite sides of the fence where crime is concerned, and I don't want to antagonise him.'

Fitch was staring at the photographs, obviously troubled.

'What worries me is that Choromansky doesn't seem to have been the type to pick up a queer. From everything I've heard, he was a womaniser.'

'Under normal circumstances, I think you'd be right. But these weren't normal. I think I've found out how he managed to give himself jaundice. It was a drug called methyl testosterone. And from what Aspinal tells me, it turns a man into a raging sex maniac. My guess is that Choromansky was bisexual, and when he couldn't find a woman – two prostitutes turned him down because they thought he was a bit kinky – he decided to make do with a man. You said yourself that the steward and his mate looked at you in an odd way when you asked if

172

Choromansky was homosexual . . .'

'But why would Spraggs kill Choromansky?'

'Well, I can suggest one reason. We know Spraggs is a sadist. And if Choromansky was another, then they were at cross-purposes . . .'

Fitch gave a snort of laughter. 'It sounds like one of those jokes – who did what to whom.' He shook his head. 'What I'd like to know is how a Russian spy got mixed up with a character like Spraggs.'

'Are you sure he was a spy?'

'Oh, there's no doubt about that. MI5 know all about him.'

'Are you sure?'

'Absolutely.' Fitch lowered his voice. 'This is all top secret of course, but I suppose I can tell you – after all, you were the first to guess he was a spy. His real name's not Choromansky. It's Krylov. I've got most of the story from Blake of the Special Branch.' Fitch allowed Saltfleet to replenish his glass; it was obvious that he felt he deserved it. 'It seems that Krylov came ashore to contact a spy in General Communications HQ. They store all the information from spy satellites – stuff about Soviet nuclear missiles in Siberia, and so on. And it seems that MI5 have known there's a spy in General Communications for some time. They've got their own double agent in Moscow. What they do, apparently, is to release false information to General Communications, and then see how much of it comes through at the other end – Blake says they call it a "dye tracer". Now they've discovered the identity of the spy at GCHQ, but they don't want to alarm him yet. The Special Branch has been watching him for months, and taking photographs of everybody he contacts. Well, a couple of weeks ago, the Special Branch man followed him into a pub in Cheltenham and saw him stick a piece of chewing-gum under the counter. Ten

173

minutes later, another man comes in and takes the chewing-gum. The photograph shows that the other man was Krylov. The agent followed him to a park, where he sat on a bench. Krylov put a newspaper down on the seat. The spy from GCHQ came and sat on the bench, picked up the newspaper, and walked off. The agent decided to follow Krylov, but Krylov gave him the slip – so he knew he was being followed.' Fitch recounted all this with enormous gusto and relish; Saltfleet had never seen him so animated. 'Blake is pretty sure the newspaper contained money.'

'And when did the Special Branch discover Krylov was dead?'

Fitch chuckled. 'When I told them.' This case was clearly doing wonders for his self-esteem. 'You should have seen Blake's face when I showed him the morgue photograph of Choromansky! Anyway, the next problem was to try and find the microfilm, or whatever the spy passed on to Choromansky, and that's what we've been trying to do most of the day. I went back on board the ship, with four Special Branch men who were supposed to be from the Port of London Authority. We said we'd found evidence that Choromansky had purchased heroin, and it was probably hidden on the ship. I daresay they're still searching. But one of the blokes is a chap called Brian Marks, and he's supposed to be a human bloodhound. If anybody can find that microfilm, he can.'

Saltfleet said: 'That sounds nice work. Scottie must be pleased with you.'

'Oh, he wouldn't admit it if he was.' But Fitch's smile made it plain that Saltfleet was echoing his own opinion.

'What are you going to do about Spraggs?'

'I thought I'd ask your opinion about that.'

'I'd suggest you get a search warrant just as soon as you

174

can. Those two photographs ought to do it. Get there early in the morning, as soon as he's left for work – he's a civil servant, so he probably has to be at his desk by nine. I'm pretty sure you'll find a lot of kinky leather gear. But what you're really looking for is photographs. Did Rice mention the name of this black boy he raped?'

'Jackie Gibson.'

'It's my guess he took photographs of Gibson. If you can find them, you've got him – you'll probably be able to get the boy to testify against him.'

'And what about Choromansky?'

'My advice would be to keep that until later. If you can get him rattled enough, he'll probably tell you about Choromansky – assuming, of course, that he knows anything.'

'Do *you* think he did it?'

Saltfleet paused before he answered. Fitch seemed to regard him as infallible, and that could not do either of them any good. He said: 'I honestly don't know. I'd say it's a fifty-fifty chance he's your killer. But even if he's not, you'll get credit for an intelligent piece of deduction. It's a lead that's got to be followed up.'

'Right.' Fitch gave him a swift sidelong glance. 'You still don't want me to tell MacPhail you gave me the idea?'

'Good God, no! I thought we'd agreed about that?'

'Yes, of course. It's just that it doesn't seem fair . . .'

Saltfleet said firmly: 'Forget it. I'm glad to help.'

'Well, you know I'm grateful. If there's anything I can do for you at any time . . .'

'Thanks. I know.' A thought struck him. 'In fact, there *is* something. You know I got a lot of help from a woman called Elfie Lefkowich. Her husband's a ponce called Joe Lefkowich – known as South American Joe – and it was Joe who told me about Spraggs. Now I gather Joe's in some kind of minor trouble on a firearms charge. They're making him report twice a day to the Notting Hill station. If you could say a word in his favour to Roy Coates or Bill Watts . . . Say you learned about Spraggs from South American Joe.'

'Am I supposed to have made a deal with this character?'

'No, nothing like that. But if Scottie wants to know how you learned about Spraggs, say Joe told you, and lay it on thick about how cooperative he's been . . .'

'All right. It's a pleasure.'

'Thanks, George. More whisky?'

Fitch looked at his watch. 'No, I suppose I'd better get along and see about that warrant.' He sighed. 'It's been a long day . . .'

'By the way, I'll tell you something else that's worth looking for in Spraggs's flat. The knife that killed Choromansky. Probably a fish-gutting knife with a retractable blade.'

'Right.'

'And could you let me have that photo back when you've got your warrant? I'd like to put it back in Moro's scrapbook.'

'I'll do that.'

At the door, Fitch cleared his throat as if he was going to say something, then grasped Saltfleet's hand, and shook it very hard.

'Thanks Greg.'

'Glad to help.'

But it was a pleasant sensation to know he had made a friend.

In the kitchen, Miranda and Josie were both wearing aprons; Josie was slicing avocado for the salad. Miranda said: 'I was just wondering whether to ask Mr Fitch to dinner.'

'No, he had to get home. I have a feeling that Fitch is a henpecked husband . . .' He helped himself to a piece of celery. 'Although I wouldn't be surprised if he answered her back today.'

Half an hour later, they had just started the main course when the phone rang. Saltfleet said: 'Let it ring.'

Miranda stood up.

'No, it might be Gerald ringing from Nassau.'

He poured Josie another glass of Beaujolais. 'I just hope it's not for me. I'm looking forward to a peaceful evening.'

Miranda came in.

'Dr Moro would like a word with you. I thought you'd want to speak to him.' As he stood up she said: 'Shall I put your dinner in the oven?'

'No, I'll only be a moment.'

He sat on the arm of the settee and took up the phone: 'Saltfleet speaking.'

Moro's voice said: 'I'm sorry to bother you at this time. But I thought I'd better tell you. Frankie says that he killed the Polish sailor.'

TEN

As he reached the corner of Ladbroke Terrace Gardens, he saw Moro waiting for him on the other side of Ladbroke Grove. With his hands thrust deep into his overcoat pockets, he looked a picture of dejection.

Saltfleet said: 'Where's Frankie?'

'He is in his room.'

'Are you sure he won't . . . disappear?'

'No. He won't disappear.' Moro said it sadly. 'He has nowhere to go.'

'What happened?'

'He simply came into my sitting-room and said he wanted to talk to me. Then he said: I'd better tell you – I killed that bloke.'

'Does he know you've gone for me?'

'Yes. *He* said he wanted to talk to you.'

As they turned into the gateway of the Institute, Saltfleet stopped Moro with a hand on his arm.

'Tell me something before we go in. Had he been talking to Dorothy?'

'I don't know. Why? Dorothy has no influence over him.'

Saltfleet smiled ironically but said nothing.

As they entered, Moro asked: 'Where would you like to see him?'

'Your office would probably be the best place.'

The rows of chairs and the Chinese screens had been removed. The only light was a single desk lamp on the desk. Saltfleet sat in the comfortable office chair beside the desk, and took out his notebook. His body felt heavy and comfortable after the meal; Miranda had refused to allow him to leave before finishing the Boeuf Stroganoff.

Frankie came in, with Moro behind him; he looked nervous and unsure of himself, like a schoolboy who had been summoned by the headmaster. He was still wearing the shabby plimsolls.

Saltfleet said: 'Hello, Frankie. Sit down.'

Frankie ignored him, staring fixedly at the carpet. It was Moro who persuaded him to sit by placing a hand gently on his shoulder. Moro sat in his chair behind the desk.

Saltfleet said: 'Now, Frankie, you say you killed the Polish sailor?'

Frankie tried to speak, but had to clear his throat. He said huskily: 'Yes.'

'Why?'

'Because . . . he was trying to kill Rosie.'

'Trying to kill her?'

'He'd got his knife against her throat.'

'And what was she doing?'

'She was kneeling in front of him.'

'And what did you do?'

Frankie made an effort to control the nervousness in his voice.

'I grabbed the knife and stabbed him.'

'Where?' Frankie was silent. 'Where did you stab him?'

'I can't remember.'

Saltfleet said patiently: 'Oh come, you must remember. Look, show me with this paperknife.' He picked up the wooden paperknife from the desk and handed it to Frankie. 'I'm the sailor, and I've got the knife against

179

Rosie's throat. Show me exactly what you did.'

Frankie bit his lip, as if trying to see through a trick question. Then he grabbed Saltfleet's hand, clumsily wrested the knife away, and brought it down in the centre of Saltfleet's chest.

Saltfleet said: 'Just there?'

'Yes.'

'That's the breastbone. The knife would have glanced off.'

'It was a bit higher . . .'

'In the throat?'

'Yes.'

'Did he cry out?'

'Er . . . yes. A bit.'

'Did you get blood on your clothes?'

'No.'

Saltfleet shook his head wearily, looking at Moro.

'All right, Frankie. You can go.'

Frankie stared with astonishment.

'Ain't you going to take me in?'

'No.' Saltfleet took a packet of Manikin cigars out of his pocket.

'Why not?'

'Because you didn't kill him. He wasn't stabbed in the throat. He didn't cry out. And you didn't get blood on your clothes. That's impossible.' He lit a cigar. 'Feel like telling me the truth?'

Frankie said sullenly: 'That *is* the truth.'

'You can go.'

'If I say I did it, why can't you believe me?' He was making an attempt to simulate anger, but was too dispirited. 'You want to get somebody, don't you? Well, you've got me. I did it.'

Saltfleet turned to Moro. 'Somebody's put him up to this.' They both stared thoughtfully at Frankie.

Frankie said suddenly: 'I can prove I did it.'

'How?'

Frankie stood up and came round to Moro's side of the desk. 'Excuse me.' He bent down and pulled open the bottom drawer. From this he took a bunch of keys. Moro and Saltfleet followed him as he crossed the room, to the case that contained the photograph of the pockmarked man with the Kaiser Wilhelm moustache. While they watched, he unlocked it, carefully raised the glass, and reached across to the group of knives that lay between the burgling tools and the coil of barbed-wire. He picked up one of the knives, and offered it to Saltfleet.

'This is what killed him.'

The knife had a wooden handle, which was as long as its pointed blade. Saltfleet took out his handkerchief, and let Frankie place the knife in it. Moro looked at him questioningly. Saltfleet held the knife gently by the handle, pressing on the yellow metal catch above the blade as he pressed the end of the blade against the corner of the case. The blade slid in. When he released the pressure, it snapped out again. Dried blood was caked around the point where the blade joined the handle, as well as a smear of mud.

Saltfleet said: 'Yes, this looks like the knife. A fish-gutting knife.'

Moro suddenly began to laugh.

'Amazing! And it was under our eyes the whole time. That was a clever move, Frankie.'

Frankie's face betrayed a flicker of satisfaction.

Saltfleet said: 'Come and sit down, Frankie.'

He wrapped the knife carefully in his handkerchief, and placed it in the desk drawer.

'So you followed Rosie when she went out on Saturday. Why?'

Frankie said promptly: 'Because she was always getting

into trouble.' He was more confident now.

'You followed her to the pub and saw her pick up the sailor.' Frankie nodded. 'What did they do then?'

'Went to a hotel. But they couldn't get in.'

'Where was the hotel?'

'Behind Notting Hill Gate. I don't know what it was called but I could show you.'

'What did they do then?'

'Went to that all-night café in Bayswater Road and had a meal.'

'Did you go in too?'

'No. I didn't want them to see me.'

'So you followed them when they came out. Where did they go then?'

'They came back here.'

Moro said: 'Back here?'

Frankie looked uncomfortable; he obviously felt that he might get Rosie into trouble.

Saltfleet said: 'She was hoping to take the sailor into her room for the night?' Frankie nodded. 'Why didn't she?'

'Harriet's light was still on.'

'So what did they do then?'

'Went across the road to the gardens.'

'And you watched them go through that gap in the fence?' Frankie nodded. 'What were they doing?'

'I couldn't see much. It was dark.'

'You said he was holding a knife against her throat. Could you see that?'

Frankie looked uncomfortable, like a schoolboy caught out in a lie. 'Yes.'

'All right. So you went and grabbed the knife and stabbed him?' Frankie nodded, avoiding his eyes.

Saltfleet picked up the paperknife. 'I'll give you one more chance. Show me where you stabbed him.'

Frankie looked at the knife, but made no attempt to

take it. Saltfleet said: 'You don't know where he was stabbed, do you?' Frankie said nothing. Saltfleet dropped the paperknife back on the desk. He placed his hand lightly on Frankie's shoulder.

'It's no good, Frankie. I know you didn't do it. You're trying to protect Rosie. You only went back for the knife.' Frankie said nothing; he sat with his hands hanging between his knees. Saltfleet sat on the edge of the desk so he could lean forward and see Frankie's face.

'Listen Frankie, this is not good sense. Suppose you convinced me that you did it. You'd go to prison for a long time. I know you'd probably get away with a charge of manslaughter, but it would still be a long time. If Rosie's charged with manslaughter, there's nothing they can do to her. At the worst, she'd be confined in an asylum for the criminally insane. And she'd probably get out after a couple of years.' Frankie was staring at him with astonishment. 'Dorothy didn't tell you that, did she?' He turned to Moro. 'Tell him to go back to his room.'

Moro said: 'Is this true, Frankie?' Frankie shook his head; he looked on the verge of tears. 'Then you are a sillier boy than I thought you were. Do as he says. Go back to your room while we try to sort this out.' He went with Frankie to the door.

Saltfleet said: 'Frankie.'

Frankie stopped, without turning round. Saltfleet said: 'Don't talk to Dorothy. She's already done enough damage.'

When Frankie had gone, Moro came back to his chair. He was looking tired, but no longer dejected. They sat in silence for a moment; Moro shook his head when Saltfleet offered him a Manikin cigar. He said: 'So it *was* Rosa.' It was not a question.

'No. It was Dorothy.'

Moro showed no surprise; he only asked quietly: 'What

makes you think so?'

Saltfleet shrugged. 'As you said when I first met you, Rosie is incapable of violence.'

Moro said: 'But Dorothy is the most sane and balanced of the three.'

Saltfleet said: 'It was Dorothy.'

'But why? Why do you think so?'

Saltfleet stood up and went to the mantelpiece. 'Because of your china dolls.' He took them down. 'Remember you told me that one of them is up here and the other down here? That the second personality knows all about the first, but the first doesn't know about the second?'

'I said that is not invariably so.'

'It is in this case. Somebody reminded me of what you said this evening. She told me of a case where one of the personalities kept hiding her moneybox. But it was no good, because the other personality always knew exactly where to go and look for it. That reminded me of something else: those bruises on Rosie's shoulders. The sailor did that. Now suppose you're right, and Dorothy didn't know what Rosie was doing, or vice-versa. When Dorothy woke up the next morning, and found her shoulders covered in bruises, she'd know that something had happened, wouldn't she? Yet she did her best to convince us that she knew nothing whatever. She even implied I must be joking when I asked her about the Polish sailor. No, Dorothy knew all right. She knew because she killed him.'

'I find that very hard to believe.'

'Then what *do* you believe?'

Moro sighed and shook his head.

'I am not sure what to believe. Rosa is the one with the mental problems. I suppose that under certain circumstances, she might be capable of . . . Could it not have been some kind of an accident?'

184

'No. He was stabbed in the heart. And it was done so quickly that he didn't even have time to cry out.'

Moro said: 'Believe me, I am not trying to defend Dorothy. As a doctor, it makes no difference to me whether the man was killed by one or the other. But if either of them did it, I think it must have been Rosa. We know she was the one who picked up the sailor . . .'

'And suppose Dorothy reappeared while Rosie was being beaten up?'

Moro considered this carefully, then said: 'In that case, I think Dorothy would have screamed. That would surely be the natural reaction of a woman who woke up to find a knife at her throat?'

'No. Not if I'm right, and Dorothy was already a spectator of everything that happened. I think Dorothy was aware of everything Rosie did that evening. She was there when Rosie picked up the sailor. She was there when they went into the garden together. What she didn't expect was the violence – to be grabbed by the throat and beaten. I think she decided it was time to intervene, before Rosie ended up dead.'

Moro said: 'Then that would hardly be murder.'

Saltfleet shrugged. 'I agree.'

He noted the shade of relief that passed over Moro's face; he knew what the next question would be.

'What do you intend to do about it?'

Saltfleet said: 'Would you allow me to try an experiment?'

Moro's face showed his misgivings. 'What experiment?'

'I want to ask Dorothy about this myself, and I want you to promise not to interfere.'

'If you prefer, I will go into another room.'

'No, I want you to be present. But I want you to promise not to interfere – not even to speak.'

After a silence Moro said: 'Very well.'

'Could you bring her up here?'

'It would be better if we went to her room.'

'If you don't mind, I'd rather she came up here.'

Moro shrugged and went out. Five minutes later, he returned alone.

'She was asleep. She will be up in a moment.'

They waited for ten minutes, each absorbed in his own thoughts. Moro was about to go downstairs to look for her when Dorothy came in. She was wearing a blue quilted dressing-gown over her nightdress, and had fur-lined slippers on her feet. Moro indicated the chair opposite his desk.

'Would you sit down, my dear?'

She sat down quietly and composedly, pulling her dressing-gown over her knees. Saltfleet thought she looked pale and fatigued. He pulled up his chair until his knees were almost touching hers. She looked at him calmly and incuriously. He said: 'Why did it take you so long to get here?'

'That is none of your business.' She spoke without animosity; he could see that she was determined to control all her reactions. He stared into her eyes, trying to beat down her gaze.

'Everything you do now is my business. Because I know exactly what happened, and you're going to tell me the truth. And you know that if you don't tell me the truth, Rosie will. That's why you're keeping her suppressed, isn't it? You can't do that indefinitely, you know. You're already beginning to tire, aren't you? Rosie wants to get out again. How do you think you'll feel after forty-eight hours of questioning in the police station?' Her gaze wavered, and he knew the point had struck home. He said: 'You told Frankie that if you let Rosie out, she'd tell me the truth. That's why Frankie decided to confess to the murder. You told him to confess, didn't you?'

186

Her eyes met his defiantly. 'That is not true.'

'But you wanted him to take the blame, didn't you?' He pulled open the drawer and took out the knife; he unwrapped his handkerchief, so she could see it. 'I'd like to make a bet with you. Your fingerprints won't be on this knife, because you wiped it clean before you told Frankie to put it in the case. It only has Frankie's fingerprints.'

Again, she failed to meet his eyes. She was unaware of how much Frankie had told him, and it undermined her confidence. Saltfleet pressed his advantage.

'So far you've been lying to me. Now I want the truth.'

She looked him in the eyes. 'I don't know what you mean.'

Saltfleet leaned forward. 'Somebody saw you walking home on Sunday morning – with blood on you.'

He observed the flicker of contemptuous amusement in her eyes. 'I don't believe you.'

'Why don't you believe me, Dorothy?' She stared back, refusing to answer. 'I'll tell you why. Because you kept your eyes very wide open when you walked back on Sunday morning. You carefully avoided the streetlamps. That's why you're sure nobody saw you.' He reached up suddenly, grabbing the collar of the dressing-gown. 'Why have you got your dressing-gown buttoned up to your throat? It's not cold?' He pulled it roughly; she tried to hold it down, and the button came off. Her face flushed angrily: 'How dare you!'

Saltfleet jerked back the dressing-gown from her shoulder; as she tried to stop him, he gripped her wrist and squeezed hard. She winced; Saltfleet had a powerful grip. 'What's this?' He had exposed the bruise. 'A love bite?'

'Let me go!' Now she was white with fury; she tried to scratch the back of his hand with her nails; he caught the other wrist, and pushed her back into her chair. She said: 'You're hurting me! Dr Moro, make him stop it!'

Moro had started to rise from his chair; when he caught Saltfleet's eye, he sat down again. He started to speak, then changed his mind.

Saltfleet thrust his face within a few inches of hers, aware of her revulsion. 'I want the truth.' He deliberately allowed one of his hands to relax; she twisted free, and struck out at him; he moved quickly and the blow caught him on the temple. In a single movement he caught her wrist, transferred both her wrists to his left hand, then slapped her face. It was a hard blow, and tears came to her eyes. Moro jumped to his feet. 'Please! Let her go!'

'All right.' Saltfleet released her hands, knowing what would happen. She was on him like a fury, the force of her charge almost overturning the chair. Then her fingers were clawing at his face, trying to scratch out his eyes. She said between clenched teeth: 'You bastard, I'll kill you for that.'

Her strength astonished him; it took both of them to hold her. She was crying with frustration as she continued to try and kick and scratch; her face was white with venomous rage. Even when Saltfleet gripped both her wrists, she continued to kick and twist.

Moro said: 'Please let her go.' This seemed to calm her. 'Now, Dorothy, calm down. I won't let him ask any more questions.' Suddenly, she seemed to collapse. When Saltfleet released her wrists, she allowed them to fall to her sides. Moro led her gently to the couch. He asked Saltfleet: 'Could you leave us alone for a moment?'

Saltfleet nodded and went out; but he took care not to close the door completely. He heard Dorothy say: 'I don't understand what he means. I wasn't there.'

Moro said soothingly: 'No, of course you weren't. He doesn't understand. Lie down. You look tired.'

'It's not true, what he says.' Her voice was sleepy.

'No. You don't have to worry. Everything is all right. Just relax and close your eyes. That's right. Just relax now. Let yourself sleep. Drift into a deep sleep, a deep sleep . . .'

Saltfleet felt something run down his chin, and realised he had a scratch on his left cheek; it hurt when he touched it. He peered in through the door. Moro had raised her hand, and allowed it to drop. Then he pulled down her dressing-gown, retrieved a slipper from the middle of the floor, and replaced it on her foot. He glanced up as Saltfleet came and stood beside him.

'You're bleeding.'

Saltfleet found a paper tissue in his pocket, and dabbed his cheek. He said: 'Well, do you believe me now?'

Moro looked down at the sleeping girl, his face troubled. 'Yes, I believe you.'

'That's how the sailor died. "You bastard, I'll kill you." And she'd have killed *me* if she'd had a knife.'

'Did you know what would happen when you slapped her?'

'I had a pretty good idea.'

'But how could you be so sure that she did it?'

'She must have got blood on her clothes. She probably burned them in the furnace, like Frankie's shoes.'

'So you've been certain it was Dorothy all the time?' He said it sadly.

'No. I started by thinking it had to be Frankie. Then I came upon another suspect – a man called Spraggs.' From Moro's face he could see that he recognised the name. 'He's the man who took the bondage pictures, isn't he?'

'Yes.' Moro made no attempt to be evasive.

'Don't you think *he* ought to be behind bars?'

Moro said quietly: 'I am a doctor, not a policeman.'

'And I'm a policeman, not a doctor.' The cigar he had

189

been smoking was trampled on the floor; he lit another. 'But there's something I'd like to ask you as a doctor. You say that Rosie used to pick up men fairly regularly?'

'Yes.'

'Do you know when this started?'

'After her last breakdown – about two years ago.'

'I had an interesting thought when we were talking about Dorothy. If Dorothy knew everything Rosie did, she must have been there when Rosie picked up those men. You could say she was a kind of voyeur.'

Moro nodded with interest. 'That is true.'

'Dorothy strikes me as a cold fish – the kind who could never give herself to a man. Could such a girl be interested in sex?'

Moro said promptly: 'Of course. Perhaps more than most.'

'So she might enjoy playing the voyeur as Rosie picked up men and let them undress her?'

'It is possible, yes.'

'And would it be possible for Dorothy to *make* Rosie go and offer herself to strangers? – to put the idea into her head and make her think she wanted to punish herself.'

Moro went and looked down at the girl's face.

'You could be right. But only Dorothy could tell us.'

'Or Rosie. Isn't it time we tried to speak to Rosie?'

Moro shook his head. 'In the morning . . .'

'No, now, while Dorothy's exhausted. She might be strong again tomorrow.'

Moro sat on the couch, and touched the girl's face with his fingertips.

'We should let her sleep.'

'Let Dorothy sleep. It's Rosie I want to talk to.'

Moro placed his hand on her forehead, and spoke close to her ear: 'Rosa, Rosa, can you hear me?'

Saltfleet went and stood by the head of the couch. Moro

continued to speak softly for several minutes. Nothing seemed to happen. The girl's chest rose and fell gently, and the face looked bloodless and lifeless. Saltfleet caught a movement; one of the fingers stirred. Moro, his face close to hers, failed to notice. Saltfleet touched him on the shoulder.

'Her hand moved.'

'Which one?'

Saltfleet pointed to her left hand. Moro smiled.

'That is promising.' He leaned forward again. 'Rosa, if you can hear me, move your fingers.' The fingers of the left hand twitched. 'Good. Now, Rosa, when I count up to ten, you're going to be wide awake, feeling relaxed and refreshed, with no worries at all. All right, let's begin. One, two . . .' He counted very slowly and distinctly. As he reached eight, she began to breathe more deeply. At nine, her eyelids stirred. Moro finished counting, then said: 'Wide awake, now! Wide awake!' The girl sighed, and slowly opened her eyes. She smiled trustingly at Moro. He said cheerfully: 'That's right. It's nice to see you back again. It's been a long time. How do you feel?'

The girl said, in a surprisingly normal voice: 'Fine, thank you.'

'And who am I?'

'Dr Moro, of course.'

Although Saltfleet had seen this before, it still filled him with astonishment. This girl was not Dorothy, and she was not Rosie, although there was a distinct resemblance to the child. She was a completely separate human being, and she had only to smile and speak a few words for this to become obvious.

Moro pointed to Saltfleet: 'And do you know who this is?'

She twisted round to look at him, and frowned, as if trying to place him. He could sense that she was short-sighted.

'No . . .'

Saltfleet smiled at her and she smiled back, pleasantly enough, but without recognition. In her smile the resemblance to Geraldine was suddenly strong; it was not in her face or her expression, but somehow in the personality itself. It seemed to support a speculation he had occasionally entertained: that human beings are cast from a limited number of moulds.

Moro said: 'You're looking better. You've got some colour in your cheeks.' It was true; all the tiredness had vanished, and she looked as if she had just awakened from a long sleep.

'I feel fine.'

'Do you feel like answering a few questions?'

'All right.' She nodded cheerfully. Moro caught Saltfleet's eye, and made an interrogative signal with his eyebrows; Saltfleet shook his head. For the moment, he wanted to watch and observe.

Moro brought a chair and placed it beside the couch; he said casually: 'I've often wanted to ask you about your eighth birthday, Rosa.' Her smile vanished. Moro took his time sitting down, giving her time to think. 'Did anything special happen that day?'

'Yes.' Her voice was scarcely audible.

'What?'

'My father . . . my father got angry with me.'

'Oh? Why?'

'He caught me in the toy cupboard with my cousin Joey.' She said it without looking at him, but her voice was firm.

'You never told me that before.'

'No . . . I suppose it didn't seem important.'

He smiled at her. 'That wasn't really the reason, was it?'

'No.' She looked up at him. 'It upset me too much. I

didn't want to talk about it.'

Moro said gently: 'But it doesn't upset you now, does it?'

She thought about this, then said with mild astonishment: 'No.'

'Do you know why?' She shook her head. 'Because you've faced up to it and got it out of your system. That's the only way to make things go away. Did your father hit you?'

'No.'

'What did he do?'

'He shook me. He shook me till I felt sick.'

'And what did he say?'

'He said I was a dirty little whore like my mother.'

'Did you know what he meant?'

'No, but I knew it was bad.'

'And does it still upset you when you talk about it?'

'No.' She added, after a pause: 'At least, not very much.' There was an honesty about her that he found very appealing.

Moro said: 'And it won't in the future. Because you're beginning to get better.' He took her hand. 'Do you know why you're beginning to get better?'

She smiled at him. 'Because you've helped me.'

'No. Because you've helped yourself.' Saltfleet could see that this puzzled her. 'You see, mental problems aren't like physical problems. If you'd picked up a bacterial infection, I could give you antibiotics, and you wouldn't have to do anything – just lie there while they did their work. But it's not the same with psychological problems. You have to help by wanting to get rid of them. And as soon as you begin to fight, you begin to get well. *Do* you want to get well? Do you want to become a normal girl?'

'If I can.' Saltfleet could sense her fear and uncertainty.

'You can.' Saltfleet had to admire Moro's confidence, the quiet conviction that seemed to make all problems seem trivial. 'I'll tell you how you can get well. The first step is to understand what caused your problems. As soon as you know that, you're more than halfway to solving them. Now tell me, what is the clinical name for your illness? Don't be afraid to say it.'

She said hesitantly: 'Multiple personality.'

'That's right. And do you know what caused it?'

She shook her head..

'I'll try to explain. You've seen those trees in parks that are surrounded by a wooden cage, to protect them while they're still young? What would happen if the cage was left there as the tree grew bigger?'

'It . . . it would be too small.'

'Yes, but that wouldn't stop the tree from growing. It would simply burst the cage. All living things need to grow and expand. That is the law of their nature. And human beings need to grow mentally as well as physically. Just as there's an oak tree inside every acorn, so there's an adult inside every baby. And just as every baby is a fully grown adult in embryo, so he's also a complete human being in embryo. But this is the really interesting thing. Because, you see, no human being on earth has ever become a *complete* human being. I'm certainly not, and I've never met anyone who was. We *all* stop growing before we reach that stage. So you're not very different from everybody else. It's all relative, isn't it?'

She nodded, smiling; her short-sighted eyes remained on his face.

'Now there's something rather special about this problem of multiple personality. It only happens to people who've had a difficult time in childhood. Do you know what causes it?' She shook her head. 'It's because when someone has been really upset or hurt, he feels totally discouraged. He doesn't want to make any more effort. He feels so low that nothing seems worth doing. Above all, he feels that he isn't *worth* anything. You know that feeling, don't you?' She nodded. 'But in your case it was a mistake. You're a bright, intelligent girl. You have an IQ above average. Yet because your father made you feel guilty and miserable, you decided to stop growing, to stop making any effort. And that's always a mistake. Because what about that person inside you, that girl you're waiting to turn into? She's there, inside you, like an oak inside an acorn. But you're refusing to let her out. You're denying her a chance of life. And finally you've made her so rebellious that she's determined to go her own way without you. She's developed into a girl called Dorothy, and she keeps pushing you out and using your body.' He took her gently by the shoulders. 'You needn't look so miserable. It isn't as bad as all that. You see, you *are* Dorothy. She's a part of you. Try to understand. Every one of us contains dozens of people. There's you before you can talk, and you at the age of seven, and you at puberty, and you when you turn into a woman. And if human beings weren't so lazy, if they had the courage to keep on developing, there might be dozens more "yous". No matter how much you develop, there are always more "yous" you might develop into. The oddest thing is that, in some strange sense, they're already there, as the oak is in the acorn. They can even communicate with you. Sometimes, if you're about to do something stupid or dangerous, you get a sudden feeling that it's not really a good idea. That's one of the "yous" up there saying: Don't do that, or you may ruin my chance of coming into existence.' He took her hands. 'Do you know why you stopped growing?'

When she saw he wanted a reply she said: 'Because . . . because I didn't try hard enough.'

'Not just that. Because you kept on *running away*. Whenever you faced a problem, you buried your head in the sand, like an ostrich. And as soon as you did that, Dorothy took over. All you have to do to get better is to stop running away. I know it's painful, but there's no other way. If you keep trying to retreat, you simply make things worse. You've got to accept that life is often difficult and painful, and start climbing again. It's nothing to be frightened about. It's much nicer being up there than down here. You feel stronger and happier and more interested in life. And all you have to do is to start taking responsibility, acting like a human being with an interesting future.'

Her eyes wavered. He said: 'I know. You're wondering if you'll be strong enough. But you don't have to do it alone. I'm here to help you. But it's *your* effort that will really make all the difference. Are you willing to try?'

'Yes.' Her voice was clear and controlled.

Moro suddenly laughed; Saltfleet thought he detected a note of relief.

'Good. Now I'm going to ask you some very personal questions, and I want you to answer them as honestly as you can. Do you mind Mr Saltfleet being present? Or would you rather I asked him to wait in the other room?'

She said quietly: 'No.'

'Very well.' Saltfleet took the opportunity to sit down; while Moro had been speaking, he had not dared to move, in case he distracted her.

Moro said: 'Now I'd like you to tell me about Uncle Greg. He's another key to this problem, isn't he?' She avoided his eyes as she nodded. 'First it was your father, telling you that you were a little whore and you'd go to hell. Then it was something that happened with Uncle Greg. What was it?'

She made a visible effort to control herself.

'He . . . he . . .'

Moro said: 'He tried to make love to you, didn't he? Did he succeed?' She nodded. 'I thought so. Tell me how it happened?'

Saltfleet thought for a moment that she was going to cry; but when she spoke, her voice was low and controlled.

'It happened one day when we were alone in the house. Aunt Vi worked at Woolworths in the afternoons. Joey was usually in the house but he'd gone somewhere. I was in the bathroom washing my stockings. Then Uncle Greg came in and started tickling me . . .'

'Were you fully dressed?'

'No. I'd taken my dress off, so as not to get it wet. Then he started to kiss me. I didn't mind that at first – he often kissed me. But this time I felt there was something different. I could feel his heart pounding. Then he took my hand and took me into the bedroom . . .'

'Your bedroom?' She nodded. 'Where was that?'

'Opposite the bathroom. He told me to lie down, and kept on saying: It won't hurt . . .'

'And did it hurt?'

'A bit. Not a lot.'

'Did you cry?'

'Not then. I cried when I saw the blood. I kept on bleeding for hours. There was blood all over the sheets . . .'

'You were afraid your aunt would find out?'

'I suppose so. But I was more frightened of the blood. I thought I was going to bleed to death.'

'What did Uncle Greg do?'

'He put the sheets in the bath, and told me to stay in bed and say I'd got a stomach pain . . .'

'And did your aunt find out?'

'Not then. But she began to suspect later on.'

'Did it happen more than once?'

'Yes. Until I left home.'

'But if you wanted him to stop, why didn't you tell him you didn't like it? He *would* have stopped, wouldn't he?'

'I didn't want to upset him.' She hesitated, thinking. 'I suppose I loved him more than my father. He was nicer than my father. My father only made me feel wicked. Uncle Greg was always kind and made me feel good. And then when . . . when that happened, I began to think perhaps my father had been right after all . . . that perhaps there was something wrong with me and I always caused trouble . . .'

'And how do you feel about it now?'

'I still feel he shouldn't have done it. It spoiled everything.'

'And you feel it was entirely his fault?' When she seemed puzzled, he said: 'I want you to try to be honest about this.'

'I *am* trying to be honest.'

'Then let me put it another way. Are you quite sure you didn't lead him to think you wanted him to make love to you?'

'No!' She sounded almost indignant.

'I don't mean deliberately. But adult males are stimulated fairly easily. A girl only has to make certain gestures, press against a man in a certain way, and the response is completely automatic. Are you quite sure you didn't do that?' She shook her head, frowning. 'For example, you used to creep up behind him and push your hands into his trouser pockets, didn't you?'

A ghost of a smile appeared on her face. 'I always did that – ever since I was a baby.'

'And sometimes you'd pretend you were going to whisper in his ear, then tickle his ear with your tongue.'

'That was just a game.'

'But you kept on doing it when you were thirteen or

198

fourteen.'

'I know.' She struggled for words. 'But I didn't feel any different – I still felt the same as when I was a little girl . . .'

'But it wasn't the same for him, because you were an attractive teenager.'

She nodded, averting her face.

'Now let's come back to the day it happened. What was your uncle doing at home at that time of day?'

'He always came home early on Fridays.'

'And why had you taken your dress off?'

'Because . . . I was washing my stockings and I didn't want to get it wet.'

'What kind of stockings were they? The thick lumpy kind?'

'No.'

'Were they attractive stockings? Nylons?'

'I suppose so.'

'The kind grown-up women wear?'

'Yes.'

'He bought them for you?' Saltfleet could see this was an inspired guess.

'Yes.'

'And you liked them because you knew they made your legs look attractive?' She nodded. 'And you knew he liked to see you looking pretty. Why did you have to take off your dress to wash your stockings?'

'I didn't want to get it wet.'

'Surely you wouldn't get it very wet washing a pair of stockings?'

'I can't remember . . . Perhaps I was washing other things as well . . .'

'And you didn't lock the bathroom door?'

'No.'

'But you knew he'd be home early. And you were in the

199

bathroom without your dress on, washing a pair of stockings he'd given you. What would you say if you heard that story about some other girl? Would you really believe she didn't *want* him to come into the bathroom?'

She said with a kind of desperation: 'You make it sound as if I thought it out deliberately.'

Moro shook his head. 'No, I'm not saying that. I'm only asking you to see it from his point of view. You were growing into a pretty girl with a good figure. But you still pushed your hands into his trouser pockets, and played tickling games, and let him kiss you. And one day he comes home from work, when he knows you'll be alone in the house, and finds you in your underwear with the bathroom door unlocked. Isn't it natural for him to feel that it's an invitation to go further than before?'

'Yes.' Her voice was almost inaudible.

'Then wouldn't it be sensible to stop blaming him?'

'I'm not blaming him.' Moro waited, looking at her. She tried to avoid his eyes, then said: 'Yes, I suppose I *do* blame him. I blame him for spoiling everything.'

Moro said quietly: 'Good. Now you're not making excuses any more.'

She coloured, and looked him direct in the eyes.

'It might have been different if it hadn't been in that house. With Joey and Aunt Vi. That made it all seem so sordid.'

'Would it have been different if you could have had him all to yourself?'

She said softly: 'Perhaps. But it was Joey I really wanted.'

Moro sighed and stood up. 'It's too late to do anything about it now. But at least you could try to forgive him. That would make you feel better.'

She said: 'I *do* feel better.'

Moro laughed, ruffling her hair. 'Good. Now do you

200

feel like talking to my friend Mr Saltfleet?'

She turned round and looked at him with curiosity. 'What about?'

Saltfleet came and sat in the chair vacated by Moro.

'Do you mind if I call you Rosa?' She smiled and nodded. 'I'd better tell you first of all that I'm a policeman.' It was obvious that this did not bother her; she was still steeped in a sense of wellbeing and trust. 'I want to talk to you about a friend of yours who's in trouble.'

Her eyes moved instinctively to Moro. Saltfleet said: 'No, not Dr Moro. It's Frankie.'

She asked quickly: 'What's happened to him?'

Saltfleet said: 'Do you remember going to the George in Portobello Road on Saturday? And Frankie followed you . . .'

Her face clouded over; she glanced at Moro with anxiety. Moro said: 'There's nothing to be afraid of. Just tell him all you can remember.'

Saltfleet said: 'You met a Polish sailor there, didn't you?' She nodded. 'And you tried to find a hotel where you could spend the night with him? Then you went and had a meal together. And you tried to bring him back here. But Harriet's light was still on, so you decided not to risk it. What happened then?'

She said: 'We went somewhere else.'

'To the gardens across the road?'

'Yes.'

'And what happened then?' She hesitated, and Moro said: 'Don't be afraid.'

'He . . . he started to make love to me.'

'How? Did he undress you?' She shook her head. 'Then what did he do?'

'He told me to lie down on the grass, and he lay down on me.'

201

'Didn't you want him to?' She shook her head. 'Why not?'

'I . . . I wasn't ready.'

'Why not? What did you want him to do?'

She looked across at Moro. 'I wanted him to shake me.'

'Shake you?' Saltfleet was startled.

She avoided his eyes. 'He had big strong hands. I kept looking at them in the restaurant. I thought how nice it would be if he took me by the shoulders and . . . and shook me and shook me . . .'

'And then made love to you?'

'Yes.'

'And did he?'

'No . . . I don't think so. I couldn't make him understand. He thought I meant shake hands.' She smiled faintly. 'Then he got angry and hit me in the face.'

'You were still lying on the grass?'

'No, I was sitting up. Kneeling.'

'What happened then?'

She shook her head. 'I don't know. I can't remember any more.'

'Try to remember. Was he still fully dressed?'

'Yes. But he'd undone his trousers . . .'

'Then he grabbed you by the hair?'

She began to cry. 'Yes.'

'You can remember him grabbing your hair. Can you remember him hitting you?'

She shook her head.

'He had a knife . . .' Moro handed her a paper handkerchief, and she blew her nose. 'He was dragging my face against his trousers. Then I think I fainted.'

Saltfleet and Moro looked at one another. Saltfleet said: 'Where was Frankie all this time?'

'I don't know.'

He placed his hand on her shoulder to make her look at him. He said: 'Rosa. The sailor was murdered. Somebody killed him.'

'Oh no!' Her look of shock was too spontaneous to be faked.

'Somebody stabbed him with his own knife. Was it Frankie?'

She was sobbing again. 'I don't . . . No. Frankie wouldn't do that.'

'But he *might* – if he saw the sailor attacking you.'

She shook her head, unable to speak. Moro came and sat on the other side of the couch, taking her hands. He said gently: 'Please try and remember.'

She mastered her sobbing. 'I *can't* remember.'

He said: 'Would you like to remember?' She looked at him without comprehension. 'Would you like me to *make* you remember?'

Saltfleet said: 'Hypnosis?'

Moro shook his head. 'That wouldn't do much good.' He took the handkerchief from the girl, and wiped the tears off her face. 'Rosa, do you remember when you first came here, I told you I could make you well?' She nodded. 'But I said it would have to be when *you* were ready. Do you know why I said that?' She stared back without speaking. 'Because I can't do it until you really want to get better. If I try it before then, you'll slip back, and it would only make things worse. Are you willing to give it a try now?'

She nodded, swallowing back tears. 'If it would help Frankie.'

'It will.'

Her lips set into a firm line. 'All right.'

'First of all, I want you to make me a promise. I want you to promise me that, whatever happens, you won't go back.' She understood instantly, and nodded. 'Will you

203

promise me that, from now on, you're going to fight?'

She drew a deep breath to clear her nose. 'Yes.'

'All right. Then I promise that I'll see you through.' She began to cry again, and he said: 'There, don't do that. Wipe your nose and sit up straight. That's better.' She blew her nose. 'Now listen, do you know why it wouldn't do any good to hypnotise you now?' She shook her head. He said urgently: '*Think*.'

'Because it . . . because it would . . .'

'Because it would only bring Dorothy back again, wouldn't it? And she's stronger than you.' She seemed to accept this as a kind of justified rebuke, and nodded. He said: '*Is* she stronger than you? Are you sure of that?' Moro squeezed her hands. 'When does Dorothy take over? It's when you're tired and depressed, isn't it? And she can do it when you're feeling ill. But when you're feeling happy and physically healthy, she can't do it. Because you're as strong as she is.' Her face made it clear that she found this hard to accept. He said: 'You think she's stronger than you? Then answer me this. Why doesn't she take over entirely, and refuse to let you come back? Don't you think she'd like to do that? Then why doesn't she? Because she *can't*. It's your body. You were here first.' She looked at him with sudden hope. 'She can only take over when you turn and run away. She can bully you because you keep on trying to retreat back into your childhood. If you stop doing that, she won't be able to get in. You can refuse to let her in.'

Saltfleet could see that she was worried, but determined to go through with it. Moro said: 'Tell me something, Rosa. How does it feel when Dorothy throws you out of your own body?'

She touched the back of her neck, just above the nape. 'I get a funny sensation here, as if I'm going to faint. Then I feel as if she's pulling me backwards.'

'Pulling you?'

'Not really pulling . . . it's too quick.'

'And what would happen if you resisted – if you pulled in the opposite direction?'

She shook her head. 'I don't know.'

Moro stood up and went behind her. He reached down and placed both hands on her shoulders, gently massaging the muscles. After a moment, she gave a sigh and relaxed. He said: 'Do you remember the phrase I use when I want you to relax deeply? What do I say?'

'It's getting dark outside.'

'And when I want you to go to sleep, I talk about . . .'

'Rain.'

'Yes, rain. Now I'll tell you what we're going to do. We're going to play a trick on Dorothy.'

She tried to look up at him. 'It's no good.'

'Why is it no good?'

She said: 'She can hear you. She's listening now.'

Moro's eyes gleamed with excitement.

'How do you know that?' She shook her head. 'Can you feel her there, inside you?'

'Yes.'

'But you couldn't before, could you?'

'No.' She reached up and pressed the back of her neck.

'Is she trying to come back?'

'Yes.'

'Listen to me, Rosa. I don't want her to come back. And you can stop her. She's tired now and you're strong She wants to come back now because she's afraid you'll get stronger still. I want you to show her that you're stronger than she is. Let's give her the opportunity to come back, shall we?' He sat down again, and took both her hands in his. She was pale and nervous. He said softly: 'It's getting dark outside.' It had no visible effect; her eyes flickered to Saltfleet and back to Moro. He repeated: 'It's getting dark outside.' This time she began to breathe deeply, and her muscles relaxed. Moro said softly: 'Rosa.'

She looked at him. He said: '*Don't let her back.*'

As he said it, an expression of shock crossed her face, as if someone had struck her. There was panic in her eyes, and her head jerked back; she seemed to be paralysed with terror. She tried to turn her head, as if to look behind her, but seemed to be unable to turn it more than a few degrees. On impulse, Saltfleet went and stood behind her, placing his hands on her neck. It was an odd sensation, as if someone was trying to pull her backwards while she tried to resist and bend forward. Saltfleet tried to help by pushing her. Moro was repeating: 'Don't let her in. Don't let her in.'

Suddenly, she twisted sideways, and he was no longer able to hold her; her convulsions carried her off the couch and on to the floor. Now she was thrashing like an epileptic; when Moro knelt beside her, she twisted so violently that he almost went backwards. Saltfleet was afraid she would hurt herself, and tried to place his hands under her head; her knee caught his face, and for a moment he saw stars. Both men tried to grab her hands, and Moro succeeded in lying across her legs. It took the effort of both men to subdue her; her strength seemed remarkable. Suddenly, the body relaxed. All three were breathing heavily. Moro said: 'Help me put her on the couch.'

The girl resisted. 'I can do it myself.' With Saltfleet's help, she stood up, and sat down on the couch.

Moro knelt in front of her, looking into her face. 'Do you know me?' She nodded. 'Who am I?'

'Doctor Moro.'

'And who are you?'

'Rosa Judd.'

For Saltfleet, the question was unnecessary; the girl was obviously Rosa.

Moro said: 'And where is Rosie?'

The girl looked puzzled. She said: 'I'm Rosie.'

'And Dorothy?'

In the silence that followed, the girl seemed to be unaware of them, as if she was trying to examine her own feelings. Suddenly she smiled.

'I think I'm Dorothy . . .'

She stood up and went over to the mirror in the corner; she said with sudden alarm: 'Dr Moro, something strange has happened. I don't look like me.'

Moro said: 'Dorothy!'

She looked round at them. Saltfleet experienced a shock. It was true that her face had changed. The lips seemed firmer, and the eyes had the direct, challenging stare that he associated with Dorothy. Moro saw it too, and his face expressed his disappointment. Then, as they watched, the girl looked bewildered. Suddenly, it was Rosa who was looking at them.

Moro went over to her and took her hand. He said: 'You are you. And you are Rosa *and* Dorothy.'

She stared at him. 'It's a strange feeling . . . being two people.'

Saltfleet said: 'Can you see into Dorothy's mind now?'

She said immediately: 'Yes.'

'Can you tell me what happened last night?'

He saw her wince. Moro said quickly: 'You don't have to say anything unless you want to.'

Saltfleet said: 'Was it Frankie who killed the sailor?'

She shook her head. 'No. It was Dorothy.'

Moro said: 'Aren't you Dorothy?'

The girl said quietly: 'Yes.'

Moro said: 'But you're Rosa too. And Rosa didn't kill him.'

Saltfleet was impatient of this interruption. He said: 'Why did Dorothy kill him?'

'She got very angry.'

'Why?'

'She didn't like the way he was behaving. She thought he was a pig. Then when he held the knife against my throat, she took over. He was trying to make me . . . do something I didn't want to do.'

Saltfleet said: 'What?'

She coloured. 'Something . . . disgusting.'

Saltfleet decided to let it go at that. He said: 'How did Dorothy get the knife?'

'He dropped it when she bit him.' A faint smile of malicious amusement crossed her face, and for a moment, they were both aware of Dorothy's presence.

'But why did she stab him? Why didn't she just run away?'

'She couldn't. He was holding my hair. That made her furious. She can't stand having her hair pulled.'

'So she stabbed him in the chest? Why did she go on stabbing him when he fell down?'

'She didn't know he was dead.'

'What did she do then?'

'She threw the knife in the flowerbed, and went out through the fence.'

'Then Frankie came?'

'No. He followed her home.'

'When did he go back for the knife?'

'Later, when she told him what she'd done.'

'Did she send him, or did he go of his own accord?'

'She sent him.'

'And then she made him wipe off the fingerprints, and put it in the glass case with the others?'

'*She* wiped off the fingerprints. Then she made Frankie put it in the case.'

Saltfleet looked at Moro; his smile was humourless.

'So that if anybody went to prison for the murder, it

would be Frankie.'

Moro said: 'What will happen?'

'If Dorothy appeared in front of a jury, she wouldn't get much sympathy. She killed in a fury, then tried to cover up the crime by laying a false trail. She'd end in jail.'

Moro said: 'And so would Rosa.'

Rosa said: 'Are you going to arrest me?' There was more than a touch of Dorothy in her direct stare.

'No.'

'Why not?' Again, it could have been Dorothy speaking.

Saltfleet said: 'It's no good arresting you for a murder Dorothy committed, is it? It's Dorothy we want. And if you don't let her take over, we can't arrest her, can we?'

She smiled, and again it was Rosa looking at him.

Saltfleet went to the drawer and took out the knife wrapped in the handkerchief.

Moro said: 'What are you going to do?'

Saltfleet said: 'To be honest, I don't know. I've got to think about it. If I don't hand over this knife, I'm withholding a vital piece of evidence. On the other hand, I don't think I'd be justified in telling Inspector Fitch I've found the murderer. Because I haven't.' He slipped the knife into his pocket. 'Let me see what I can do.'

Rosa leaned forward and kissed him on the corner of the mouth, exactly as Geraldine would have kissed him if she wanted to say thank you. He looked into her face.

'I can't promise anything.'

But he knew it was untrue; he had already promised himself.

ELEVEN

Two nights later, the Indian summer came to an end with gales and heavy rain. When he woke up the following morning, the wind had dropped, but the rain drummed steadily on the bedroom windows. In the street below, the gutter was full of dead leaves. In the bathroom as he shaved, he could hear the noise of rain running down gutters. He used a safety razor instead of his usual electric shaver; during weekends and holidays, the warm water and scent of shaving foam underlined his sense of relaxation. He was wiping off the remaining foam with a sponge when he heard the telephone ring. A moment later, Miranda called upstairs: 'It's Inspector Fitch. He wants to know if he can come and see you after breakfast.'

'Yes, of course. We're not going out until eleven.' He had promised to take Miranda to the Chinese Exhibition at the Royal Academy.

Miranda was frying thick rashers of ham with mushrooms. Outside, the patio was covered with sodden leaves, and the garden chairs had blown over in the gale. The sky was a uniform slate grey. He said: 'I wondered what had happened to Fitch. We haven't seen him for a couple of days.'

'That means the case is going well. Otherwise he'd be round twice a day.' Miranda was inclined to become mildly satirical when she felt her husband was being exploited.

'I hope so. Poor old Fitch has reached the time of life when he could do with a break.'

She poured him fresh orange juice and coffee.

'Geraldine rang after you'd gone to bed last night. She wants to know if she can take next week off from school and come and stay here.'

He unfolded the *Telegraph*.

'What did you say?'

'I said I'd have to ask you.'

'I don't like her taking time off from school in the year she's taking her O-levels.'

'That's almost another year.'

'All right. If you think it's a good idea.'

She looked at him curiously.

'I thought you wanted to get her away from this boyfriend?'

He laid down the newspaper.

'That's not quite true. I wish it had never happened. I wish she'd waited a few more years. But we can't put the clock back.'

'No, I suppose not.' She broke an egg into the pan. His attitude puzzled her. 'You mean you don't mind about Charlie?'

He said with mild exasperation: 'Of course I mind. But we've got to be practical. We can't lock her in a chastity belt. If she wants to come and stay here a week, it means she knows we're worrying about her. And I suppose that's all that matters.'

'That sounds very liberal.'

'Not liberal. Just philosophical. Moro said something the other day that struck me – something like: every living thing has to grow and expand; that is the law of nature. Rosie's father tried to stop her growing, and look what happened.'

Miranda seemed to find the comparison odd. 'There's a big difference between Geraldine and Rosie!'

'I know. But Moro's right all the same. What do you suppose would have happened if Rosie's father hadn't tried to frighten the life out of her? She certainly wouldn't have turned into a nymphomaniac. She's not the type. I realised that when I talked to her. What she wants out of life is love and affection and security. She wants to be cared about. Just like Geraldine.'

She placed his breakfast in front of him.

'So what shall I tell her about next week?'

'Tell her to come, if she wants to. In fact, I'd like her to meet Rosie. It might be good for both of them.'

He had retired to the sitting-room, and was reading the back page of the *Telegraph*, when the telephone rang.

'Mr Saltfleet. This is Roberto Moro.'

'Ah, hello. Glad to hear from you. Is everything all right?'

'There is something I would like to speak to you about.'

'Go ahead.'

'I would prefer to see you. Would it be possible for you to come here?'

He looked at his watch. 'Later on, perhaps. I'm waiting for a visitor.'

'Could I come and see you there?'

'Yes, of course. Do you know where it is?' Saltfleet gave him the address. 'Nothing wrong, I hope?'

'Not seriously. But it is something we have to discuss.'

He heard Fitch's car draw up outside as he hung up. He opened the door before Fitch could reach the doorbell.

'Hello, George, everything all right?'

'Yes, fine.' In spite of the rain, Fitch looked cheerful and animated. 'You're well, I hope?'

Saltfleet took his damp hat and coat; for some reason, Fitch kept on his gloves. They went into the sitting-room.

Fitch was carrying an old attaché case. He said: 'First of all, a little appreciation.'

From the case he took a brown paper bag; it proved to contain a two-quart bottle of whisky.

'Good God, what's this for?'

'All your help.'

'But I can't take this!'

A bottle of Bell's was a traditional gift to a policeman who has performed some small personal service; but it was usually presented to the CID room and opened on 'diary day', the afternoon when detectives make up the diary of their movements for official scrutiny and expense claims; Saltfleet had his doubts about accepting a double-size bottle from a fellow officer for his personal consumption.

'I'll be very upset if you refuse.' Fitch spoke with a genial confidence that Saltfleet had never seen in him before. He decided to stifle his scruples.

'Well, that's very kind of you. Will you have one now?'

'Only if you do.'

'It's a bit early. But perhaps a very small one . . .'

They touched glasses. 'Cheers.' The smoky liquid tasted raw on his palate at half-past nine in the morning; he drained it in one gulp like medicine. Fitch sipped his own with obvious appreciation.

Saltfleet said: 'Anything interesting happening?'

'Aha!' Fitch placed the attaché case on the table. 'I've brought something to show you, although I'd be in trouble if anyone found out.' He took from the case a white bag of the kind used by Exhibits Officers. 'But I thought you ought to see this.' He tilted the bag. A knife slid on to the tabletop; it was the wooden-handled fish-gutting knife that had killed Choromansky. Saltfleet felt an involuntary contraction of his stomach at seeing it again.

Fitch picked it up carefully with his gloved hands, holding it by the end of the blade and the end of the handle.

'This is what we were looking for.'

'Choromansky's knife?'

'That's right.'

'Where did you find it?'

'The gardener found it yesterday when he was sweeping up the leaves.'

'In the garden?' Saltfleet went to the window. He wanted to keep his face turned away from Fitch; he disliked acting.

'How did the police miss it?'

'It was down among the bushes at the Ladbroke Grove end. I reckon what happened was that Spraggs threw it in the flowerbed, realised it might have prints on it, and went back for it. Then he wiped it clean of fingerprints, and tossed it over the railings as he made his way back.'

'You're sure it was Spraggs?'

'Pretty sure. He takes size eleven shoes, like the footprint in the flowerbed.'

'Did you find the right pair?'

Fitch scowled. 'No. I think he's destroyed them. The type we're looking for were crepe-soled, and Spraggs didn't have a single pair.'

'You got your search warrant, then?'

'Oh yes, no problem. By the way, you wanted this back.' From his inside pocket he took an envelope; it contained the photograph Saltfleet had taken from Moro's album.

'Thanks.'

'Yes, we got the warrant, and the landlord let us in with his passkey. We found the room he used for his parties. You've never seen anything like it. He had this projector with revolving coloured lenses. When you switch it on, it projects colours on to this faceted crystal hanging from the ceiling, which also turns round. You've never seen anything like it. Thick velvet curtains that don't let in a ray of light. And when we turned this projector on, it covered the walls with these nasty, crawling colours. It made *me* feel funny at ten in the morning, so I can imagine what it did to kids who were full of pills.'

'Did you find any pills?'

'Oh yes, plenty. Marihuana, glue, amphetamines, heart tablets, LSD – you name it. Also a bit of cocaine. So we've got him for possession of dangerous drugs. We found whips and chains and dildoes, and that leather harness arrangement that's in that photograph. And all kinds of photographs – incredible photographs. You wouldn't believe them. Would you believe it's possible for a man to get his whole arm, up to the elbow, up somebody's anus?'

'My God!'

'So we've pulled him in. He's a really nasty piece of work – I'd love to see him put away for twenty years.'

'Any evidence about the murder?'

Fitch pulled a wry face. 'No.'

'Then how are you sure it *is* him?'

'Everything points to it. The photographs show he's got a thing about knives – one of them shows him writing his initials on somebody's belly with a kind of stiletto. He can't provide us with an alibi for Saturday night – claims he spent the evening in his room reading. That's about as likely as Jack the Ripper going to Sunday school.'

'You need a witness who saw him with Choromansky.'

'Yes, we're working on that.'

'How about the boy he assaulted? Has he agreed to testify?'

'Yes. We've got statements from the boy and his

mother.'

Saltfleet said thoughtfully: 'I don't want to discourage you. But I wouldn't be too hopeful about a conviction.'

'Why not?'

'To begin with, his obvious defence will be that the boy went there voluntarily, knowing what he was letting himself in for. He'll probably claim the boy accepted money. As to the cocaine, they'll probably accuse you of planting it there.'

'I know.' Fitch shrugged gloomily. 'I'm just hoping we can get hold of some of the other boys in the photographs and get them to testify. If we can just get a bit more evidence . . .'

Saltfleet changed the subject. 'What about the spy at Cheltenham?'

'Aha!' Fitch picked up the knife from the table. 'I've got something interesting to show you.' He took a toothpick from his pocket, and pressed its point against a brass nail-head on the knife handle; with his thumb, he pushed on the base of the handle. It slid back like the lid of a pencil case. Inside was a small compartment, an inch long by an eighth-of-an-inch deep.

'Was there anything in there?'

Fitch looked at him with satisfaction. 'Microfilm.'

Saltfleet laughed with pleasure. 'That's marvellous. So at least you've proved Choromansky *was* a spy.'

'*And* Price – that's the chap in GCHQ. He was stupid enough to leave a bit of a thumbprint on the microfilm container – not much, but enough for identification. The Special Branch picked him up yesterday afternoon. He'll be charged today or tomorrow.'

Saltfleet slapped him on the shoulder. 'You *have* done well. I reckon this will mean promotion.'

Fitch tried to hide his pleasure, but was not enough of an actor.

216

'MacPhail dropped a hint in the same direction . . .'

'Chief Inspector Fitch! We ought to drink to that . . .'

There was a ring at the doorbell; Saltfleet peered through the curtain and recognised Moro. He was glad of the interruption; more whisky would have made him sleepy.

'Excuse me.'

Moro looked surprisingly smart and dapper in a tweed overcoat and a deerstalker hat; he was carrying a very large umbrella. As he took Moro's coat, Saltfleet suddenly remembered the knife, and hoped Moro was a good enough actor not to betray that he had seen it before. But a glance at the tabletop revealed that Fitch had already put it away.

Saltfleet said: 'Inspector Fitch, this is Dr Moro.' The name obviously meant nothing to Fitch.

Fitch said: 'I won't disturb you any more. My regards to your wife.'

Saltfleet helped him on with his overcoat.

'Let me know what happens.'

'I will. Oh, by the way . . .' He paused at the door. 'About this chap South American Joe . . .'

'Yes?'

Fitch winked. 'I had a few words in the right quarters – told them how helpful he'd been. The charge is going to be dropped.'

'That's good of you, George. I'm very grateful.'

'That's all right. Glad to help any time.' Observing his jaunty step as he crossed the pavement, and the vigorous, economical swing with which he closed the car door, Saltfleet thought: How a little success can improve a man . . . The reflection gave him real satisfaction; he had an innate objection to defeat.

Moro said: 'He is working on the case?'

'Yes, he's in charge of it.' He thought Moro looked

217

tense and nervous. 'Why?'

'Rosa wants to talk to him.'

'What!' Saltfleet stared at him in amazement.

Moro sighed with embarrassment. 'Please try to understand. She is faced with a difficult problem. She has agreed that from now on she is going to fight back. She is going to try to prevent Dorothy from ever taking over again. But for that she needs optimism – she needs to believe in the future. With that man's death on her conscience, how can she do that?'

'But she hasn't got that man's death on her conscience.'

'Nevertheless, she feels responsible. She picked him up. She took him to the place where he died. It was her hand that killed him. Now she feel she carries a guilty secret.'

'So what does she want to do about it?'

'Naturally, she wants to bring it into the open.'

'You mean she wants to stand trial?'

'If that is necessary.'

'And do you agree with her?'

'That is why I have come to you. I need your opinion.'

'My opinion is that it would involve some unpleasant complications. To begin with, the fact that I've connived at a felony by not arresting her two days ago.'

'Ah no. There is no question of involving you. She would simply say that she had decided to confess what she knows – without mentioning that you already know about it.'

Saltfleet considered this carefully. He said: 'There's another problem – the knife. I got rid of it by throwing it into the garden. Now it's been found. We'd have to persuade Frankie to say he threw it there.'

Moro looked troubled. 'She does not want to involve Frankie.'

'She'd *have* to involve Frankie. Unless she insists that

218

she went back and took the knife from the flowerbed and wiped off the fingerprints. And if she admits to all that, she's going to raise some strong doubts in the mind of the jury. They'll find it hard to accept a plea of diminished responsibility from someone who thinks things out as carefully as that.'

'Then what do you suggest?'

Saltfleet thought about it, then said: 'I suggest you point out to her that it's going to be impossible not to involve Frankie, and that if she involves him, he'll be charged as an accessory after the fact. I know she wouldn't want that.'

Moro shook his head with exasperation. 'I know. But what worries her even more is that somebody else might be charged with the murder one day.'

Saltfleet looked up quickly. 'Are you sure that's what's worrying her?'

'Of course. We have talked about it again and again.'

Saltfleet laughed. 'In that case, you can tell her she has nothing to worry about. Inspector Fitch is quite convinced that the killer is your friend Spraggs. He's hoping to charge Spraggs with sexual assault on a teenager. But he's not going to get a shred of evidence about the murder. And I'm pretty certain the rape charge isn't going to stick either. My guess is that Spraggs will end on probation.'

Moro said quickly: 'Are you sure of that?'

'Absolutely sure. As far as Fitch is concerned, the murder is now solved, but he can't prove it. He's not going to look any further for the killer. The case is closed.'

Moro's smile showed relief. 'Would you come back and explain that to Rosa?'

'Of course I will. Let's go now. I've promised to take my wife out this morning.' He fetched Moro's overcoat and hat. 'Before we go, there's something I'd like to ask you – a question that's been bothering me for days.'

'Yes?'

'What are the hopes of a long-term cure? You say Rosa's going to fight back. But how long does she have to go on fighting?'

'That is difficult to say. The most important thing is to persuade Rosa to fight back, so that Dorothy no longer has it all her own way. As Rosa gets stronger and more confident, Dorothy will begin to feel "squeezed", as they say. When that happens, I shall try to integrate the two personalities under hypnosis.'

Saltfleet said: 'That's another problem that bothers me. You seem to be quite sure that Dorothy is a part of Rosa's total personality. But she doesn't strike me as a part of anything. She strikes me as a totally different person. You might as well try and integrate you and me under hypnosis.'

Moro made an expressive gesture.

'I know a respectable parapsychologist who holds the same opinion. He believes that many cases of multiple personality are cases of what used to be called "possession" – possession of the personality by an alien spirit. I have to confess that there have been times when I have agreed with him.'

'Then how can you talk about integrating Dorothy and Rosa?'

Moro said: 'Allow me to ask you a question in return. You feel that Spraggs deserves to go to prison. How will you feel if he escapes with probation?'

Saltfleet said promptly: 'I shan't lose any sleep about it.'

'Why? You believe he is guilty.'

'Because you can't always bring a case to an ideal conclusion. You have to accept second best. That's what police work's all about.'

Moro said gravely: 'And that, my dear sir, is what psychiatric work is all about. I cannot guarantee that I can cure Rosa. But I know I have to make the effort. Does that answer your question?'

Saltfleet sighed. 'No. But I suppose it will have to do.' He handed him his umbrella. 'I'll come back with you and talk to Rosa.'

APPENDIX
ON MULTIPLE PERSONALITY

The curious psychological anomaly known as 'multiple personality' has been recorded by doctors since the early nineteenth century. One morning in 1811, Mary Reynolds of Pennsylvania woke up to find that she had lost every vestige of memory, including her own language. She had to be taught again, like a child. Five weeks later she woke up one day in her previous personality, with no memory whatever of the past weeks. And for the remainder of her life, her relatives were never quite sure which of the two Marys was going to wake up in the morning.

The two Marys were totally different people: 'Mary One' was a dull girl with depressive tendencies; 'Mary Two' was merry and mischievous. And eventually, in middle life, the two Marys more or less blended together. In discussing the case in my book *Mysteries* I have suggested that it was almost as if the human personality is made up out of a construction kit: 'Mary One' had used up the serious 'bits', and 'Mary Two' had to make do with merriness, flightiness and a complete lack of caution. Mary One hated nature, Mary Two loved it, and so on . . .

As more and more cases were recorded, it became clear that most cases of multiple personality began with a severe shock. In 1877 a French boy named Louis Vivé was stunned with fear when attacked by a viper; he had a 'hysterico-epileptic' attack that lasted fifteen hours, and when he recovered, was another person. Louis One was a quiet, well-behaved boy who had paralysis of one side of the body; Louis Two was a loquacious delinquent who preached atheism and the violent overthrow of the state, and who was paralysed down the other side of his body – the right. Doctors discovered that they could transfer the paralysis from one side of the body to the other by stroking him with steel; the moment it was transferred, Louis became his 'other self'.

The case of 'Christine Beauchamp', recorded by Dr Morton Prince, has become a classic. Christine, whose real name was Clara Fowler, had an unfortunate childhood; her mother died in great pain and her father was an alcoholic. She transferred all her admiration to a certain friend of her father's. When this man made some kind of attempt at sexual assault, Christine 'split', and was suddenly taken over by a vivacious, mischievous child who called herself Sally. Christine was quiet, submissive and easily fatigued; Sally was noisy, merry and in robust health. Her idea of a joke was to walk miles into the countryside around Boston, then allow Christine back into her own body, so she had to walk home. Sally was stronger than Christine, and could 'take over' whenever she liked. Under Prince's hypnosis, a third personality emerged, a far more self-possessed and balanced young woman who seemed to be quite different from the other two. When Christine was cheerful and optimistic, Sally felt 'squeezed'. Prince was convinced that all these personalities were a part of the girl Christine *should* have become if her growth had not been stunted by misery and shock, and finally effected a partial cure by 'integrating' the personalities under hypnosis. Christine married one of Prince's assistants, and became a more or less normal person – except for occasional relapses.

It is interesting to note that both Louis Two and Christine Two (Sally) suffered from speech defects. This suggests one solution to the problem of multiple personality (which I have explored in my book *Frankenstein's Castle*). Modern brain research has revealed that the two halves of the brain – left and right – seem to have completely different functions; the left deals with logic and language, and the right with intuitions and pattern-recognition. The left brain controls the right side of the body and vice-versa. It was discovered that epileptic attacks could be cured by severing the knot of nerves that joins the two halves of the brain, the corpus callosum. And a 'split brain' patient becomes, in some senses, *two separate people*. One split brain patient tried to hit his wife with his left hand (connected to the right brain) while the right tried to defend her. A patient who is shown a 'dirty' picture with his left eye only (connected to the right brain) blushes; asked why he is blushing he replies, 'I don't know'. This suggests that the person we call 'I' lives in the left half of the brain; that 'other' person is a stranger. Christine One and Louis One and probably Mary One were all the 'left brain' personalities; the delinquent and/or mischievous personalities seem to belong to the right.

But in that case, where did Christine's *third* personality – the self-possessed young woman – belong? And the question becomes even more baffling when we consider the equally celebrated case of 'Doris Fischer', recorded by Walter Franklin Prince. Doris 'split' when her father snatched her out of her mother's arms in a drunken frenzy and hurled her to the floor; Doris lost consciousness of herself, and only recovered it the following morning as she came downstairs, when she experienced a clicking sensation in the back of her neck.

Soon she began losing her memory for hours at a time, and during this period a lively and mischievous girl who called herself Margaret took over. Doris was always getting into trouble for things that Margaret had done. And Margaret could literally 'pull' Doris out of her own body at will. When Doris was seventeen, her mother died under highly unpleasant circumstances, and yet another personality took over – a tired, dull girl whom Prince called 'Sick Doris'. A year later Doris slipped and fell on the back of her head, and yet another personality appeared, a kind of child who had a photographic memory of all Doris's early years. Prince also discovered that if he woke Doris up in the night, he encountered an altogether more balanced and mature personality, which he called 'Sleeping Doris'. So Doris Fischer was a compendium of five personalities.

The odd thing was that they appeared to form some kind of hierarchy. 'Sleeping Doris' was at the top, and knew all about the lower four. Margaret came next, and knew about the three below her. Doris knew about the two below her, and so on. This, again, seems common in cases of multiple personality – as if the personalities were arranged in the form of a ladder. This led me, in *Mysteries*, to suggest a 'ladder of selves' theory of the structure of personality.

In practice, this meant that Margaret could 'drag' Doris out of her own body when she felt inclined, and that 'Sleeping Doris' could drag Margaret out when she wanted to. One day, Margaret dragged Doris out suddenly as she was talking to Prince, and Doris's face was suddenly replaced by that of the mischievous Margaret. Sleeping Doris was so angry that she grabbed Margaret and dragged *her* out. Later that day, Margaret returned, and said to Prince: 'You know, Doctor, there's somebody else in this body. When I'd dragged Doris out this morning, somebody came and dragged *me* out!'

By making Doris more cheerful and optimistic, Prince was able to slowly eliminate the lowest of the personalities. They slowly disintegrated; 'Sick Doris' even went for a farewell walk with Prince and said a touching goodbye before she 'died'. Margaret began to get younger and younger until she became a small child, then a baby; finally she went blind. And although she had the strongest possible objection to 'dying', she eventually faded out. The highest of the five, 'Sleeping Doris', never faded out. But then, she was never any trouble. Moreover, she claimed that she was not a part of Doris, but a spirit who had been sent by Doris's dead mother to help her in her struggle against Margaret. Although we may reject this notion as absurd, it is only fair to add that Doris's subsequent history, as recorded by Prince, tends to support 'Sleeping Doris's' claims.

One of the most famous cases of the twentieth century was recorded in the book *The Three Faces of Eve* by C. H. Thigpen and H. M. Cleckley (1957). The real name of 'Eve' was Christine Sizemore. At the age of six she became intensely jealous of her newly-born twin sisters; one day, to her amazement, she 'came to' and found herself being violently beaten for attacking them as they lay in their cot; it was the first appearance of 'Eve Black'. In her teens she married a racing driver, who could only achieve an orgasm by pounding her with his fists. Later still, she made an only slightly less disastrous second marriage, and 'Eve Black' began making more frequent appearances. While 'Eve White' was a priggish, born-again Christian, Eve Black was a mischievous and fun-loving stranger, who smoked, drank and liked virile males. Thigpen and Cleckley, her doctors, helped her a great deal. But they also incurred a certain resentment by writing a best-selling book about her case which became a film. A third personality, 'Jane', now emerged – more mature than either of the two Eves – and it was Jane who met and married a kindly man called Don Sizemore. But Christine still felt insecure – they lived in a mobile home – and the result was the emergence of a whole host of new personalities; (in her book *Eve*, Christine Sizemore describes about thirty).

One of the most curious things about the Sizemore case is that the two Eves had quite different physical characteristics. Eve Black was allergic to nylon, which brought her out in a rash; when Eve White took over, the blotches promptly vanished. When one personality was being put to sleep with anaesthetic, another took over which was totally unaffected by it.

One of the most sensational of all books on multiple personality was *Sybil* by Flora Rheta Schreiber. Sybil was also badly treated as a child – her mother was an intensely neurotic woman who used to strip her, hang her from the ceiling and insert lighted matches in her vagina. Sybil split into fourteen personalities, all quite distinct; they included a writer, a painter, a musician, a builder and a carpenter. And one of the oddest things about these personalities is that some got on well together while others loathed one another. They behaved exactly like fourteen real people.

. In an appendix to her book, Dr Schreiber describes two other cases and the medical tests carried out on them. In one case, the personalities showed four quite distinct sets of responses to word association tests; in another, an EEG machine (for measuring 'brain waves') revealed that the different personalities had quite different brain patterns. Yet brain patterns are as distinctive and unique as fingerprints.

The oddest of recent cases is that of Billy Milligan, arrested in 1977 in Columbus, Ohio, for rape. When a social worker came to interview him, he explained that he was not Billy but David, and that Billy was asleep 'in here' – pointing to his chest. David was eight years old. And little by little, it became clear that Billy was a compound of twenty-three different personalities. Billy – like all such cases – had had a traumatic childhood, and claimed he had been raped and beaten by his stepfather. The first of his 'other personalities' took over when he tried to throw himself from the roof at school. These other selves included a suave Englishman who spoke with an impeccable English accent, read and wrote Arabic and wore glasses; a powerful Yugoslav who spoke Serbo-Croat; a con-man; an electronics expert; a three-year-old child and her thirteen-year-old brother; and an anti-social lesbian. Daniel Keyes's book about the case, *The Minds of Billy Milligan*, is perhaps the most astonishing record of multiple personality ever written. Eventually, it was discovered that it was the lesbian who had committed the rapes, and another of the personalities who had turned Billy in to the police.

Here again, there was a 'superior' personality, who was referred to as 'the Teacher'. According to the Yugoslav, Billy was a child prodigy when he was little – all the personalities in one – but because of his difficult childhood, never had a chance to develop his potentialities. It was the teacher who taught him to be a weapons expert, taught another personality to be an electronics expert, and so on. But how the teacher 'taught' the Yugoslav Serbo-Croat is not explained.

In *Mysteries*, I suggested a theory of multiple personality that seems to be supported by the Milligan case (which occurred while I was writing the book). My theory was that we are *all* fundamentally 'multiple personalities', beginning with the baby and the child, and slowly developing into more complex selves. If, for some

228

reason, we abruptly cease to develop – through some trauma that undermines self-confidence – all those potential personalities are stunted and repressed. And some accident or violent shock may give one of them the opportunity to 'take over'. This suggests, of course, that in some mysterious sense, our 'future' personalities are already there, in embryo, so to speak, and that they *also* develop as we mature. We 'move' from personality to personality, as we might climb a ladder. The Beethovens and Leonardos got further up the ladder than most of us; yet even they failed to reach the top, as we can see if we study their lives.

Such a theory of personality is hard to grasp, because it is natural for us to regard the 'me' who now looks out of my eyes as the one and only inhabitant of the brain. But then, it would have been just as difficult for the seven-year-old 'me' to imagine the 'me' who is now writing this book. In other words, it is arguable that the phenomenon of multiple personality is so baffling simply because most of us are blinkered by a mistaken notion about the permanence of the present 'me' – in exactly the same way that we tend to think of the present moment as far more permanent and unchangeable than it actually is. If human consciousness was powerful enough to grasp the reality of our lives, we would recognise that personality is as real and permanent as a column of smoke rising from a bonfire . . . We all experience different 'selves' according to our circumstances and whom we happen to be talking to; assertive people make us feel ineffectual; gentle people make us feel strong; admiring people make us feel admirable; contemptuous people make us feel contemptible, and so on.

Yet while there is undoubtedly a great deal of truth in this notion, it simply fails to explain how two personalities can be so utterly unlike. And, above all, how one can be *unknown* to the other. I may, for example, behave quite uncharacteristically when drunk; but unless I am very drunk, I can still recall that other 'me'. In 1917, the psychologist Cyril Burt investigated a case in which various people received obscene letters signed with the name of a well-behaved and inoffensive little girl named May Naylor. Under hypnosis, May revealed that she *had* written the letters; she was virtually a Jekyll and Hyde, taken over periodically by a dirty-minded and vengeful little girl. As is usual in such cases, May's childhood had been traumatic; her mother had been constantly unfaithful to her father, and May had sometimes witnessed her having sexual intercourse; the father had divorced his wife and married again. May had apparently weathered all these storms; but the Mr Hyde alter-ego had developed.

All this we can understand, with the aid of our knowledge of the left and right brain and the Freudian 'unconscious'. What is so hard to understand is why May remained totally ignorant of having written the letters. Yet Burt eventually succeeded in integrating the two girls, so that the vindictive letter-writer simply vanished.

Max Freedom Long, a modern anthropologist who studied the secret religion of the Huna Indians of Hawaii, gradually came to accept the Huna belief that man has three souls or 'selves': a 'low self', a 'middle self' and a 'high self'. The 'you', the normal ego, is the middle self. The low self corresponds roughly to the Freudian unconscious. The high self is a kind of 'superconscious' mind, as much *above* ordinary consciousness as the 'unconscious' is below it. In his classic work *The Secret Science Behind Miracles* (an offputting title for one of the most remarkable books of our time) Long analyses various cases of multiple personality – Mary Reynolds and Christine Beauchamp among them – in terms of

Huna beliefs, and reaches the highly unorthodox conclusion that such cases actually involve a kind of 'possession' by an invading personality.

Such a notion will strike most of us as totally unacceptable. Yet it must be admitted that there *is* a certain amount of evidence for it, at least in certain cases. In 1877, a girl named Lurancy Vennum, of Watseka, Illinois, fell into a very deep sleep which turned into a trance; various personalities began to speak through her, and one of them, a disagreeable old woman, began to 'take over' so often that her family thought of having her committed to an asylum. Lurancy had, in effect, become a 'medium'. Spirit mediums usually have a 'control', a 'spirit' whose business is to act as master of ceremonies or chairman, and control the 'spirits' who wish to use the medium to speak. Lurancy soon came under control of a being who called herself Mary Roff, and who said she had died (at the age of eighteen) twelve years earlier. Lurancy now virtually *became* Mary Roff. Taken to Mary Roff's home (in the same town) she left no one in any doubt that she was really Mary, recognising people she had known during her lifetime and showing a detailed knowledge of Mary's life. She explained that she could only stay for four months. During that time, she lived with the Roffs as their daughter, and they had no doubt whatever that this *was* their daughter in a different body. On the exact date she had foretold, Mary took leave of her family, and Lurancy returned to her own body – now perfectly normal and healthy.

Another well-authenticated case, described by Dr Ian Stevenson in *Twenty Cases Suggestive of Reincarnation*, is that of a three-year-old child, Jasbir Lal Jat, who 'died' of smallpox. Hours later, he revived, but had become a different person; he claimed to be the son of a Brahmin from a nearby village, who had died from a head injury.

Taken to the village, he recognised relatives, was able to guide his companions unerringly to various houses, and showed a detailed knowledge of the affairs of the Brahmin's family. They had no doubt that he was their dead son, and allowed him to spend his holidays with them.

The 'spiritualist' view, of course, is that the personality survives bodily death, and that it can, under certain circumstances, communicate with living people through the agency of a 'medium', whose body provides a temporary mouthpiece for the 'spirit'. In 1977, such a case made legal history when a man in Chicago was found guilty of murder on the evidence of a 'spirit'. A Filipino nurse named Teresita Basa was stabbed to death in her apartment, and the intruder stole jewellery. Two weeks later, a colleague of the dead nurse, another Filipino named Remy Chua, went into a trance, and a strange voice declared that it was the dead Teresita Basa, and that she had been murdered by a black named Alan Showery, who had come to her apartment to repair her television. She described the murder, said that Showery had given certain pieces of jewellery to a girlfriend, and listed various friends who could identify the jewellery. After this had happened several times, Remy Chua's husband went to the police; the jewellery was found in the home of Showery's common-law wife, and Showery admitted to killing the nurse when he went to repair her television. The defence tried to have the case dismissed on the grounds that the testimony of a 'spirit' could hardly be accepted as reliable; but Showery was found guilty nevertheless.

There is, of course, no fundamental contradiction between Long's 'possession' view of multiple personality and the notion of psychologists like Morton Prince and Cyril Burt that it is simply a matter of a 'damaged' personality which fragments into two or more parts. The Doris Fischer case seems to provide evidence that supports both views; the 'personality fragment' theory seems to fit the childish personalities who finally 'withered away', while the 'spirit' theory seems to apply to the balanced and mature 'Sleeping Doris', who was more 'grown up' than Doris herself had ever had a chance to become. The Jekyll and Hyde personalities of May Naylor or Louis Vivé may be simply a more extreme version of the left-right brain split that is common to all of us, while cases like Lurancy Vennum and Jasbir Lal Jat may be genuine mediumship or 'spirit possession'. It would certainly be a mistake to rule out totally either possibility. It is also interesting to note that in many cases, such as Pierre Janet's patient Leonie (discussed in my *Mysteries*) or the 'Miss First' case (discussed by Freedom Long), a secondary personality appeared when the subject had been placed under such deep hypnosis that the heartbeat had almost ceased, and the patient was therefore in the same state of 'deep trance' as a medium.

A case discussed by the psychologist Jung provides an interesting cautionary tale about oversimplification. At the age of fifteen, Jung's cousin Helene Preiswerk began experimenting with automatic writing, and one day fell into a trance and began to speak in a different voice. Soon a number of 'spirits' were speaking through her mouth, one of whom claimed to be her grandfather. The most remarkable of these intruders was a woman who called herself Ivenes, a mature woman of considerable intellect, who went on to propound a brilliant and complex mystical philosophy. Jung's cousin, a quiet and shy girl, blossomed under the attention she received; but the later seances became increasingly disappointing, and when she admitted to Jung that she had deliberately

233

'cheated' at one of them, he lost all interest in her. She died at the age of twenty-six – still rather less mature than her alter-ego Ivenes. Jung later evolved the interesting theory that she somehow knew that she was fated for an early death, and 'Ivenes' was her attempt to compensate for this. When he discussed the case in his first published work, *On the Psychology and Pathology of So-called Occult Phenomena*, he treated it as a case of multiple personality due to hysteria and sexual repression; that is to say, he dismissed his cousin as a kind of super-Walter Mitty. A decade or so later, when Jung stumbled upon the mandala symbol (mandala is Sanskrit for circle) and decided that it was an 'archetypal' religious symbol, he recalled with astonishment that it had figured largely in the mystical philosophy of 'Ivenes'.

In middle life, Jung became increasingly convinced of the reality of the paranormal – he spent a highly disturbed weekend in a haunted cottage in 1920 – and attended seances. It must have struck him that his cousin was not a case of multiple personality, but of simple 'mediumship'. But to admit as much would undoubtedly have caused a storm in the world of medical psychology; he seems to have been forced to adopt an attitude of 'double-think'. In an essay on the 'Psychological Foundations of Belief in Spirits', written in the 1930s, he interprets spirits as 'autonomous complexes' (or personality fragments). In a cautious postscript written in 1948 – when he had begun to admit openly to his deep interest in the paranormal – he comments that he has purposely confined himself to the 'psychological side of the problem' and avoided the question of whether spirits exist – the nearest he ever came to an admission that his earlier views had been mistaken. In the same postscript, he stated, untruthfully, that he had had no experience that might prove it one way or the other; for elsewhere,

234

in a preface to a book called *Ghosts, Reality or Delusion*, he describes his hair-raising weekend in the haunted cottage, when he had been awakened at one point to find half a head looking at him from the other pillow.

On the whole, it seems best to avoid the Jungian dilemma by admitting that it seems virtually impossible to produce a wholly-satisfying explanation of multiple personality either in psychological or 'occult' terms, and leave it at that.